The Fixer

D A Latham

Copyright © 2016 D A Latham All rights reserved.

ISBN 13: 978-1530590193
ISBN-10: 1530590191

No part of this book may be reproduced, scanned or distributed in any printed or electronic format without permission.

Please do not participate in or encourage piracy of copyrighted materials in violation of the author's rights.

DEDICATION

To my dearest, darling Allan

CONTENTS

Chapter 1	1
Chapter 2	17
Chapter 3	21
Chapter 4	37
Chapter 5	42
Chapter 6	54
Chapter 7	57
Chapter 8	69
Chapter 9	72
Chapter 10	78
Chapter 11	81
Chapter 12	101
Chapter 13	104
Chapter 14	116
Chapter 15	119
Chapter 16	127
Chapter 17	132
Chapter 18	139

Chapter 19	152
Chapter 20	167
Chapter 21	179
Chapter 22	192
Chapter 23	204
Also by D A Latham	208

CHAPTER 1

Sarah

The days which irrevocably change a person's life rarely announce their arrival with much fanfare. Sarah's day began badly, with her alarm clock failing to wake her at six a.m. in order for her to get herself properly together and ready for work. It normally took two coffees and at least an hour of preparation to present herself as a polished professional. That morning she had just fifteen minutes.

She stood in front of the mirror, cursing. She knew that if she didn't get a move on, she'd be late, which wouldn't go down well with Mr Hitchcock, her manager, who was a stickler for punctuality. She was starting a new project that Monday morning, so she really needed to be on time and playing her "A" game. Unfortunately, Having chosen that morning to oversleep, it meant she'd have no time for coffee. Irritated, Sarah yanked her hair into a ponytail and grabbed her bag, flinging it over her shoulder before racing out of the door. Of all people, she should be the most organised, given that she was a fixer, or rather, a glorified nanny for the top talent at Laker Brothers, the biggest film studio in the world. Her real job title was Executive Assistant: a rather prim, corporate moniker for what could essentially be a rather dirty, immoral job.

She was the person who sorted hotel rooms, found the stuff requested in stars' riders, and generally wiped their noses. She was a mixture of PA, mummy, and often pimp, catering to the whims and desires of overpaid, spoilt, and largely egotistical actors. It was actually a great job, her dream job, and she never had two days the same. Her previous charge had thankfully flown back to LA two days before into the safe care of her LA equivalent. It had left her just one day to get her laundry up to date, see her poor, neglected friends, and clean her little house in Fulham before her next assignment arrived. The last one had been a twenty four/seven job, a spoilt and demanding actress whom Sarah had been glad to see the back of.

In the grand scheme of things, it didn't sound like a particularly important way to earn a living, but it was extraordinarily well paid, with great perks, and fixers wielded a certain amount of power within their worlds due to their budgets, plus the lure of providing celebrity clients to the various businesses around London. Backhanders and bribes were commonplace, depending on the star level of the celebrity involved and the size of the fandom which followed them. Sarah was a particularly well-connected fixer and usually looked after "A" listers.

Clive Hitchcock was already in the spacious, open-plan office by the time she got there. "Morning Sarah. Looking forward to meeting your new charge?" He smirked as she rolled her eyes. She regarded all the stars she looked after as pretty ordinary, although usually bearing extraordinary self-confidence. Sarah had never met anyone that she'd want to be best friends with.

"You know the answer to that one Clive. So who have I been assigned this week?" She asked, pleased that he hadn't mentioned the fact that it was five past nine. She knew that they had at least five actors arriving, but casting was often a last-minute affair, so things often changed at the last moment.

"Actually you've got him for the next three months. He's filming here, and in Italy, all this summer. His name's James Morell. Played the lead in Cosmic Warriors. You must know who he is."

"Rings a bell," she said nonchalantly. "From what I know, he's just a pretty boy. At least I get a bit of eye candy while I'm working." She knew from bitter experience that film stars were pains in the butt; no matter how nice the outer packaging, it often concealed narcissistic personalities. Still, she reasoned that it was better to have a nice view if this James Morell was going to treat her like a dogsbody.

Clive sent the file over with Mr Morell's requirements. Sarah printed it off and flicked through it. She was to get his London home ready, to get it cleaned and stocked. She needed to sort him a car and driver for the duration of his stay, all of which was easy enough. "Where's the rest of the file?" She asked. "There's no rider, no special requirements, doesn't even say what household staff he wants." The LA fixer was clearly getting lazy, not sending through the normal reams of instructions, detailing the myriad obscure requests that most stars required.

Clive glanced up from his screen, "I don't think he wants any, but he might change his mind when he finds out what's on offer. Just work with what you have. His flight arrives tomorrow morning at eight. Don't forget to tip off the paps."

Part of Sarah's job was to liaise with PR and the publicists to make sure stars were always kept in the public eye and presented in the best possible light. She had one day to get everything ready, which was not a lot of time, but she'd managed worse deadlines with far more detailed riders. She picked up the phone to start on her list of calls. She started with a call to the estate agent holding the keys to his house in Kensington, which had been rented out while Mr Morell had been contracted to film for almost a year in the States. Sarah discovered that he was, in fact, British and had lived in London while travelling regularly to LA in order to audition and eventually break into the closed world of Hollywood. Her day ended up a whirlwind of phone calls, taxi rides, and organising the interns to run myriad errands. She fell into bed at midnight and was up again at four to get herself ready and over to the airport to do the meet and greet.

James Morell stared at his watch yet again, willing the time to pass. He hated flying alone. He had nobody to talk to, nobody to settle his anxiety at hurtling through the air in a metal cigar, and nobody to share his death if it crashed. He took another sip of champagne and tried to watch a film. He was ensconced in the luxury of first class, on a comfy flat-bed, surrounded by top-of-the-range entertainment, food, and drink. He barely noticed it all, having become accustomed to the finer side of life. He debated whether or not he should shower and get changed before dismissing the idea. He was landing early in the morning, so didn't expect any fuss. He just hoped that Laker Brothers had arranged for him to be met at the airport, otherwise he'd have to schlepp over to the taxi rank and get a cab home. His fixer had told him that someone called Sarah would be there to meet him. He hoped there were no screw-ups, although with his LA fixer's track record, anything was possible.

By the time James landed, his house was prepared, his fridge filled, his measurements sent to the various designers who wanted to dress him, clothes collected and hung in his wardrobe, a car and driver, and security sorted. Sarah was to meet him at the first class area of Heathrow at eight and brief him on the way back to his Kensington home.

Now, she was used to the various actors that Laker Brothers employed. They were usually handsome, charismatic, and fit. She liked to think she was immune to pretty faces. In her opinion they usually just covered up an asshole personality. She'd looked after quite a few in the past, and after a moment to get over their looks, Sarah was perfectly capable of being the professional around them.

She got there a little early and sat reading through her notes as she waited. She hoped his plane wouldn't be late, as there were a load of paparazzi waiting outside, which would quickly attract a large crowd of onlookers, curious as to who would be arriving.

Nothing prepared Sarah for the first sight of James in the flesh, striding down the corridor. His masculine beauty simply took her breath away. She stood frozen, clipboard in hand, just drinking in the sight of him. *'I am so screwed,'* she thought, as he beamed a devastating smile and halted in front of her. "Are you Sarah?" He asked, surprised that Laker employed such a pretty fixer. Most of the ones he'd come across had been middle-aged and rather grizzled, prized for their abilities to magic up even the most outrageous requests and deal with the most disastrous calamities. "Pleased to meet you, I'm James Morell."

He didn't really mean to use his "sexy" voice, but this gorgeous brunette with the liquid brown eyes was just too mesmerising to bark at in a businesslike way.

Sarah just stared at him for a moment before eventually mentally slapping herself, closing her slack jaw, and forcing herself back to the job at hand. "Yes, I'm Sarah. Nice to meet you. Your car's this way. Please follow me. There are photographers at the entrance." She quickly turned on her heels, desperate to hide the fact that she was blushing furiously. He trotted along beside her as they strode towards the exit, both reeling from their initial reactions to each other.

They headed through a walkway towards the exit, where Sarah had stationed a battalion of paparazzi ready to snap his arrival in the UK. James caught sight of himself in the mirrored glass running along the wall. His skin looked grey, and his dark, curly hair was wayward and bouffant, not his usual well-groomed appearance and not how he wanted to look in pictures that would be shared across the net. "I look like shit after the flight," he groaned before his brain had gone into gear. He could've kicked himself for sounding so vain in front of her.

She braved a glance at him, fully aware that she'd blush again and feel stupid for being such a sap. "You look OK to me," she muttered, turning away so he wouldn't see the pink flush rising from her neck.

Flashbulbs started going off the moment they stepped outside. Sarah steered him through the mass of paparazzi, then had to wait while he posed for pictures with a few fans who had gathered. He began signing autographs, secretly rather pleased that so many people had turned out to catch sight of him. It didn't occur to him that they'd been sent there specifically.

"We really need to get going," she huffed. Reluctantly, he said goodbye to the people screaming out his name and followed her out of the concourse and into the VIP car park. "Bob will be your driver and security," she told him. He smiled and shook Bob's hand, taking the burly, cynical driver by surprise. He was used to the asshole stars too. Most looked straight through him.

During the drive to his house, she ran through all the services he could request that would be accommodated by the studio. To her surprise, he refused most of them, only saying yes to a personal trainer. James had no desire to be stifled by a houseful of staff, as he'd experienced it in LA and had hated both the loss of privacy as well as the lack of autonomy that having housekeepers and butlers inflicted. He also didn't want to appear helpless in front of such an obviously bright young woman.

When he declined the services of a personal stylist, she smiled at his comment that he could manage to dress himself. He stared at her, trying to fathom why her smile made him glad to be back home and why she was affecting him so much. James was used to beautiful women around him, used to the way they reacted to his face and physique. Sometimes they were a welcome diversion, sometimes an irritant that his security needed to deal with, but very few actually held his interest. Sarah somehow seemed different. She wasn't like the tall, thin models and actresses he usually met, being petite and curvy. As she loosened her jacket, he caught sight of the swell of a decent-sized cleavage. This instantly captured his interest, but it was more than that, it was her confidence, her quiet capability. She was clearly…different.

She interrupted his musing. "I can arrange some company for you, either female or male, whichever you prefer." It was all part of the normal spiel that she had to give each of the stars she looked after. With the abundance of camera phones, the studio couldn't allow less-than-discreet liaisons for their charges. For some reason, those words coming out of her mouth sounded almost offensive. When his LA fixer had offered the same "service," he hadn't been the slightest bit bothered.

"Certainly not," he bit back, startling her. "Sorry, but I won't be needing anything like that. I prefer my relationships to be a little more…traditional." He fixed her with his intense gaze, trying to see into her psyche, which she found a little disconcerting, as was his intense focus on everything she had to say. Generally stars treated Sarah as though she was part of the furniture, so she wasn't used to dealing with such rapt attention. She took a deep breath to steady herself.

"Oh, OK. Will you be having anyone joining you during your stay?"

His face betrayed a sadness. "No. No, I won't." She decided to drop the subject, moving on to his itinerary and travel dates. "So will you be babysitting me all summer?" He asked, smiling. It was at that moment that Sarah began to suspect that he might be flirting with her.

"Yes. I've been assigned to you for your entire stay in London and while you're travelling to Italy," she told him, while praying that she could get over his extraordinary good looks and get her professional composure back. Her palms were sweaty, and her body was responding just sitting next to him. She breathed in his lovely scent and felt another blush rise up her already overheated neck, which James noticed immediately and was gratified to see. He decided to take charge.

"Well, we'll just have to get to know each other, Sarah, seeing as we'll be in close quarters for the next three months. I'll take you out to dinner tonight." It wasn't really a request, more a statement, but coming from him, it didn't sound impertinent. She told herself it was perfectly normal for stars to dine with their fixers, even though she knew it was highly unusual. Something told her he wasn't a man who'd take "no" for an answer. Besides, she found him unusually appealing.

"OK."

He beamed his film-star smile and settled back in his seat, while she attempted to recover her professional composure by running through his schedule for the following few days. He groaned when she told him about a photo shoot his agents had signed him up for. "I hate those things. I know they're important, but I always feel awkward," he confided.

Sarah laughed. "You're probably the most photogenic person on the planet. How'd ya think the rest of us mere mortals feel?"

"Oh, I don't know, a beautiful woman like you must take an amazing picture."

'*A charmer too. I'm really screwed here,*' she thought. "Thank you for the compliment, but I assure you I don't," she told him, rather primly.

"Now, I don't believe that for one moment," he said, "with your cheekbones and flawless skin, not to mention those big brown eyes, I'd expect the camera to adore you." He stared at her, drinking in her startled features, waiting for her reaction.

"I have no desire to be on your side of the camera," she told him. "I've seen enough screwed-up starlets to know it's not a life I'd aspire to."

He didn't answer. She wondered if she'd offended him.

He gazed out of the window for a while, as they sped towards Kensington, "I miss London. As much as I love LA, there's no place like home is there?"

"Even on a grey, miserable day like today?" Sarah laughed. It was forecast to rain, and the whole sky was blanketed by dark clouds, giving everything a grey, dingy appearance. James wondered if all his sweaters were still in storage. He hadn't needed them in LA.

"Especially on a day like today," he grinned. "Bright blue skies every day become tedious after a while. Everything in LA conforms, you know: perfect weather, perfect houses, and all the women look like models with the ubiquitous long blonde hair and fake bodies." He thought for a moment, "Yeah, I've missed London."

They arrived before Sarah could question him further as to why he'd got fed up with gorgeous people, weather, and homes. His house was on a small residential street in Kensington. It was white, stucco fronted, with glossy, black railings marking the perimeter. She rummaged around in her handbag to hand him his keys, but he fished a set out of his jacket pocket and hopped out of the car, clearly eager to get inside. He'd missed his home more than he'd care to admit. It had been his only significant purchase after his first blockbuster, and to James, it was a solid embodiment of his success in a way that plaudits or awards could never compete with. He'd always reasoned with himself that in the fickle world of acting, his career could end at any time, but he'd always have his house.

Sarah thought his home was lovely, modern, and nicely furnished. Bob placed his bags in the hall, and asked if James wanted them taken upstairs. "No thanks, just there's great. I'll sort them out in a bit." He turned to Sarah, "The first thing is some English tea. I've missed it more than you'd believe. Join me?" It was an effective but gentle way of dismissing Bob, who smiled thinly before turning to leave.

Sarah followed James through the long hallway, waving goodbye to Bob. She watched as James moved around his luxurious kitchen with a practiced ease, filling the kettle, and pulling out cups. It was a large room, taking up the entire rear half of his house and fitted out with off-white units and granite worktops. It was the type of kitchen beloved of moderately successful stockbroker's wives, managing to be both slick and traditional at the same time. He opened the fridge and examined the contents, noting that there was a terrific selection. "I take it you filled it up?" She nodded, nervous, praying she'd not forgotten milk. "You've done a great job, thought of everything by the looks of it." Sarah breathed a sigh of relief, then mentally slapped herself for caring so much.

He beamed a knicker-combusting smile. "Sorry, I shouldn't be surprised. You do this type of thing all the time don't you?"

"Yes. Yes I do." It was a struggle to get the words out; she was so mesmerised by the perfect planes of his jawline that she could barely concentrate. To try and regain control, she pulled his file out of her bag, to run through some of the PR requests.

Fixers work closely with the PR department. They make sure that their stars are seen in the right places, with the right people, and wearing the right clothes. Every detail is planned and scrutinised so that they're one step ahead of the celeb sites. It would probably surprise people how meticulously everything is organised so they never see the stars wearing the same outfit twice, or in the company of non-entities. Laker Brother's PR department was widely acknowledged as being one of the best and most detailed in the business. It was also the department that Sarah had cut her teeth in, so she was generally "on message" without too much of their involvement.

"They want to see you out and about in London. They'd like you to go out with your co-stars, maybe a family meet-up, and have requested that you get papped being a man-about-town. Think you can manage that?" She glanced up to see him frowning.

"Am I really controlled that much?" He asked. "I don't mind meeting my brothers or going out for dinner with Harry, my co-star, and his wife, but the rest of it, is it really necessary?"

"You have an image to keep up," she explained. "PR monitors public opinion, and they want to see more of you, preferably in a less formal setting. Don't worry, you'll have security." She wondered what his problem was.

"It's not that it's just..." He paused, "It's so false. I'm going to be catching up with friends while I'm here, so I'll make sure we go somewhere public. Should satisfy the pimps at PR." James knew the game, he'd been around long enough to understand how stardom was created and maintained, but this "businesslike" Sarah was... disappointing. He wondered how to get her to snap out of PR mode and get her blushing again. He was also falling asleep, having been unable to sleep on the flight due to a rather selfish businessman tapping away at his keyboard half the night, then a couple having an argument during the remainder. He drained his cup, savouring the taste of fresh, hot, British tea made with good, hard London water.

"Hmm," she said, non committal. "Now, Tom Ford and Giorgio Armani will be dressing you. Their people sent over a selection. I hung it all in your wardrobe. Please don't wear anything else in public. Your workout clothing will be Nike and nothing else. They've sent over a large selection." Sarah ticked stuff off her list as she went. She was just about to run through his shooting schedule, when he interrupted her.

"I don't want to be rude, but I need a shower and some sleep. Can I pick you up around seven?"

Embarrassed at bombarding him when he was clearly jet-lagged, she nodded her assent.

"Where shall I pick you up?" He asked. Sarah scribbled down her address on the back of her contact card and handed it to him.

"Shall I book a restaurant?" she asked, rightly figuring he'd be asleep fairly quickly. Besides, she could get a table in just about any restaurant in London at short notice.

"Yes, please. Wherever you like, I don't mind," he said, before yawning loudly. Sarah smiled and said her goodbyes before letting herself out.

Back outside, she took a deep breath. She was hot, flustered, and affected by that man, all very unusual behaviour for her. Inside the house, James sat and scrubbed his hands over his face, trying to work out what it was about her, and wondering if it was the jet lag that'd rendered him so vulnerable. As he let the hot water of the shower pour over him, he couldn't shake the image of her out of his head, nor the sensation that he'd found *her*, his mythical Aphrodite.

Back at the office, Clive didn't even look up. "You're back early."

"He's jet-lagged. I'll meet up with him again later. I've got some admin and calls I can be getting on with." Sarah pulled out her phone and booked a table at The Ivy. She liked it there, and the lure of being able to put it on expenses meant she couldn't resist. Glancing over, she could see Clive's eyebrows had shot up.

"If he's going to The Ivy tonight, make sure the paps know. It's a prime opportunity. Who's he going with?"

"Only with me. We've still got stuff to run through."

"Make sure you tip off the paps then, and Sarah? Try and look your best. The fans won't know that you're his babysitter, so we might as well get some mileage."

She tried not to be horribly offended at the suggestion that she wouldn't pass muster as a celebrity girlfriend. Just to make sure, she booked a blowdry at the salon down the road that afternoon. If she was gonna be papped, she'd make damn sure she looked her best.

It took five changes of outfits to decide what Sarah would wear to dinner that night. As much as she tried to keep running the mantra "It's not a date, it's a client" through her head, she knew full well that she found him extraordinarily attractive. As she stared at her reflection in the mirror, she could see that she looked polished, even glamorous, but no amount of clever dressing could disguise the fact that she was petite and a bit curvy. The little voice in her head told her that he couldn't possibly be interested, and that she shouldn't get her hopes up as he was way out of her league. The worst thing she could do would be to flirt and make a fool of herself.

Meanwhile, James was digging around in his wardrobe full of unfamiliar clothes, wondering what he should wear as he had no idea where they'd be going. *'Just another example of why I hate not doing things for myself,'* he thought, as he called Bob to pick him up, the irony of which was rather lost on him.

He arrived dead on time that evening. Sarah's breath caught as she opened the door. He was fresh from the shower and dressed in a simple, fitted black shirt and black trousers. "Hey Sarah, you look amazing," he murmured, taking in the sight of her in a lace-covered, fitted black dress, which showed off her curves to perfection. Smiling, she grabbed her bag and followed him to the car.

"There might be photographers, so I thought I'd better scrub up," she told him. "I booked a table at the Ivy. Hope that's OK?"

"Great. I've not been there for ages, and I really want some English food," he said, flashing her that devastating smile, "and you scrub up beautifully. We can convince them that you're my new girlfriend. Get the studio off my back."

Sarah should have been pleased, but inside she was a little disappointed, wondering why he needed a fake girlfriend when he could take his pick of real ones. She stared out of the window while she tried to phrase the question she needed to ask. "If you're gay, James, you can tell me. I won't be shocked or surprised. I do this for a living you know, so I often deal with closeted film stars." There'd been at least three of her charges that she'd had to cover for, carefully constructing fake relationships for their public personas. It wasn't an approach that she personally agreed with, as she had seen the intense pressure it had put the "stars" under, but she understood why they did it.

"I'm not gay," he snapped, startling her. "Everyone seems to think I am, and I'm not."

"So why do you need a fake girlfriend then?" She challenged.

He thought for a moment and was just about to start speaking, when they arrived at the restaurant. The moment they got out of the car, the flashbulbs went off, momentarily blinding them both. Sarah felt his arm snake around her waist, his hand gripping her hip firmly, forming an instant physical connection. For James, it had been a primal, instinctive reaction; a desire to protect her from the aggressive photographers. His response even took him by surprise.

Sarah's body reacted instantly. Everything south of her waist tightened viciously. She leaned into him, closing the gap between them as they posed for pictures. He felt warm and solid, a strong, steadfast man. He also smelt adorable, a mixture of citrus notes and fresh mint. She breathed in deeply as the paps yelled questions at them. James didn't say a word, just steered her round and into the lobby, where he stopped again for more pictures.

After a few moments, they made their way into the restaurant, both a bit dazzled by the flashes. "You OK?" he asked her.

"A bit blind, but otherwise alright. You?"

"All in a day's work for me."

They were shown to a quiet little table at the back of the room. Sitting down, Sarah glanced around, recognising a couple of famous faces, but nobody as "A" list as James. She turned her attention back to him. He was reading the wine list, seemingly not remotely interested in star spotting.

"Red or white?" He asked, not taking his eyes off the list.

"I prefer red, but I'm not fussed, if you prefer white," she replied.

He ordered a bottle of Merlot, and sat back to read the menu. "You were about to tell me why you needed a fake girlfriend," Sarah asked. In a normal setting, it wouldn't be any of her business, but as his handler, she needed to know. She wondered if he had "quirks" she'd have to organise someone to accommodate. She'd had to source a dominatrix for a client before, and finding prostitutes was a fairly normal occurrence.

He groaned, "OK, here's how it is. You imagine having this so-called pretty face," he pointed at himself, "and a good job, paying great money. Women fling themselves at you all day every day. Only here's the thing, Sarah, they all want the image, the outer packaging. None of them have any idea about the man inside. I question their agendas constantly. You know, whether they're gonna sell their stories, spill to the press."

"What Titanium Rod's really like in bed..." she said. He laughed.

"Exactly. You imagine if I'd had too much to drink one night."

"Titanium Rod was anything but," she was catching on. He roared with laughter.

"It's never happened yet, but yeah, you get the picture."

"That's why we offer discreet escorts to our stars, so that kind of thing doesn't happen. They all sign watertight NDAs."

"I really don't want to use prostitutes, thank you," he snapped. Sarah wondered if she'd offended him. "I'll find the woman I'm looking for one day. Until then, I'd rather not settle for second best."

"If you don't let anyone in, or assume all women have ulterior motives, then it's never gonna happen," she snapped back, annoyed that he assumed all women would be after his fame or money. It was a bit rude, and made him sound like a typical pompous star. Up until that point, she'd thought he was different.

They were interrupted by the waiter. After they'd ordered, she fully intended to start going through the work stuff that she'd brought, as there was still quite a bit to do.

"I don't think all women are after my money or fame," he said quietly. "That didn't really come out right."

"Clearly," she replied. "Anyway, we need to run though your diary for the next three months. I need to organise a hotel in Rome while you're filming. You have a choice of three." She handed him the printouts. He barely glanced at them.

"I really don't mind where I stay. Will you be coming out there?"

"Yep. I'm assigned to you for the next three months."

"In which case, you can choose where we stay. Pick the best one."

Sarah laughed, "I'll be at the Italian version of a Travelodge. Only the actors get the five-star treatment."

"Well in which case, one of my requirements is that you're in the same hotel as me, preferably on the same floor." He smiled tentatively. She scribbled a note in her pad, fully intending to book the Grande Vizente, which had an award-winning spa and a rooftop restaurant. She'd already pored over TripAdvisor to find the top three hotels. With the studio paying, it'd be rude not to indulge. She prayed that they'd have two rooms available. Sarah was about to move onto discussing his workout regime when he interrupted.

"So you know all about me, down to what shoe size I am. It's only fair for me to know about you. Where are you from Sarah?"

"I'm from Hertfordshire originally. I moved to London after uni. Mainly because I'd got the job at Laker Brothers."

"What uni did you attend?"

She paused, before replying "Cambridge. I studied psychology. I interned at the head office, in the PR department, and was offered a job. A few promotions later, here I am."

He looked shocked. "A Cambridge degree? And you're wiping actor's noses for a living?"

"I'm paid a hell of a lot more than I'd get working in the NHS," she pointed out.

"Even so. Wouldn't you prefer a job that actually utilised your degree?"

"Not if it meant living in poverty, I wouldn't, no." She was getting a little annoyed. "Anyway, this isn't about me. We need to sort your diary, if you don't mind?"

He ignored her. "Are you single, married?"

She ignored the question. "Rod McDowell has been assigned as your personal trainer while you're in London. He operates from Equinox in Kensington Church Street. Bob will pick you up at 7 a.m. each morning to take you there." He groaned. "He'll be back from his holiday in a day or two, but I arranged for one of the gym employees to look after you starting tomorrow."

"I asked if you were single or married. Don't dodge the question." His voice had changed to being playful, teasing.

"I'm single, at the moment." Sarah admitted. She was always single, primarily because she worked strange hours, often in the bubble that surrounded the "A" list actors and actresses in her care. It was almost impossible to meet nice men, let alone sustain a relationship. Her last boyfriend had dumped her almost a year previously, fed up with constantly being dropped to run around after a particularly difficult actress, who'd had a fairly serious psychological issue and didn't like being alone.

"That's good to know," he said, before smiling a sphinx-like smile.

The food was exquisite, and they both ate heartily. James

The Fixer

seemed to relax and regaled Sarah with funny stories from the Cosmic Warriors set. In turn, she made him laugh with some of the tales she often told about fun experiences she'd had while working on various shoots. The evening seemed to flash by, and all too soon it was time to go. He couldn't remember when he'd last enjoyed a woman's company so much.

The paps got them again as they were leaving. James immediately grabbed her waist, and held her close as the flashbulbs blinded them. "Who's your girlfriend?" One of them yelled. James didn't answer, he just flashed his film-star smile and steered Sarah towards the waiting car. They jumped in and slammed the door. Within seconds, Bob had pulled away into the traffic.

Sarah lay back into the leather seat, slightly blinded by the flashes. James squeezed her hand, an affectionate gesture meant to reassure her. "You OK?" he whispered, before he slid up the privacy screen, cutting them off from their driver. He desperately wanted to be alone with her, to try and gauge whether he could make a move or not. She was difficult to read, having not flung herself at him or flirted outrageously like most women did.

"I'm fine," she told him. Inside, she was a bit shaky, whether from the paparazzi or the fact he was holding her hand, she couldn't be certain.

"You did amazingly well. You're clearly a natural," he mused. She could see him smiling in the glow that the street lamps cast through the car windows. It struck her that he hadn't taken his eyes off her all evening and was again staring at her. It should've put her on her guard, or even made her uncomfortable, but she sensed that there was something genuinely kind about him. She could tell that he was as normal and decent a man as one could ever find in Hollywood. At that point, she'd even have gone far enough to say that he stood out amongst the stars she'd previously met as probably the most well adjusted.

"We've certainly put the cat amongst the pigeons," she remarked. Sarah just hoped she wouldn't be waking up to a mass rally of his fans deeming her too ugly for their god. James's fans were well known for being a bit extreme in their devotion to their idol.

"They'll all be wondering who the beautiful woman is," he said kindly.

It only took fifteen minutes to get to Sarah's place. She was almost sad to get home so quickly, as she'd enjoyed James's company and found him to be a lot more fun than she'd expected. As they pulled up outside, she reminded him that Bob would pick him up at seven.

"So when will I see you again?" He asked. Inside he was having a furious debate with himself as to whether or not to make his move. It reminded him of how he was aged fifteen, taking his date home from the school disco in the back of a taxi. The thought amused him.

"Tomorrow. I'll be accompanying you to the Heat interview," she told him. She was just about to hop out of the car, when his arm snaked around her waist, and he pulled her close, crushing her to his chest. His eyes bored into hers, asking for permission before his lips met hers, softly, slowly, before he deepened the kiss. His tongue grazed her lips, before pushing in to meet hers, shyly at first, then becoming bolder, more demanding. It went against every rule in the book, but at that precise moment, Sarah didn't care.

She softened into him, lightly holding his waist, feeling the firm ripples of his precisely-toned muscles. Eventually he pulled away and stroked his hand down her cheek. "You have no idea how lovely you are, do you?"

She shook her head, mute. Everything about the man screamed perfection. He looked, tasted, and smelt divine, as though the gods had listened to a woman's pleas and created the most exquisite male specimen.

He planted another, chaste kiss on her lips before pulling back. "Until tomorrow Sarah, and I honestly can't wait."

"Tomorrow," she parroted, breathless. In a dream state, she opened the car door and got out, testing her legs before standing upright. She took one last glance at him. He blew her a kiss.

Sarah walked up to her front door in a daze, questioning herself as to whether or not that had actually happened. As his car pulled away, she touched her tingling lips, and came to only one conclusion; she was totally, utterly screwed.

James felt triumphant as the car sped over to Kensington. Easy lays and hungry starlets held no fascination compared to the bright, intelligent woman who'd made him feel like a schoolboy again. He would have Sarah, he decided.

CHAPTER 2

Anna

It was thrilling to wake up in a different continent, thought Anna, as she dressed in desert combat gear that she'd bought from an old army surplus store in Illinois. She laced up her army boots with practiced ease as they were similar to the hiking boots she wore at home. She'd purchased new ones especially for her vacation, knowing they'd be trekking across some difficult, rocky terrain. She also wanted to look the part.

The smells and sounds of Africa assaulted Anna's nostrils as she waited for her father to join her for breakfast on their second morning at the Wapopo Lodge in Zimbabwe. The reds and oranges of daybreak streaked the sky as she listened to the last fanfare of unseen and unknown nocturnal creatures as the light licked across the treetops. Branches rustled as animals either made their way to their sleeping quarters for the day or woke up from their nighttime slumber. Loud screeches could be heard from deep inside the dense undergrowth, the greeting calls of impossibly glamorous birds. The air smelt like a curious mixture of forest floor, hot sand, and barbecue.

Anna and her father were part of a select group of big game hunters, the wealthy, successful American elite who could pay upwards of fifty thousand dollars each for ten days hunting on the Moranghi game reserve, with the promise of bagging a trophy or two each during their stay, which would be decapitated, stuffed, and mounted on a polished plinth before being shipped to them in the United States, where the poor unlucky corpses would end up in a wood-lined room, a gruesome place full of what these people rather laughably called "trophies."

The group was made up of eight people, including Anna and her father, Ricky. All of them took their hunting seriously and were well-practised in the art of stalking prey and handling high velocity rifles, having honed their skills in the forests and plains back home. Going to Africa was the next step up, elevating their status, in their minds, to that of a "great white hunter."

Anna's father had given her her first rifle when she was just ten and had spent hours with her teaching target practice in their backyard in Illinois. In fact, her only really happy memories from her childhood were when he lined up tin cans along their old back wall and the two of them played shooting practice. She'd loved it when she'd hit her target and prompted a hug from Ricky.

He was delighted that she'd turned out to be a good shot, able to handle weapons with ease. The most important thing to her was pleasing her daddy, gaining his praise and his approval. The second most important thing was pleasing their church, Soldiers of the Illinois Pentecost.

She'd had a weird childhood. Her mother had disappeared when she was three. She'd tucked Anna into bed one night, kissing her forehead gently and sitting by the bed until Anna had fallen asleep. By the morning, she'd gone. Her daddy had been tight-lipped about where she was, but had patted Anna's head and let her eat pizza for tea, which was a rare treat as they normally ate what he'd hunted in the surrounding woods. From then on, it was just him and Anna.

He'd never told her how he'd squeezed the life out of her mother while in a drunken rage, or that she lay buried deep in the earth below a factory he'd built shortly afterwards, cemented securely into the foundations. Ricky'd had a large, extended family of aunts, uncles, and cousins, who'd disliked his wife, and who were delighted to accept that she'd run away during the night with a fancy-man. Anna's mother had no family to question his story. His sisters and brother had assisted with Anna, minding her alongside their own children, so she never felt lonely growing up. Ricky was able to expand his business, building factories on the outskirts of their land and turning it into a commercial centre, aided by influential people from their church. Ricky became a significant benefactor, and his influence in their town grew.

Financially successful, Ricky was able to indulge Anna, both in the material sense, but also by spending a lot of time with her, teaching her to enjoy the same pastimes as he liked, which mainly consisted of hunting, shooting, and killing. He took her out into the wilds to hunt deer and wolves, smiling as Anna used squirrels for target practice, feeling it was a reflection on his parenting, just how good a shot she was.

A couple from Wisconsin, the Weintraubs, joined Anna at the table, pouring themselves cups of hot coffee and helping themselves to bread, eggs, and the sausages made from the antelope Rick'd shot the day before. "Morning Anna, your husband not up yet?"

Anna shook her head. "He won't be long. He's after a Wildebeest this week for his trophy collection, so he won't laze about in bed for too long." She never corrected people when they assumed her father was her husband, as it made things easier. He looked young for his thirty-nine years, she looked old for her nineteen years. "Here he comes now." They all smiled as her father strolled over to the table in full camouflage gear. He took his hunting seriously too. One thing they both shared was the thrill of the kill. Ever since Anna was little, she'd felt elated at having power over the dumb animals, having learnt that from Rick. It was just another reason for him to love her and claim her as his mini-me.

They set off straight after they'd eaten, their guide driving them out onto the plains behind the mountains into prime wildebeest country. The Weintraubs, preferring to hunt bigger beasts, had taken a separate jeep, so it was just Anna and Rick, along with their guides, who let it be believed that they could barely speak English.

Out on the plain, the guides spotted wildebeest tracks, so they followed for a while, scanning the countryside for tell-tale signs of a large gathering. Rick saw a giraffe lumbering slowly through the trees. "Theres a big 'un for you, baby girl." He motioned for the driver to stop.

Anna clicked off the safety catch of her rifle. It was a high powered one, so she knew she was well within range. She rested the butt in the crook of her shoulder, a familiar sensation to a regular hunter such as Anna. The giraffe was in her sights, too busy pulling leaves off the tree to take much notice of the jeep. They could see it was male, probably an old bull, its size indicating it had reached a good age, probably due to its strong, solid rear hooves, capable of breaking a lion's back if necessary.

"You want a clean kill, not the head though, make sure you don't damage that pretty face of his," Rick whispered.

Anna felt the sweat pool on her upper lip as she lined up the sights, aiming for where she thought the heart would be. With her heart pumping and the adrenaline rushing through her body, she squeezed the trigger.

The bullet hit the giraffe before the sound did, a loud crack that reverberated for miles around the plain, bouncing off the surrounding mountains. The lumbering animal stood stock still for a moment before both the noise and the effects of Anna's bullet startled him. They watched as it reared up, attempting to run away, but its legs crumpled underneath it as it tried to put one hoof in front of the other.

The guides shouted at Anna in their own language, trying to urge her to shoot it again, put it out of its misery, as she hadn't achieved a clean kill. She lifted her rifle and shot at it again. This time the bullet hit its side, sending it toppling onto the scrub. "YES!" she screeched, elated at her achievement.

"You got it baby," her father said as the guides drove them over to inspect the corpse. What they didn't know was that it took a full three minutes for the poor creature to die. Three minutes where it lay on the ground, not knowing what had happened or how it got there. It had spent its life avoiding the predators, yet it had a fire burning in its body which had come from nowhere and had rendered it helpless.

"One for the album baby-girl?" Rick said, holding aloft his camera. Anna leapt out of the jeep and ran over to the giraffe, laying down beside it at the exact moment that its soul left its body. She grinned as Rick took a whole bunch of photos, changing poses so that she could select the best ones for her Facebook page once they were home. She didn't notice the guides roll their eyes or their disapproval as they called for a pick-up jeep to collect the prey. She was way too busy basking in the approval of her father who was snapping her sitting astride the corpse, rather like the way models do when selling flashy motorbikes or expensive sports cars. Rick turned to the guides; "Tell them to cut off the head and mount it for us as a souvenir," he barked. They nodded silently. "Anna, hold the head up next to yours. That's it, smile baby."

CHAPTER 3

Sarah

Sarah didn't sleep at all well that night, constantly turning over the details of that kiss in her mind. She was torn between being delighted that he seemed to want her, and horrified that she'd let her guard down and behaved in such an unprofessional way. 'He was James Morell, every woman in the Western world idolised him, yet he was flirting with me,' she thought, feeling stupid for even trying to resist. Eventually, she gave up, and got up early. She tried to take her mind off things by catching up with some mundane chores, telling herself that she'd need to be organised to deal with the next three months of looking after James. Truth was, she spent most of that morning making sure she was impeccably groomed, just in case he hadn't been drunk and genuinely liked kissing her. She even spent a good fifteen minutes flossing her teeth.

Sarah stared at herself in the bathroom mirror, trying to analyse why James was flirting, trying to see what he saw. She regarded herself as decent-looking, some would even say pretty, but not extraordinary. Her brown hair was shiny, but not luscious, and her skin was clear, but not perfectly dewy like the models you see in cosmetic adverts. If she compared herself with the majority of her peers, she'd be a nine out of ten, but held up against the supermodels who surrounded celebrities, especially a leading man such as James, she felt as though she'd probably come in at about a five or six. It was a sobering thought. She wondered if James had an extensive beauty regime. He hadn't asked for a facialist to be employed or expensive products to be sourced.

James, meanwhile, was sweating it out at the gym. He'd also struggled to sleep, having slept most of the previous day, sending his body clock haywire. The mental imprint of Sarah touching her lips in shock after he'd kissed her kept playing like a gif in his mind and making him smile. He was still smiling when he'd emailed the head of the studio, Danny Laker, who was a good friend, and made sure that Sarah didn't get into any trouble at work. He even included the line, *"I'm pursuing her as hard as I know how, so it really won't be her fault when she gives in to my considerable charms,"* which made the recipient shake his head as he read it, and wonder what had got the normally level-headed James Morell so excited.

Sarah wasn't due to pick James up until lunchtime for his interview, so she went straight into the office to sort out the Italy trip and check out the list of questions he'd be asked that day. She began with the interview, which had been read though and emailed to one of the interns by PR, who'd printed them off and placed them on her desk. Rather stupidly, she hadn't read any other emails or looked online at that point.

She read through the list, checking the answers he'd been instructed to give. They were mostly innocuous, relating mainly to his role as Titanium Rod and other details about the Cosmic Warriors set. Only one related to his private life, asking if he had a girlfriend. PR had written that he was to say "no," and that he was looking for the right woman. Sarah scowled slightly before handing it back to the intern to attach it to an email, and send it to him at james@cosmicwarriors.com, smiling at the address.

"Hey Sarah, have you checked out the sites this morning?" Clive said, as he walked into the office. "Seems like you caused a bit of a stir. They're all asking who the mystery date is. Plus, and this is a biggie, they're not ripping you apart like they did the last one." She'd been so wrapped up in thinking about their kiss, she'd forgotten about the paps at The Ivy.

Sarah clicked onto the gossip sites, only to be faced with pictures of the two of them arriving and departing the restaurant. Their body language looked comfortable, even intimate. They actually weren't bad photos, and Sarah was glad she'd gotten her hair done. She read through the comments, smiling at the outlandish guesses, and wincing at the hatefulness of some of the posters, who clearly had a bit of a crush on him. Not one person guessed correctly who she was.

"Genius move, taking him out like that," said Clive, "shut up the speculation about his orientation, and got him on every gossip site going. The kiss in the car at the end was inspired."
She froze.
Then she clicked through the pictures.
Sure enough, there it was, a grainy image of their clinch. Sarah racked her brain to figure out how, and then recalled a motorbike going past. '*The paparazzi must have followed us.*'

A seed of doubt planted itself firmly in her mind, thinking that maybe James had realised they'd been followed and staged that kiss to get the studio PR off his back. She resolved to ask him about it later.

James was also staring at the pictures, wondering if Sarah had set the paparazzi up to follow them. He quickly dismissed the idea, knowing full well he'd kissed her and not the other way around. He was glad he'd alerted her boss though. He quickly skimmed through the rest of his emails, only opening the one from her office, bearing the list of questions. Reading through them, they all seemed pretty straightforward until he reached the one asking if he had a girlfriend. When he saw that he was instructed to say no, and that he was still looking for Ms Right, he scowled. Under the impression that Sarah had written his instructions, his heart sank slightly. Not really knowing how best to handle the situation, he simply replied: "Remove question 9, I don't want that one left in."

Sarah had just booked their rooms at the Grande Vizente, when her email pinged. Clicking it open, she found the email from James, requesting the removal of the girlfriend question from that day's interview. It was a cold, impersonal email, with no hint of playfulness. Sighing, she emailed "Heat" to request the question be removed, and got on with booking flights. '*I should've known better than to think a man like him would be interested in me. I'm way too ordinary for someone with his charisma,*' she thought despondently, angry at herself for getting taken in by him.

Sarah and Bob picked James up at mid-day, having braced herself to face him again. She'd decided not to mention their kiss, having spent the morning convincing herself it had all been staged for the cameras. "Hi Sarah. Busy morning?" James said, after opening the door. He smiled warmly. Sarah attempted to appear unaffected. Inside, she was churning, instantly hyper-aware of the effect his beautiful face had on her. She shuffled awkwardly on his doorstep, not making any move to step inside.

"Yeah. Sorted that hotel, and our flights on the 20th July," she told him, trying to gauge his mood.

"Excellent. Where have we gotta go for this interview?"

"Covent Garden." She watched as he grabbed his keys and wallet and followed her out of the house and up to the waiting car, automatically holding the door open for her.

The journey over was an exercise in surviving sexual tension. In the close confines of the car, she could smell his delicious scent, and was hyper-aware of him sitting next to her. "Are you alright Sarah? You seem very quiet," he asked. He'd made no move to touch her, nor had he put any distance between them as he was a bit perplexed by her coolness towards him.

"Yeah, I'm fine." She paused. "Did you see the gossip sites this morning?"

"I did." He decided not to mention that he'd printed off some of the better photos of the two of them.

Sarah took a deep breath. "Were you aware that we were being followed?"

He regarded her intently. "Of course not. Were you?" There was a trace of annoyance in his voice. Just the fact that she thought he'd set them up like that annoyed him more than was reasonable, after all, no harm had been done.

She shook her head, "No."

"Are you in trouble at work because of it? If you are, I can fix it. Your boss's boss is a good friend of mine."

"No, my boss was delighted. He thinks we staged it, you know, for the photographer."

"I see."

That was it, no soothing words, no "it'll be alright," just an "I see." Somehow, to Sarah, it felt worse. She decided that he must have been drunk.

"Don't worry, it won't happen again," she snapped. She watched annoyance flash over his beautiful face. He huffed a bit, then turned to stare out of the window for the rest of the journey, while Sarah busied herself sending an email, mainly so that she didn't have to speak to him. She was cross with herself for breaking her own rules and allowing an asshole actor to get too close. She was also still open to the possibility that he might be gay.

James, meanwhile, was wondering why Sarah's boss would think their kiss was just for show. He made a mental note to give Dan Laker a call and make sure her job was safe. Dan was a decent guy, but a bit forgetful when it came to passing on messages.

They drove along in silence until Bob pulled up outside the offices and slid out of the car. "You memorised those questions?" Sarah asked, never really trusting actors to put the grunt work in, as in her experience, most of them were lazy buggers.

"Of course I have," he replied. "I always do my homework."

They walked into the Heat offices, their bodies at least three feet apart and a chill wind blowing between them. Sarah knew a few of the journalists there, as she'd often accompanied actors to their interviews and photo shoots, and PR was a fairly small world. "Sarah," squealed an excited, rather high pitched voice. "I knew it was you in those pics! Am I allowed to name you? It's only a matter of time before someone does."

They turned to see Susie Delaney beaming a smile. Sarah and she had known each other since uni, and they were quite good friends. "Hi Suze, can we have a coffee after this interview? I need to give it some thought." Sarah said, causing James to frown.

"Sure. You know where my office is. See you in a bit." She flashed a smile at James, then trotted off in her impossibly high Manolos.

"So are you gonna let her name you?" James muttered as they waited for the lift.

"Probably, with some edits. I can do damage limitation if she's on side," Sarah replied.

He looked quizzical. "Damage limitation? What can possibly be damaging about two people going out for dinner and kissing goodnight?" Annoyance flashed across his face again. She wondered why.

"I'm your handler, in case you hadn't noticed. I'm paid to fetch and carry, organise stuff, wipe your nose, and supply you with anything you need. I can be your pimp, your dealer, and your fixer. What I can't be is 'involved.'" Sarah kept her voice low, aware that they were in the offices of rapacious journalists.

He frowned and looked thoughtful for a moment. As the lift doors opened, he flashed his movie star smile, "Oh, yes you can."

Before she could answer, he was shaking hands with his

interviewer, the infamous Greg O'Brian. He was one of the most militant gay men Sarah had ever met, part of the activist scene in London. She groaned inwardly, knowing full well it would be a tricky interview, as he liked to constantly promote his gay agenda.

They were filming it for their website, as well as transcribing it for the magazine. James was shown to a chair set in front of a Heat-branded backdrop. He sat quietly while a makeup artist brushed some powder over his forehead and nose. Sarah prayed that Greg would go easy on him.

"And here we have the Titanium Rod himself, James Morell, everyone," Greg began, shaking James's hand. The first few questions were easy enough. Greg was sticking to his script and not causing any problems. Sarah began to relax.

"So James, the costume. It was quite a departure from the ones in the comic books?"

"Yes, the team decided on an updated version, to reflect a more modern-day outlook and utilise the most advanced modern materials." Sarah glanced at Greg's assistant's clipboard, to see that additional questions had been put in. She frowned at James.

"Did you have to wear a sock?"

She could see his confusion, "I'm sorry, what do you mean, 'a sock'?"

"To fill out the latex bit of the suit." Greg started laughing at his own puerile joke. He gestured towards James's crotch.

"No, man," snapped James, visibly annoyed.

Sarah stepped in. "That wasn't on the list of questions, Greg." She snatched the clipboard from his assistant's hand and scanned it. "Nor was 'are you gay?', 'Who were you with last night?', or 'How much did you make last year?'" She was furious, but James just seemed amused at it all.

"Sarah, stop being such a control freak. They're the things people wanna know, not 'what is the Titanium suit made of?'" Greg drawled, not taking her terribly seriously. She saw red.

"Interview's over," she announced. "If you can't be trusted when I deliver our top talent to you, Greg, then you won't get any more exclusives." Greg sat up straighter, clearly annoyed at being challenged.

"Very feisty, Sarah. Think I might just have to do some naming and shaming this afternoon, although it pains me to participate in a bearding exercise," he snapped, rather spitefully.

"Right, that's it," said James, pulling off his microphone. "I'm not listening to you talking to her like that. You don't have my permission to use the footage."

Greg put up his hands in a gesture of surrender. "OK, I'll stick to the script. Just thought your fans would like some juicier questions. You've told the same Cosmic Warrior stories over and over." James shot him a disdainful look and walked out, with Sarah close behind.

She struggled to keep up in her heels, as he stomped down the corridor to the lift. "Will you slow down?" She called out.

He turned to face her, fury written all over his lovely face, which for some strange reason simply changed it from boyishly handsome to dangerous and rugged. "Sarah, I'm gonna go home for a while and cool down. I suggest you go do your 'damage limitation' with your friend. I'll see you later on."

"You haven't got anything else scheduled for today. Just call me if you need anything. Otherwise I'll see you tomorrow at ten for the 'Men's Health' shoot."

"Fine," he barked, before pushing through the stairwell doors, clearly not wanting to share an elevator. Sarah sighed. She didn't blame him for being angry. Greg had been totally out of order. She watched him stride away, his sturdy, broad shoulders stiff with tension, as the doors swung closed behind him.

She made her way down to Susie's office, only to find Greg sitting in there looking a bit shamefaced. "I've already told her what happened," he began, "to save you the aggravation of going through it all again."

"Why did you just do that?" She demanded. "You know full well Premier Artists and Laker Brothers won't let you within fifty feet of any of their stars again once they hear about this."

"I wasn't necessarily going to ask those questions," he bleated. "I was gonna gauge how chatty he was, and if he'd loosened up enough, maybe slip one or two in." Sarah didn't believe a word of it.

"You practically asked him if he's got a small dick," she spat. "That was totally inappropriate, and you knew it."

Greg stared at the floor, in no doubt as to how much he'd screwed up. Eventually, Susie spoke. "It's done now. We'll scrap the tape. Do you want us to do some strategic identification of you regarding those pictures?" She was holding out an olive branch.

Having them owing a favour could be very advantageous. Sarah decided to milk it for all it was worth.

"Please. Something along the lines of me being a secretary, and it was a first date." She turned to Greg, "Think you can manage that? If this is controlled, I might just be able to talk James out of mentioning this whole sorry affair to his agent. Capiche?" He nodded.

"We'll get to work on it straightaway. Just be aware that he's got some fans that'll be jealous no matter what. We can get the interns to monitor the forums and try and calm down any rabid posts, but ultimately a lot of women are gonna be pretty envious." Susie was blunt and to the point. They all knew how it worked, and that there was the distinct possibility she'd be ripped apart. If she was correctly identified, it could damage James too and cause the gay rumours to resurface.

"Did you know you were being photographed?" Greg asked.

Sarah shook her head. "Neither of us did."

"So, this thing, with you and James…"

"It's not a thing," she snapped, interrupting him. "I barely know him. We just both had too much to drink, that's all. It won't happen again."

"Now that would be a shame," Greg smirked. "Every man, woman, and beast would want to jump that particular set of bones. Is he a good kisser?"

"Like I'd tell you," She said, throwing him a disdainful look. If it hadn't been for the fact that Greg's talent in life was steering the gossip blogs and being the front man for the biggest one in the world, she'd have cheerfully stuck two fingers up, and refused to ever deal with the idiot again. At least he owed her one, and with the threat of not allowing access to some of Hollywood's top actors ever again, he would behave himself with her for a while. The three of them spent the following hour drafting a press release.

They decided that she'd be portrayed as a naive secretary who had caught James's eye and he'd taken her out on a first date. Since his arrival in the UK had been well documented, it would be perfectly believable. Greg kept all the details about Sarah deliberately vague, while appearing to have tracked her down like a bloodhound. They hoped that by giving up a little bit of info, they could throw the more rabid fans off the scent and satisfy the more rational ones. Her heart was in her throat when he pressed the button to make it live.

Back in the office, Sarah checked the gossip sites, and set up some Google alerts. She watched the aftermath of Greg gently outing her, portraying her as a sweet little secretary, upon whom James had set his sights. She read through the comments, wincing at the ones stating that, in their opinion, James could do better, and smiling at the ones that thought she looked like a nice girl, and prettier than his previous girlfriend. Nobody appeared to have discovered that she was his fixer, which would have been a PR disaster. She was interrupted by her phone ringing. She glanced at the screen and saw that it was James.

"You let that pillock name you in the press?" He said, without preamble.

"Yes, in return for ripping up that tape, a grovelling apology, and a promise never to pull a stunt like that again," she told him. "Greg's an influential blogger. He's spinning this for me and hopefully squashing it quickly before it becomes a big deal. Did you tell anyone what happened this afternoon?" She held her breath.

"Not yet, why?"

"Because it would really do me a big favour if you didn't," she told him. "It's also in your own best interests. If it gets out that I work for you, all the 'closet accusations' will rear their ugly little heads again. This way we're both being protected."

"Machiavellian little thing aren't you?" James was impressed.

"That's why I'm a fixer," Sarah replied. "Keeping a lid on stuff is what I do best." She could hear bleeps telling her that she had other calls coming through, but she ignored them. "Are you out tonight?" She asked, snapping back into professional mode.

"No. Why?"

"Just wondered if I needed to put Bob on stand-by, that's all." She'd never had a charge not need anything for a whole afternoon and evening. Stars just didn't sit at home by themselves for any length of time, at least not the ones Sarah was used to looking after.

"Are you out?" He couldn't help himself, it just blurted from his mouth.

"No. I need to do some chores. If I'm not needed, I'll take a night off."

Sarah could almost hear his smile down the phone. "I'll see what I can come up with. Wouldn't want your little charge getting himself into trouble, now would you?" His voice took on a sexy, purring quality, which lightened his threat to find something to keep her busy, and away from the ironing she really needed to get done. In spite of herself, she smiled.

"I'll see you later on," he purred, before ending the call. Sarah sat, dazed for a few minutes, before her phone ringing jolted her out of her daydream.

The calls continued all afternoon. Sarah pulled in every favour she'd ever been owed to keep the celeb sites on her side. In a lot of respects, it did James a huge favour, putting him at the top of almost every celebrity gossip site. It also fully squashed the Datalounge brigade, with their shrill accusations that he was closeted. As long as her real identity was concealed, it was a pretty decent result all round.

James was also sitting in front of his laptop, watching the proceedings from his kitchen, where he had been taking out his frustration on some steak. He had to hand it to her, she was a great fixer and seemed to be handling everything flawlessly. Like most celebrities, he loved being big news, so being on the front page of the big five celebrity gossip blogs at the same time sent a thrill through him. Portraying her as a sweet little secretary had been genius, as it gave even the most fanatical of his followers a sort of false hope that one day they too could be that "normal" girl he'd date.

In his opinion, Sarah was anything but "normal," having handled a difficult and potentially damaging situation with great judgement and aplomb, on a par with some of the best, most sought after fixers in the movie world. After allowing himself a few moments to daydream about having a partner whose sole purpose in life was to smooth his over, he set about devising a way to get her alone and off guard. He had a standard seduction technique that had never failed him, so with that in mind, he set about making his signature dish...

Sarah was exhausted by the time she walked through her front door. She kicked off her heels and threw down her handbag. The house seemed too silent and lonely, so she switched on the TV and flicked the channel onto the news. The noise was comforting, reminding her that she wasn't alone in the world, as she knocked up some beans on toast. She didn't have much food in and no wine at all. Her organisational skills seemed to run out when it came to her own wellbeing. She sat down to eat, when she heard her handbag chirp. Pulling her phone out, her tummy flipped when she saw it was a text from James.

Are you free this evening?

She immediately texted back, ***Yes, is there something you need?*** praying he wasn't just after some work-related item, or worse still, an escort. It was at that moment Sarah realised that she wanted him to want her. She held her breath as she stared at her phone, willing him to reply, her food forgotten about. After a few moments, it chirped again. Her hands shook slightly as she opened the text.

I'd like to see you. Can you come over?

She replied; ***Sure, just let me quickly eat, and I'll be there.***

She looked at her sad plate of beans, the toast going soggy from the juice. ***Don't eat, I'll cook***

She didn't need asking twice. It took her only ten minutes to have a quick shower, throw on some clean clothes, and fly out the door, all thoughts of chores forgotten. She wanted that man, and it was starting to dawn on her that he wanted her too.

During the taxi ride over, her confidence began to wane slightly. That little voice in her head warned against getting too excited, goading her that he was still an asshole actor, and was probably just a bit bored on his own. By the time she'd got there, she'd convinced herself that it was probably just a work thing, and he wanted some scheduling organised, or a kind ear to listen as he ran through a script. He was starting filming the following week, so he probably had pages of lines to learn. Sarah mentally chided herself for dropping everything and racing over, even though it was her job.

It was one of the myriad reasons she'd never got involved with any of her charges. She had no choice but to see them and respond when they clicked their fingers. If you threw in the awkwardness of a one night stand, it would make her job a million times more difficult.

Meanwhile, James was lowering the lights, checking on dinner, and opening some wine. For all his affable, easy-going exterior, he was a determined man, who, once his mind was set, would go all out to achieve an objective. He hadn't become one of the most successful and highly paid actors in Hollywood for nothing. In fact, his drive and ambition were almost legendary.

Sarah's taxi pulled up outside, and she scanned the street for nosy neighbours or stalking fans. Satisfied that she wasn't being watched, she paid the driver and hopped out. She scuttled up the path to discover James waiting at the door, beaming a wide smile. "Thanks for coming," he said. The sight of him in just jeans and a tight, white T-shirt caused her tummy to flip.

"No problem at all," she said as she followed him through to the kitchen, where she was surprised to discover that he'd cooked for them both. Sarah sipped some wine as he dished up pasta, meatballs, and salad. "You cooked that all from scratch?" She asked, knowing that she hadn't included ready-made ones in his food order.

He blushed slightly. "I find cooking relaxes me. I was pretty angry this afternoon, so I came back here and took it out on some steak." He watched her take a mouthful, groaning as the flavours hit her palate.

"This is gorgeous," she told him. He beamed his film-star smile at the compliment.

"I'm a man of many talents," he murmured. Sarah's belly squeezed at the inference, before she mentally shook herself and resolved to get a grip. "I have a lot of other tricks up my sleeve," he purred, fully aware of the flush working its way up her neck as she tried not to imagine what those other "talents" could possibly be. Just seeing her reaction pleased him inordinately.

While Sarah was trying to get her blush under control, she stole a glance at his hands, wrapped around his glass of wine. His fingers were long but strong-looking, not slender like a piano player or feminine in any way, just enough to give her the impression that he was a dexterous individual. Her belly squeezed again, and she felt the heat rise back up her neck. Sarah tried not to look at him, concentrating on her salad.

They chatted about her "outing" on the gossip sites that afternoon, with James confessing that he'd been reading what had been written. "That must be quite weird, having people watch your every move. It'd drive me nuts. It's why I've never wanted to be famous," She told him, glad the conversation was back on safer ground. She got her blush back under control.

"I don't know if I'll ever get used to it. I just regard it as the downside of my job. I always feel sorry for the woman I'm with though, because every detail is scrutinised, everything criticised."

"Someone on IMDB said I had 'man hands'," Sarah sniffed, "I wasn't too impressed with that assessment." He laughed and grabbed one of her hands across the table, examining it closely. Compared to his, hers looked tiny.

"You have beautiful hands. Delicate and pretty, there's nothing manly about them," he said, keeping hold of it. Sarah left it there, enjoying the sensation of his skin on hers. He smiled tentatively, and took a sip of wine. "You shouldn't ever be bothered about the opinions of people on the Internet. They'd criticise even if you were a top supermodel. Even I get pulled apart if I take a mildly squinty picture."

"Does that ever happen though?" She teased.

"Absolutely. I get accused of being bald if my hair's gone a bit fluffy, and anytime I've been snapped looking mildly cheesed off is interpreted as my closeted lifestyle getting on top of me. Nobody would ever believe it's because I got a parking ticket or missed a call."

"Well, I'm hoping they'll all shut up about me soon," she said, although glancing down at their entwined hands, it didn't appear that he was giving up anytime soon.

"My last two girlfriends couldn't cope with it. After a while they got paranoid and upset at all the vicious comments. At least you're in the business and understand what to expect."

Sarah reeled at his statement. It sounded as though he thought she'd be girlfriend material. She wondered if she was reading too much into it. "I'm not usually on that side of the camera though. I'm normally the one steering the gossip. I'm not sure about being on the receiving end." She gently pulled her hand away and continued eating.

"They were both actresses, used to scrutiny, but neither of them had the strength of character to deal with it," he mused. "I can tell you're a very grounded, intelligent woman." James smiled tentatively at her.

During the meal, Sarah thought about the prospect of losing her privacy. Being with someone like James would mean having the whole world watching her every move, which was a fairly serious downside, given that she'd seen up close the effects lack of anonymity could have on a person.

"I'm sure you've spent today weighing it all up carefully," he said. "I've seen firsthand what a detail-orientated person you are.

I'm certain you know exactly what you're doing to me. You already know how far you want to take this."

He seemed momentarily unsure, vulnerable even. As perfect and beautiful as he was, Sarah realised he was still a man, with all the normal emotions everybody experiences. It was his version of pursuing her, albeit in his strange, restricted world.

"I wouldn't be here if I didn't want to be." She said it to reassure him, even though it wasn't strictly true. Her job was to jump to his demands, although she'd never had a client want to get closer or request THAT before.

After eating, they took their wine glasses and the remainder of the bottle into the sitting room. James pressed play on his sound system, and the strains of Adele singing that she "nearly had it all," softly filled the room. Sarah sat down on the large, squashy sofa. James sat next to her, tucking his feet underneath himself and turning to face her. His close proximity seemed to have its usual effect, making her feel slightly light-headed.

"So what's my agenda for tomorrow?" He asked, snapping Sarah out of her dream-like daze and back into work mode.

"Bob's picking you up at seven for your training, then the Men's Health shoot in Clerkenwell directly afterwards. You have dinner planned with your agent at eight tomorrow night at Nobu."

He groaned, "So that's pretty much all day taken care of. Am I diarised like that every day?"

"Yep. You're in demand at the moment. Ride it and enjoy it. You'd be more worried if you were sitting in here every day with the phone not ringing."

"I know, it just doesn't leave much time for... fun though." He traced his finger up her bare arm, sending tingles through her entire body. She shivered with the sensation. He was watching her reactions intently through hooded eyes, knowing exactly what he was doing to her. Without speaking, he leaned over to kiss her, his cool lips grazing hers, gently at first, testing her reaction, seeing if she would pull away, even the tiniest bit. He felt her whole body soften as he gently grasped her shoulder.

He deepened the kiss, his tongue meeting Sarah's in a sensual dance. She tasted of red wine and Sarah, a heady combination. She felt him tug her towards him, and his muscular, powerful arms enveloped her. He felt strong, secure, as his chest pressed against hers, overwhelming her with his masculinity. She ran her fingers through his thick curls, marvelling at how soft and luxurious they were, while their tongues engaged in an erotic dance.

Breathless, she pulled back. "We shouldn't be doing this," she murmured. "I'm your handler, and this could make things… difficult."

He smiled, "I'd never let that happen, and yes, we should be doing this… and more."

"More?" she squeaked. Even though she'd spent all day dreaming about him, when actually faced with his advances, she was terrified— well, terrified and turned on, if there was such a thing.

"Much more, everything in fact. I can't take my eyes off you Sarah, you must have noticed?" She nodded, mute. "What I want is to see your beautiful face when I make you come. I want to hear you scream my name as you lose control. I think you want me too."

Just his words, spoken in his rich, deep voice were mesmerising to her. She was desperate for him and horny beyond belief. Still mute, she nodded her assent. He'd very effectively cast his spell.

Sarah squealed as he pushed her onto her back and slid his body over hers. He nestled one leg between her shamelessly open ones, and threaded his fingers through hers, to hold her hands beside her head. She could feel his heart beating as he kissed her. Hers was thumping so hard she thought it would leap straight out of her chest. He pressed tiny kisses along her jaw before working his way back to her lips, taking his time to get fully acquainted with her soft skin and gentle perfume. James fought the urge to move too fast. He needed to make sure she was entirely helpless in the face of his seduction. With that in mind, he nibbled lightly on her lower lip, savouring the moment.

Every cell in Sarah's body seemed to ignite, as though, like Sleeping Beauty, they'd been dormant all her life and suddenly awakened. She ached for him to make love to her, to feel him inside her, and to see lust in his sparkling blue eyes.

He released her hand so he could stroke her face. He pulled back to look at her. "You are just so beautiful, so pretty," he murmured, before leaning in for another kiss. She was totally captured by his mesmerising presence. He ran his hand down her side, over her ribs in firm, confident strokes, culminating in him cupping her breast. *'Hmm, so James is a breast man,'* she thought.

The Fixer

He shifted slightly, making her aware of the hardness encased in his jeans. Sarah marvelled that she could have such an effect on him, as she felt the heat radiating off him in waves. She breathed in his lovely scent. He smelt of fresh water and body wash, subtle but unique. His kisses became more urgent as his hands roamed over her. "I really want to make love to you," he murmured between kisses.

"We shouldn't," she breathed. "I'm supposed to be working for you."

He pulled away, leaving her momentarily bereft. He kneeled upright, gazing down at her. "Is there any rule against it?" he asked, his voice more normal.

Sarah shook her head, "Not as such, no, but…"

He cut her off. "Do you want it?" She didn't answer, too nervous to make the decision. "Do you want to feel me inside you, pleasuring you until you come?"

Sarah nodded, too nervous to speak. She was soaked, and her clit was throbbing so hard it hurt. She knew she'd kick herself for the rest of her life if she turned down James Morell. "I'm scared," she admitted.

"You're only scared because you know that I'm gonna turn your world upside down," he stated. He was confident to the point of cocky. Unfortunately he was also right.

CHAPTER 4

Anna

Anna uploaded the photos of their holiday to Facebook first, then Instagram, before finally tweeting a few to her Twitter followers. She sat back and waited for the likes and comments to come flooding in. A lot of her online friends were members of the extreme hunting online community, and more locally, her gym buddies and fellow church members all hunted too. She knew they'd be impressed that a glamorous little blonde could handle a high-powered hunting rifle.

"Anna, I'm home," yelled her dad as he walked through the door. "We're going to Matt and Jen's for dinner tonight, so you need to start getting ready."

"OK," she shouted, taking one last glance at the screen before closing it, thrilled to see that she'd already got forty likes and several shares on Facebook.

That evening they ate at Ricky's brother Matt's place. It was primarily so that Ricky could show off about their hunting trip, having printed off the photos so he could pass them around. Matt and his three sons all liked to hunt too, but being the less financially-successful arm of the family, had to restrict themselves to local trails and cheaper rifles. There was no way that he could pay fifty thousand dollars a head for a go at big game. Matt had often wished that Rick was a bit more generous with his money, especially after all the help they'd given when Anna was small.

Their father had left each of his sons an identical amount of land and money. Rick had developed his portion, which had made him wealthy, but he'd objected when Matt had wanted to do the same, as it would have spoilt the view from his house. Rick had always been a tricky son-of-a-bitch, and had managed to talk the church elders into renting some of Matt's land for a small sum each year. It was enough for the family to survive, but effectively scuppered any of Matt's dreams of developing his land any further.

"Can't see that shooting a giraffe is hard," sneered Nat, the youngest of Anna's cousins in that particular branch of the family. "I thought they were large and slow. I'd have been more impressed if you'd shot a gazelle."

"We were a long way away," Ricky replied. "It was no more than a pin-head in Anna's sights. You'd never have hit it."

"Well, next year we might be joining you in Africa," said Jen, serving up some hash. "Matt has some exciting news, don't you Matt?"

"Sure do. Some fancy film director's sounded me out about renting some land down in the mountains for a film shoot. They also want to rent this house for six months too. I told them three hundred thousand, and they accepted it." He puffed up his chest proudly, pleased that he'd finally got one over on Rick. His brother would have to put up with his view being disrupted for six months.

"Sounds good," said Ricky. "What film is it?"

"Cosmic Warriors 2."

Anna's belly flipped. She was waiting to see Cosmic Warriors 1 when it came out in the cinema, primarily because her favourite actor, James Morell, was the leading man. "So will the actors be staying here then?" she asked, trying to sound nonchalant. Her Uncle shook his head.

"I think they'll stay in town. The director, Martin, sounded out the Hubbards about hiring their entire hotel. They're holding their breath, hoping it all happens too." He turned back to Ricky, "Did you know that Illinois gives filmmakers special tax breaks?"

Ricky shook his head, rather annoyed that the director hadn't approached him too. He also guessed that the family would end up staying in his house for the duration, which would be intrusive and noisy. Anna didn't notice her father's less-than-impressed mood, too excited about the prospect of meeting James Morell. If she was really smart, she figured, she'd be able to position herself to be in daily contact with him. She needed to get home and start her research in order to be ready for his arrival in a few months.

The rest of the evening crawled past interminably slowly. Her aunt seemed to be clearing away the dinner things at a snail's pace, taking her time fetching the crockery for Anna to wash up. Rick was in no hurry either, as he was happily regaling the boys with tales of Africa, especially after bagging a large lion for his trophy room by bribing the guides to lure it away from the reserve and into the bush, where he'd eventually killed it.

That night, Anna drew up a plan of action to put her into direct contact with James Morell. She would join the gym she felt he would most likely use, then get a job there. The other option would be working at the Hubbard's hotel, which she really didn't fancy, as domestic labour wasn't her thing. Old man Hubbard had a reputation at their church for being a dirty old man with wandering hands, and there'd even been rumours that he'd gotten a young girl pregnant before she'd mysteriously disappeared. The church elders had smoothed it over, but people had still gossiped.

She sat up till two in the morning researching the gyms where Mr Morell had previously trained, whom they were affiliated with, and their methods. She discovered that only staff were ever allowed contact with celebrities, as generally the gyms he'd used had to close to the public while he was in attendance. It meant that she needed to get a job, as opposed to the occasional cardio class she helped out with when the regular staff at her country club were on vacation or off sick. Despite Rick spending thousands on courses for her, Anna had never felt the urge to work full time, or even study particularly hard. Girls in their church married young and had families in order to create more little Soldiers of the Illinois Pentecost and carry on their good work.

It wasn't a community that everyone understood. It was more low-key than the Mormons, less extreme than the Amish, and didn't cause controversy like the Westboro lot. The Soldiers were good, God-fearing folk who worshiped every Sunday at church, read the Bible, and believed that the good Lord, Jesus, would save them from the Reptilian shape-shifters currently controlling the U.S. government, who'd been sent by the Anti-Christ himself. The Soldiers prepared themselves for the coming battle against the Reptilians and the aftermath of the struggle, as they expected food, weapons, and ammunition to be in short supply.

As good soldiers, they were expected to master all the survivalist skills which would be needed to repopulate the planet after Armageddon. Anna had excelled in the hunting and shooting classes, although her mastery of agriculture had left a bit to be desired. As with all the other preppers, they had a bunker filled with food, ammunition, and guns underneath their yard, which Ricky checked and added to on a weekly basis.

CHAPTER 5

Sarah

Sarah was shaking as James led her upstairs to his bed, not because she didn't want what was about to happen— she wanted it badly; wanted him. She was terrified, afraid of being naked in front of him, and worried about being gauche or clumsy.

He could sense her reticence, so he took total control of her. He undressed her slowly, caressing each piece of newly-exposed skin, kissing her all over, making sure she could see how delighted he was with everything he uncovered. He paid a lot of attention to her nipples as he'd released them from the confines of her bra, so when he slid her knickers down her legs, she was fully prepared for him to touch her. She wasn't entirely prepared for him to do it with his tongue though. He lapped at her greedily, taking her to the edge of an orgasm, before stopping abruptly, causing Sarah to whimper her frustration. He knew exactly what he was doing to her as he pulled away, his face glistening with her juices.

"My turn," he murmured, as he began to undress. Sarah watched mutely as each item came off. She knew that he had a finely-toned body, as there were enough shirtless pictures of him published. She was totally unprepared for the first sight of him naked. In her opinion, the angels must have blessed him the moment he was conceived, as he was male perfection, better than a Greek god. He smirked at her shocked expression, as it wasn't the first time a woman had gazed at him in total awe.

James was glad he'd gotten her ready, making sure that Sarah was wet and unbearably horny as he nudged his large, wide cock into her. It wouldn't have fitted unless he'd prepared her first, as it was the largest she'd ever experienced. It filled her totally, with that delicious stretching sensation that only a well-built man can inflict. He groaned as her body enveloped him, pausing a moment to let her get used to his size. He started to move, gently at first, then Sarah heard her disembodied voice shamelessly begging him to go faster. "Your wish is my command," he murmured in his deep sultry voice, as he slammed into her, each thrust pushing her further into oblivion. All concerns about him being a client were firmly shoved out of Sarah's head, as she gave herself over to the pleasure he was inflicting.

He took total control of her body, making love with both passion and tenderness, alternating between taking her hard and fast, then slowly, wringing maximum pleasure from her. He was more sexually confident than she was. He showed her exactly what her body was capable of, taking her to heights she'd never before experienced, riding her through her orgasm, prolonging it to the point that a fresh one rolled through her, causing her to arch off the bed.

"Suck me," he'd demanded, only to see Sarah scramble to her knees and cram his engorged cock into her mouth. She hadn't questioned or hesitated. He only let her suck for a few minutes before grasping her shoulders and pushing her back onto the bed to plunge into her again, causing her to scream as another orgasm tore through her.

For James, it was a dream come true. Sarah was the sexiest, most sensual woman he'd ever experienced. Her willingness to please, her languid touch, and her absolute submission to him sexually was an enormous turn-on.

As her climax began to subside, he sped up before pressing in deep and letting go. His perfect, sculptured lips parted in a groan. Even his "O" face was beautiful. He slumped onto her chest for a moment before lifting his head to kiss her deeply, a tender, grateful kiss which felt to Sarah as though it was a thank you, which in a lot of ways, it was.

James's heart was hammering in his chest as he lay down beside her, propped up on his elbow, his free hand casually stroking her tummy. "I knew we'd be good together," he murmured, before planting another, more chaste, kiss on her lips.

"That was... amazing," Sarah managed to say. She was rewarded with a smile.

"For a first time," he added. "The next one will be even better, now that we're intimately acquainted."

James saw her belly squeeze at the thought of doing it again. "Still horny are you? I do like a greedy girl." His hands slid down to the apex of her thighs, making her jump. In a moment of bravery, Sarah grasped his dick, and was astonished to discover that it was as hard as titanium, despite his orgasm only five minutes before.

He groaned as she took his nipple into her mouth, flicking it with her tongue until it formed a tight little bead on his hard, muscular pecs. She proceeded to kiss her way over his taut stomach, and slowly down his happy trail, moving his massive erection aside so that she could press wet kisses right down to the base and over his balls. Sarah wanted to kiss every inch of him, taste every part of his finely-honed body. In her opinion, she would never find a more perfect specimen of manhood, so she was determined to make the very most of him while she could.

He gasped as she took his cock into her mouth and sucked gently on the tip. she ran her tongue over every part of it, licking the satiny-soft skin, tasting the beads of pre-cum that leaked out of him. He watched her, spellbound.

She felt him writhe, so sucked more greedily, running her lips rhythmically up and down the shaft, taking him in as deeply as she could, relishing the pleasure she was inflicting on him. Hearing and feeling how much she pleased him was intoxicating to Sarah. To her, at that point, he was a supreme alpha male, a man so perfect that the rest of womankind worshipped his beauty from afar.

He growled before she felt him grasp her shoulders and lift her on top of him, giving her the impression that he found her weightless. Sarah was wet and horny when his cock slipped into her, hitting her sweet spot. As they began to move, she watched him struggle to hold back as he thrust into her, his cock rubbing repeatedly over her G-spot. It became frenzied fast-fucking, the sort that is led purely by animal instinct.

Sarah was utterly helpless when her orgasm hit, tearing its way through her body, relentlessly shaking her to the core. James came about thirty seconds later, holding her hips still in a vice-like grip, pressing her down onto him. In the soft lamplight, his beauty was otherworldly. Sarah drank in the sight of him in ecstasy, trying to memorise the moment.

He made love to her four times that night in total, in four different positions. He teased her with his tongue and fingers until she begged for him to salve the ache she had for him. There were little interludes between, where they would recover, just talking and sharing thoughts and secrets about their lives, both fighting to stay awake in case the night ended. "Tell me your deepest, darkest secret," he'd implored her. She'd thought for a moment.

"I nicked five pounds off my dad once and spent it on cigarettes. Trying to be part of the 'in crowd' at school."

He laughed. "What happened?"

"I smoked one and promptly threw up all over the boy I liked's shoes. It wasn't my finest hour," she admitted. "Tell me yours."

He debated whether to tell her about the cult he'd been part of for a while, but dismissed the idea. It was an episode of his life that he was deeply ashamed of. "I used to blame my brother for eating the sweets," he said. "Mum used to get them for only one of my brothers. I wasn't allowed them, so I used to steal them and blame Jonathan. She didn't punish him as much as he was smaller and cuter."

"Why did she only buy them for one of you?" Sarah asked.

"It was just the way she was. The oldest two were grown up and Miles was her favourite. Apparently I was an accident and Jonathan was her 'last chance' baby. I think I was the only unwanted one."

"That's such a shame," Sarah said, squeezing him a little tighter. She kept her horror at his admission to herself.

As the light began to peek through the blinds, Sarah dozed off in his arms.

She was awakened rather abruptly by the shrill ring of a mobile. She opened her eyes to see a pair of twinkly blue ones gazing into hers. James was ignoring the phone too, mainly due to being comfortable and warm, wrapped around each other, their legs entwined, as though they just couldn't get close enough. "It's probably Bob," he said, making no move to untangle himself.

"Shouldn't you answer?"

"He'll be banging on the door in ten minutes," he said before sighing loudly and snuggling back into her. He nuzzled her neck, growling softly. Sarah was torn between being the professional nag and the bad influence. She rolled the concept through her mind for a few moments, while revelling in the sensation of his lips on her skin.

"You need to get up," she reminded him, although she was rather enjoying the cuddle. He groaned and rolled onto his back, annoyed that morning had come so quickly. It seemed that Sarah wasn't throwing off her professional duties even for a day.

"You're right. Can you make sure we're both free this evening? I want to see you." He swung his legs out of bed. Sarah gaped again.

"What are you staring at?" He asked, smirking.

"You. Mr Male Perfection." She ogled him shamelessly as he pulled on his track suit and a vest. He sat on the bed to pull on his socks and trainers, wondering why she was so quiet.

"You didn't answer my question about tonight," he pointed out.

"You're meeting your agent at Nobu, remember?" Sarah reminded him. He pulled a face.

"Book an extra place then. You can come with me."

"I'm not usually present when people meet their agents," she told him, which was broadly true, although she spoke frequently to his agent while diarising.

"Well, you will be tonight. I'd also like you to check my schedule and book us both a weekend off together. I want some time alone with you." He leaned over to plant a soft, chaste kiss at the corner of her mouth. "I'll be finished with this workout in about two hours. I'll see you back here?" He sounded unsure, as though worried that she'd disappear.

"I need to go home, shower, and get ready. You have a photoshoot at eleven."

"I'll pick you up from yours at nine. We can get some breakfast before we go."

With that, he blew her a kiss and was gone. Sarah heard the front door slam, and him saying good morning to Bob. She glanced at the clock; it was seven in the morning. They'd had two hours' sleep. He'd looked amazing. She knew she'd look a wreck.

James sat back in the car to eat a banana and a protein drink, and thought about their night together. Sarah had been a revelation. Her soft, smooth skin, her perfect curves, and her gentle, sensual nature had all been better than he'd imagined. Her feminine, submissive manner was, in his opinion, the perfect wrapping of a fierce intellect and a quick wit. He turned to Bob; "How well do you know Sarah?"

The Fixer

"Well enough. We've worked on quite a few assignments together... Why?" Bob replied.

"What's she like?"

"In general? She's alright. Bit uptight about deadlines, but she's very efficient," he said, before turning his attention to getting a parking space right outside Equinox. "There you go. What time shall I pick you up?"

"Eight-ten please," said James, who was resigned to meeting another new trainer, who no doubt would want to push him to the limit, just to say he'd made the famous James Morell puke. He accepted that maintaining his physique was part of the job, but on that particular morning, he just wasn't feeling it. His heart sank when an overly-muscled meat-head in lycra tights and a cropped vest strutted over.

"Hi, I'm Rod. You must be James?"

James nodded.

"I don't know what pussies have been training you up till now, but your biceps need to be a lot bigger. You'd better prepare to be trained by a proper professional." Rod stood in a superior stance, with his arms crossed against his inflated chest and a sneer on his face. James wanted to roll his eyes. Every trainer he'd come across was the same, all thinking they could make a name for themselves by pumping him up like a steroid-inflated bodybuilder.

"I've had some great trainers, thanks," he muttered. "I'm sure you must've been emailed my routine." He prayed that Sarah hadn't forgotten it.

"Yes, but there's some changes I'd like to make," Rod began.

"No changes," James snapped. "You can just spot for me on the bench press if you're not willing to implement my normal workout." He stared Rod straight in the eye, daring him to object. Chastened, Rod nodded.

"Follow me please. The weight room is through here."

Back at James's house, Sarah made herself a coffee to get herself moving, and pulled on her rather wrinkled clothes. Sipping at her drink, she walked around the house, checking it out. She actually did what every self-respecting woman would have done in that situation-- she had a good snoop.

After raking through some drawers, through his wardrobes, and looking under his bed, she had to concede that it was all rather disappointing. James didn't seem to have lots of "stuff." She found some family photos, but that was about it. Sarah also discovered that his laptop was password-protected, and wasn't going to give up its secrets easily. Aware that she was crossing into stalker territory, she closed the lid.

After a short time, she gave up, hopped into a taxi, and went home to get ready and try and cover up the lack of sleep evident on her face. As she showered, she thought about what she'd done, namely broken her own, and possibly her employer's, rules about getting involved with a client. The truth of it was that she didn't actually care.

James and Bob picked her up shortly after nine. A copious amount of Touche Éclat had covered up her lack of sleep pretty successfully, so she didn't feel too bad. James smiled warmly as she joined him in the back of the car, surreptitiously squeezing her hand as she said hello.

They were dropped off outside a little café in Clerkenwell, opposite the studios where James had his shoot. "Bob didn't suspect a thing," he told her as they sat down. "I'd rather not have to keep this secret, but I can understand you wanting to be discreet." His gaze was steady, sincere. Personally, he'd have liked to shouted from the rooftops that he'd found his Aphrodite, but ultimately it would have to be her choice.

"Just for now," she replied. "It's all very new, and if I'm just a little summer fling, I'd rather it wasn't discussed all over the world."

His stomach sank. "Why would you think it's just a fling? Did you not think last night was special?" He wondered how many other movie stars had gotten their hands on her.

Sarah thought about it. "It was incredible. You were incredible. I just want to take it a day at a time. I don't normally get involved with my charges. It's all a bit new to me."

"You've never had a night of passion with any of Hollywood's famous Lotharios?" He was incredulous. She shook her head. "Not even DiCaprio?"

"He was a typical star. Had me racing round all over London, sourcing obscure foodstuffs, and Ayurvedic yoghurt. Drove me mental. There's no way on God's green earth I'd have jumped into bed with him. Anyway, to him I was just 'staff'."

"So if I'd have asked for posh yoghurt, I'd have been ruled out?" He was grinning at her, relieved he hadn't asked her to find Spirulina pannacotta, which he'd been eating in LA.

"Yeah, probably." Sarah smiled back.

They were interrupted by a bored-looking waitress, who perked up immediately when she recognised James. After taking their order and having a photo taken of her and James with her mobile, she disappeared with a dreamy smile on her face. *'You don't know the half of it,'* Sarah thought, rather smugly, her mind wandering back to the early hours.

"What about Fassbender?" James asked, dragging her from her erotic thoughts.

"Too much of a nelly. Used more skincare than I do, and moaned about 'draughts' in his hotel room."

"Clooney?"

"Too old. He's the same age as my dad."

"Bomer? He's a heartthrob." James knew he was fishing, but he wanted to know.

"Likes the boys."

"So I was honoured then?" He was grinning again.

"Yep. I'm a fussy cow."

"I'm glad. So was I your first actor?" He held his breath.

"Yes, you are. And I'm glad too. I have no desire to be known as a Hollywood groupie."

He beamed his devastating smile at her, which was like looking at the surface of the sun, totally dazzling, and released the breath he was holding.

Sarah found it hard to believe that this beautiful man wanted her as much as she wanted him, but after experiencing a night of his lovemaking, she was almost ready to accept that they had something special between them. Something in him called to her on a deeper level than just his extraordinary good looks. It was more like a recognition that somehow they should be entwined. She tried to shake that thought and concentrate on her bagel, noting that the waitress was hovering with the coffee pot far more than was necessary. James didn't notice, Sarah figured he was probably used to it.

The photo shoot went without a hitch. James was patient and accommodating, and he simply followed the photographer's instructions without complaint. He was well-practiced at modelling, and always found that following the photographer's instructions got the shoot over with much quicker than trying to interfere. It gave Sarah ample opportunity to just ogle him and drink in his lovely features. She also used some of the time to get on with some work, returning calls and emails, and sorting out his schedule. He was in massive demand, but she managed to block out a weekend in early July for them both, before they flew out to Rome.

Thankfully, they sped through the shoot quickly, which meant they had time for a little lunch in a small bistro nearby. Afterwards, James went home to read through some scripts, and Sarah managed to get a few chores done in her own house before getting ready to go out that night.

It felt strange to Sarah to be alone. In a short time she'd become comfortable around James in a way she'd never done with previous clients. They shared a similar sense of humour as well as similar backgrounds. It felt as though she'd known him forever. It kind of worried her. She was used to being a single girl, unencumbered in life. Falling in love wasn't on her agenda, but she found herself thinking about him constantly as she Hoovered through her little house and did her laundry.

James's agent, Alan, was a nondescript, middle-aged man with grey hair and a bit of a weight issue. His only extraordinary feature was his personality. He was jovial, entertaining, and charismatic as he chatted throughout their meal. Even the normally dour waiters were charmed, and brought them out little "extras" to taste. Sarah had spoken to him a few times on the phone when organising James's diary, but after meeting him in the flesh, she was utterly charmed.

James was relaxed in his company, and listened intently to the myriad offers which had come forth following his Cosmic Warriors appearance, including one to model underwear for Calvin Klein, which impressed Sarah. Alan counselled him on which jobs to accept, and which to turn down, as they would conflict with his "clean, wholesome" image. James's career was clearly going strong, Alan was a safe pair of hands.

"So Sarah," he boomed. "You're the young lady I saw on all the gossip sites the other day? Lovely photos by the way. Not giving you too hard a time I hope?" He sounded genuinely concerned.

"Apart from the accusation of having 'man hands,' they've been quite kind, although it is all being tightly controlled at the moment. I was owed enough favours to get a lot of the celeb sites on side." Sarah replied, surprised that he'd remembered. The fans had thankfully forgotten, having been adeptly steered onto other subjects by some fake accounts she'd created for the purpose.

"Excellent. I have to say, you make a stunning couple. Let's just hope they leave the two of you alone." He turned to James, "Let's hope this one doesn't cut and run as well, eh?"

James laughed. "Sarah's made of strong stuff. I hope she doesn't run off as well."

"Treat her well Mr Morell. Good women are hard to find," said Alan, smiling broadly and giving Sarah a rather theatrical, oversized wink.

The rest of their evening was filled with good food, far too much wine, and good conversation. Sarah had really liked Alan, and he seemed to bring out the best in James, although he was a bit of a devil for plying them with alcohol. It was midnight by the time they got back to James's house. Sarah was exhausted from only two hours of sleep the night before.

"Shall I go home?" She said, as their taxi pulled onto his road.

"No way," he replied. "Are you tired?" She nodded. "Then we go to sleep and save the wild sex for the morning. I'm shattered too." He squeezed her hand and kissed her softly on the cheek. He really didn't want to sleep alone or pass up the thought of some sleepy sex. Propping each other up, the pair of them swayed as they staggered up the path to James's front door.

Within five minutes of getting back, they were snuggled up together in that delicious place between lucidity and sleep, each idly wondering how it was that they felt so comfortable in each other's arms in such a short space of time. Sarah just needed to silence the little devil whispering in her ear that it *'couldn't possibly be real. He couldn't possibly want ordinary little me, when he could have almost any woman in the world.'* She felt his heart beating as he pulled her in tighter, and she relaxed. For at least another night, he was hers.

She was awakened early by James caressing her. Having woken early, he just couldn't resist touching her after gazing at her sleeping body for what had seemed like hours. She'd looked so relaxed and peaceful that he couldn't stop himself from pressing tiny kisses down her shoulder, gently bringing her out of slumber. His silky, warm body pressed against hers, letting her feel his arousal. "Good morning," she muttered, before rolling onto her back to give him free access.

Their lovemaking was languid and sensual that morning. James wasn't in any rush as he kissed every inch of her body, revelling in the taste of her smooth skin. He slipped inside her gently, enjoying the warm, slow pace of wake-up sex before pushing her into a long, soul-shaking orgasm. He held her tight as she shuddered and shook around him, her climax going on and on. James gazed into her eyes as he finally let go, his perfect mouth forming an "O" as he pressed in deep.

"I could get used to waking up like this," he said, as she lay in his arms, comfortable and boneless. Sarah turned to face him. He had a faraway look in his eyes. A tiny part of her worried it was getting too serious, too fast, but the loudest voice in her head told her to enjoy the ride and stop worrying about the future.

"I'll need to go home to my own flat one night soon. There's stuff I need to catch up with," she told him. He snuggled in a bit closer, not wanting to let her go. He found her presence strangely soothing.

"I'll stay there with you then." It was a simple statement, but one loaded with meaning. He didn't want to be alone, but he hoped she didn't think he meant it as a random "not wishing to be by himself," like the actress she'd told him she'd babysat. It was more a declaration that he wanted to be with her as much as he could. He watched her face as she processed his words, the little V-shaped frown that appeared between her brows when she was thinking hard was adorable to him.

"Shall I make us some coffee?" he said, mainly to break the silence. He was rewarded by a beaming smile.

"Have you got time?" Sarah glanced at the clock. Bob would arrive soon.

He quickly made her a coffee before getting ready for his workout. Sarah drank it sitting up in bed watching him dress. "You should leave some clothes here," he said nonchalantly, "save you keep having to go back to your house to get ready. It's nearer to your office here."

"I'll think about it," she told him. It all just felt a bit too fast to her. She was in danger of falling head-first in love with him, knowing that he'd be leaving after the summer and heading off to Illinois to film the Cosmic Warrior sequel. He noticed she was deep in thought as he came over and wrapped his big arms around her.

"Don't overthink it, just go with the flow. Let 'us' happen

Sarah." Her eyes flicked up to his face. Amid the perfect features, she detected his concern. "I'll be forced to remind you just why you like me so much..." his voice took on a mock-stern tone. She giggled as he pushed her back onto the bed before kissing her hard; a deep, probing, needy kiss, designed to show her how much he desired her. She softened into him, moaning softly as his perfect mouth communicated with hers. They heard Bob knock on the door. "Fuck Bob," murmured James.

Sarah pushed him away gently. "I'd rather you didn't," she said. "Besides, I need to go to the office. I have a stack of stuff to take care of for you before I accompany you to your costume fitting at eleven."

"I'll come straight to your office after my workout," he said, grinning widely.

He turned up at half nine, while Sarah was on the phone. She felt him walk in before she even saw him, she was so attuned to his presence around her. He smiled and nodded as she held up a finger to indicate she'd be with him in a minute. To her horror, he used the time to introduce himself to Clive, shaking his hand warmly and asking quietly if Clive had got the memo from Danny Laker. "Yep, got it," muttered Clive, as he tried to ignore a few of the interns gazing at James in total adoration. He wondered what it was like to be that handsome, rich, and famous. He was quite certain he wouldn't be chasing around after a fixer when he could have supermodels falling at his feet, even though he thought Sarah was quite pretty.

Sarah finished her call and watched as James perched on the edge of the desk, his muscular thighs bulging nicely in his sweatpants. "Good workout?" She asked.

"I can safely say that Rod McDowell is a sadist," he said, smiling at her. "The bastard had me doing squats until my legs shook. I need a massage, otherwise I'll ache tomorrow."

"Would you like me to book one?" She asked, reaching for her phone. He shook his head.

"I know exactly who I'd like rubbing my thighs, and it's not a masseuse." He had a naughty glint in his eye. Sarah glanced around the open-plan office to see that one of the intern's mouth had dropped open.

"James, You are so... naughty," she chided, smiling despite herself. "Did you only come here to get me into trouble, or is there something you need?"

He tilted his head down and looked up at her through his long, dark lashes. It was a look that she decided to christen his naughty boy look. "We have an hour and a half before we need to be at my fitting," he whispered.

"Your point is?" She teased.

"We could…" Clive walked over into earshot at that precise moment. "Go get some breakfast while you tell me my schedule?"

"You don't have to pretend on my account, Mr Morell," said Clive. "You can cut the sexual tension between you two with a knife. All I ask is that you get some press milage out of it."

Sarah felt the blush work its way up her neck. Clive just grinned at her discomfort. All her concerns about her affair with James compromising her career melted away. She decided to allow herself to run with their budding relationship, safe in the knowledge that her career would be protected.

CHAPTER 6

Anna

Quinsville was a small, rather scruffy town deep in the remote countryside. It was hemmed in by large hills on three sides, which restricted access somewhat. The town was built in a sheltered area back when lumber was a prime commodity. Unfortunately, it had fallen on hard times when lumber prices had plummeted, which meant that the town had a rather forlorn and neglected feel. The commercial centre that Rick had built was on the opposite side of his acreage, and was pretty much self-contained, so hadn't had much effect on townsfolk who didn't work there.

Anna pulled up outside the unprepossessing industrial unit, just fifty yards away from the Hubbard's hotel. Her SUV stood out like a sore thumb, being way too shiny and new compared to the muddy and dented trucks dotted around the parking lot. She glanced up at the scruffy sign on the front of the building which said "Bart's Gym." Satisfied that she'd found the right place, she pushed open the door and made her way into the lobby.

Anna was no stranger to gyms, but being picky about her surroundings had meant she'd eschewed this rather hard-core place for a swanky fitness studio five miles away in Logan, mainly because it also had a spa and a pool. Having done her research, she was sure that James Morell would pick Bart's for his training due to one of the trainers being affiliated with the chain of gyms which trained all the Hollywood stars.

A massive, bearded man looked up from his paperwork, "Hi miss, can I help you?" He looked her up and down, appraising her well-toned figure. He thought he recognised her from church, but couldn't be totally sure as he normally sat at the back.

"Are you the owner?" Anna asked the man-mountain, trying to keep her voice light and breezy. He nodded. "I'd like to join up please," she said. "I want to try the Match-fit program." She glanced over at the huge sign above the door announcing that they offered the hard-core training regime.

"Yep, I'm Bart," the man said, grinning at her. "You're more than welcome to join up missy, but I warn you, we ain't got no fancy changing rooms or pool here. It's all about strength and grit."

"Sounds perfect," Anna lied, cringing inwardly. She'd keep her spa membership going as well, just in case, she decided. "Sign me up."

Bart showed her around the gym, which he referred to as a "box." To Anna's dismay, it was mainly home to free weights and mats, with rudimentary apparatus. He outlined the Match-fit philosophy as they walked around, which seemed to consist of being superhumanly strong as well as extremely fit. Bart told her that training should focus on interval training, but using heavy free weights to build her strength.

There were a number of men training, one straining to pull himself up on bars with large weights tied around his waist. Another man was bench pressing vast barbells. They all ignored her at first, only becoming interested when Bart introduced her as a new member.

"Hey guys, this is Anna, just joined today. Anna, this is Jess, Sonny, and Mitch." They all nodded at her. Anna was delighted, as Mitch was the trainer she'd identified in her research as the most likely to be employed by Laker Brothers for James.

She beamed a smile. "Hey guys, mind if I join you?"

Anna could barely move the next day, having impressed the men by keeping up, albeit with much lighter weights. As she soaked in a tub of hot water and bath-salts to try and soothe her protesting muscles, she felt strangely triumphant that she'd managed to get talking to her prey quite so easily. He'd given up a fair bit of information, letting on that he had indeed been approached by a "major studio," boasting that he'd been head-hunted to train a Hollywood star. Anna had made sure she sounded suitably impressed, expressing her admiration for his over-muscled physique by breathily asking to feel his biceps.

When she discovered that they were also soldiers of the Illinois Pentecost, her acceptance had been complete.

CHAPTER 7

James Morell considered himself to be a fortunate man. Lady luck had smiled down upon him more times than he could count. He was aware of his good looks and regarded fellow actors who pretended not to notice their own attractiveness to be frauds. The only area he considered himself to be a bit of a failure was in his personal relationships. His mistakes, he felt, had been due to taking the easy option of dating fellow actresses. His theory at the time had been that they would understand the lifestyle and the pressures of living life in the public eye. The reality had turned out to be somewhat different. Not even the most beautiful women in Hollywood had helped fill the emptiness he felt inside, or cured the persistent fear of failure that dogged him in his quiet moments.

He'd found their neediness and insecurity annoying and their lack of common sense tiresome. In his mind, Sarah was bright, clever, and totally immersed within his life. He admired her ingenuity, whether it was the way she expertly handled his schedule, or the way she'd managed to steer his fan forums into believing that she was nothing more than a rumour. She was happy to fly under the radar and keep her anonymity, which he found refreshing.

"Don't go home tonight," he found himself saying, cringing inwardly at himself. He felt happier, more relaxed when Sarah was around. On the odd occasions she'd gone home to catch up on chores, he'd found himself listless and lonely, wondering what she was doing.

Sarah smiled at him across the breakfast table. "It's six in the morning, and you're talking about tonight already?"

"I like waking up with you," he murmured before taking a sip of his coffee. "I forgot to mention, I asked Mum if you could join us on Saturday. She thinks it's a great idea. She's really looking forward to it." He'd braced himself for his monthly phone call to his mother. She was a loud, domineering woman, who barely let him get a word in edgeways as she talked at him, usually in great detail about people he'd never met. She spoke about them nastily, telling him the ways they'd slighted her, as if he knew all her neighbours intimately. She conveniently forgot that he'd left home at eighteen, preferring to live in cheap, shabby, shared rooms in London. Anything had been better than the family life he'd endured back home.

"You want me to meet your parents?" Sarah asked in a voice two octaves higher than normal. He nodded, amused at her reaction. "But you're going there for the weekend."

He nodded again. "I don't really want to be a whole two days without you. Is that such a bad thing?" He asked, giving her what he hoped was a winsome smile. Sarah wasn't immune to his charm, but she wasn't as much of a pushover as other women had been. He could cope with his mother if she was there, he decided. Plus his mum tended to behave better when there were other people around.

"OK," she said, "on one condition."

"Which is?"

"You meet mine and show that lovely smile to my mum."

"It's a deal." he beamed at her. "Cute smile huh? She'll be putty in my hands."

Sarah swallowed her toast. "She might be, but my dad won't."

"Don't worry about that," he said airily. "Dads always like me. Its because I'm a gentleman."

Sarah snorted her coffee out through her nose, causing her to fish around in her bag for a tissue. "I don't think Dad would consider what you did to me last night to be the act of a gentlemen," she giggled.

"We won't mention that," he smirked, thinking back to the previous night when he'd had her in the restroom in the restaurant, while his brother had been seated at their table just twenty feet away. He'd joked that it had just been an aperitif, a pre-cursor to the long, slow session they'd have once they were safely home. It wasn't his fault that he couldn't keep his hands off her. His brother Jonathan had liked her though, and had remarked that Sarah was the "best one yet." She'd already met and charmed his eldest brother and his partner during a dinner at Mezzo, while they were over visiting from Australia, so James felt quite safe taking her home to meet his folks.

What he really craved was time alone with her. There was just never enough. It made him glad that she spent most days with him, organising his workload and fending off pushy execs. He was in enormous demand, which was good from a career perspective, but in reality meant that he was pulled in five different directions simultaneously. He relied heavily on Sarah to cut through the crap, prise the time wasters off of his shirt-tails, and make sure he was in the right place at the correct time, wearing the outfit that he was supposed to.

"I'll need to disappear for a couple of hours this afternoon," Sarah announced, breaking into his thoughts.

James pouted. "Why?" he asked.

She sighed loudly. "If I'm going away this weekend, I need some clean clothes and a bag packed." She'd barely been home for a week, too swept up in the madness of James's world to allow something as dull as laundry to spoil her fun.

"OK, but before I forget, can you hire me a car and book ferry tickets please? We'll be leaving around nine tomorrow morning. I'll drive."

"I'll do it while you're at the gym."

That afternoon, Sarah dutifully delivered James to his meeting and skipped off, promising to see him at eight that night. She hopped into the passenger seat of the car and asked Bob to stop off at the dry cleaners on the way back. "Did they have to surgically remove him from your hip this afternoon?" Bob growled as he headed over to Fulham.

"Yeah, something like that. I'm running out of clean clothes and my house is like a pigsty."

Bob nodded. "He's quite the smitten kitten isn't he? I'm not criticising, just observing."

"Never thought you noticed anything," Sarah remarked, a little snarkily. It made her edgy when people from work mentioned anything, despite James's reassurance that she wouldn't get the sack.

"I notice everything," Bob replied, "and I think you two are cute together. Just don't forget what he is."

"I won't," Sarah snapped.

Her little house was covered in a thin film of dust which hung in the air, made visible by the afternoon sun. Sarah changed into tracksuit bottoms and an old vest and set about cleaning up. She'd just put the second washload into the machine when there was a knock at the door. Glancing at her reflection in the mirror that hung in the hallway, she saw that she was sweaty from Hoovering, and her hair was dusty. She quickly wiped the smears of makeup from under her eyes and opened the door.

James had missed her the moment she'd gone. Her absence caused an irrational sense of loss deep within him. He'd fought with himself as to whether he should go over to her house or leave her to it, telling himself it was only a few hours. Despite this, the moment he got into the car, he heard himself asking Bob to take him over to Fulham. To make it seem a bit less pathetic, he stopped off and picked up some fresh milk and some flowers for her, just in case she wanted a drink. He held his offerings out in front of him as she opened the door, half-expecting her to scowl, be cross that he'd interrupted her, or worse, accuse him of not letting her have time off. Instead, she broke into a broad smile that lit up her face.

"I was desperate for a cup of tea," she said, "and the flowers are lovely."

She stepped aside to invite him into her little house. He walked through, gauging the furnishings to see if they'd give up their secrets about their owner. Sarah's house was small, basically a two-up, two-down, but it was in a fantastic location and was nicely furnished. "Have you had this place long?" he asked as he followed her into the kitchen, which although much smaller, was fairly similar to his.

"I bought it at the beginning of last year," Sarah told him. She was inordinately proud of her home, even though she had an eye-watering mortgage. Buying alone in central London wasn't easy at the best of times. Even flats were hard to afford, so when a run-down terraced place had been given to a local agent by an old lady's family after her death, Sarah had been fortunate to be given first viewing. Sometimes knowing a lot of people had its perks. Her dad and two uncles had soon got it ship-shape, and her mum was a dab hand at interior decorating.

"It's lovely," he said appreciatively, glancing around at the decor. Despite its size, the pale colours gave it an elegant, airy feel. He could imagine her curled up on her trendy, griege sofa, flicking through Tatler to find out which places were "in" with the beautiful crowd. "I thought I'd come and give you a hand."

Sarah arched an eyebrow. "You want to help me do my laundry? Too late pal, it's in the machine."

"So what shall we do while we're waiting?" he purred, his eyes hooded. He blinked slowly at her. "Your nipples are poking through your vest at me," he murmured as he snaked his arms around her waist, pressing her against the sink unit. Her body responded immediately, softening into his grasp.

"What are you suggesting?" she asked, her eyebrows raised. He slipped the shoulder-strap of her vest down her arm.

"I was thinking…" he purred, before kissing his way down her neck and onto her now-bare shoulder. They were interrupted by Sarah's phone ringing.

"Damn," she exclaimed before diving over to her handbag to answer it. James sighed loudly as she switched her attention to whoever was calling. "Yes, he's here," she said, frowning slightly before handing her phone to James. "It's Alan asking why your phone is switched off."

"I turned it off because I never get a moment's peace," James announced loudly into the phone.

"Sorry about that, complain to all the people who want to give you their money." Alan was sarcastic. "While you were with your accountant earlier, counting all your dosh and figuring out how to hide it from the taxman, I was negotiating on three more deals for you. How do you fancy being the face and voice of Hengarath Whisky?"

Sarah left him to it and carried on dusting her lounge. By the time James had finished, she was ironing the first washload, while the second load hummed round in the drier. "Sorry about that," he said sheepishly. "Your phone needs charging now."

"OK. Is there anything Alan's gonna need me to organise or schedule?" she asked. James shook his head and went to make her a drink. As the kettle boiled, he ruminated on the fact that she hadn't flipped out at his agent interrupting. Almost all other women needed a level of attention that he'd been unable to give. Sarah understood the lifestyle, knew that fame and its trappings required constant work to remain in the public eye. Even so, he had to break it to her that he'd just ruined their night off together by agreeing to meet up with Alan and an executive from the whisky company who were prepared to offer an obscene amount of money for a series of ads and a few voice-overs.

"Well?" she pressed.

"Tonight... sorry. Blame Alan, he pestered until I agreed to it." He noticed her lips press into a thin, grumpy line. "He asked if you'd come too."

"I see. Come where? Or am I expected to book a table as well?"

James handed her the tea he'd made, hoping it might perk her up. "He mentioned that he really wanted to try that new grill place in Beauchamp Place, but couldn't get a table. I don't suppose…"

"Oh for God's sake, pass me my phone please," Sarah huffed, her eyes twinkling, betraying herself. Five minutes later, she'd snagged a table and emailed Alan with the good news. All that remained for her to do was tip off the paps and arrange to arrive separately round the back entrance. There was absolutely no doubt that she was part of team Morell.

The following morning, James drove the hired BMW down to the south coast to catch the ferry to his childhood home on the Isle of Wight. He was in an extremely good mood, partly due to wrapping up the whisky deal the previous night, and partly because he was looking forward to introducing Sarah to his parents.

He knew they'd like her. His mum, Marion, was a housewife who looked after their farmhouse, cooked roast dinners, and baked cakes for the women's institute. His dad, Harry, pottered around in his greenhouse a lot, tending to his vegetables and growing flowers for his wife to arrange. In short, they were ordinary, unpretentious people who had successfully raised a family of five sons, all of whom had grown into fine, upstanding men, four of whom had met girls just like Sarah. For the first time, he'd have done as well as his brothers.

His mother had made a huge fuss, insisting they rested after the drive. So he ended up sitting in front of the TV with his feet up on the rather well-worn, leather pouffe, sipping hot, fresh tea made in a traditional teapot, while his dad asked about the journey down, discussing which "A" road was best and which was besieged by roadworks. It was the type of slightly self-conscious conversation that dads all over the country have when welcoming their adult offspring home, which was comforting in itself.

Sarah was given the guided tour of the garden along with a full report on all the neighbour's habits. James's mother, Marion, seemed particularly bedazzled by Sarah's career, lapping up stories about famous film stars, as though her own son wasn't part of that world.

James thought it ironic that his mum had been slightly disappointed that Sarah only dealt with A-listers and not her favourite soap actors, who were, in his mum's opinion, far more famous than mere Hollywood people. Sarah seemed to understand and delighted his mother by emailing a gossip blog contact to get the lowdown on whether two Emmerdale actors were genuinely having an affair, or whether it was just a made up story for "Soap star" magazine. Marion had been thrilled when Sarah read out the reply that the two people in question had indeed been caught snogging at a party, and at least one of them had been served divorce papers as a result.

"Isn't she lovely?" his mum had whispered when Sarah went to the loo. "Such a pretty girl too."

"It's not often that the clever ones are attractive," his dad joined in. "She's got a good head on her shoulders. much more suitable than that histrionic American woman we met in LA."

"Oh yes, she was hard work," his mum agreed. "Sarah seems like such a nice, steady sort of girl. That last one was too flighty for my liking. Let's hope that this one doesn't ditch you after five minutes too." James felt the familiar burn of indignation.

Later that evening during dinner, Marion asked if James had met Sarah's parents. "They're coming to London next weekend to see 'Mamma Mia,' so we'll meet them for dinner," Sarah told her. James blinked, surprised.

"You didn't tell me it was next weekend."

She nodded. "I did, plus I booked out Friday evening in your diary. Didn't you notice?" He shook his head.

"James!" admonished his mother. He held his hands up in a gesture of surrender.

"I know, I need to pay more attention," he admitted. His mother gave him a hard stare, while his dad tried unsuccessfully to conceal a smirk. "This lamb is lovely," he said, changing the subject.

"Are you a good cook?" Marion asked Sarah, making James cringe inside at his mother's lack of tact.

"Not bad," Sarah said, smiling. "I can't make gravy like this though. Yours is delicious, you must show me how you make it."

Marion beamed at her, delighted that she was taking an active interest in looking after her boy. It was so transparent that James wanted to laugh. He wondered if Sarah was mortified at his mother's blatant fact-finding.

Sarah was too busy watching proceedings with rapt interest. The little sneers, the put-downs when Marion thought that Sarah wouldn't notice. It was plain to see that the family was dysfunctional. Sarah's dissertation for her degree had been "The Effects of a Narcissistic Mother on the Family." She realised that she was viewing a textbook case.

Being in James's home and seeing his childhood bedroom made Sarah strangely homesick, not for her own home in London, but her childhood one in Hertfordshire. Both her and James's upbringings had been filled with the same rituals, the same values, and the same social norms. Both their mothers had brought them up on roast dinners and home-made puddings with custard that would stick you to your chair. For all his success and position in life, Sarah realised that he was remarkably similar to her, simply by virtue of their social class. As she lay there that night, in his rather cramped four-foot-six bed, she thought about her own childhood, wondering if he'd feel the same if he saw her parent's smart home in a leafy village near Hertford, or if he'd recognise the Marks and Spencer crockery so beloved of middle-aged ladies due to the ease of replacing pieces lost to butter-fingers.

He snuggled into her, slipping a leg in between hers, but not making a move to touch any of her erogenous zones. It was an unspoken understanding, no sex in your parent's house, drilled in to teenagers used to having to leave bedroom doors open when first crushes came over to listen to music or "collaborate on homework."

"Sorry about Mum," he whispered. "She just gets a bit excited when she thinks she might get me settled once and for all."

"Wait till you meet mine," Sarah whispered back, "Mine has a daughter. One daughter who she honestly believes needs a man to look after her." She said it to make him feel better, to cover up the uneasy truce that she'd sensed between him and his parents. She understood why he'd wanted her there. She was clued up enough to understand that narcissists were often charming to outsiders.

"Can't wait," quipped James, wrapping his arm around her waist and giving her a squeeze. Sarah lay in the darkness, contemplating the evening. His mum hadn't upset her in the slightest with her questions. If she'd have been a mother, she'd probably have asked the same things. The desire to see offspring "settled" had always puzzled her though. It was a phrase her own mother often used, usually to Sarah's annoyance. Surely it was better to wish your offspring a life of excitement? A rollercoaster ride to the grave as opposed to wanting them "settled," which made Sarah think of a tree, planted forever with no opportunity to change the view.

Sarah woke early the next morning, disturbed from her sleep by James emanating heat as he wrapped himself around her in the small bed. She tried to throw some of the covers off, thinking it was maybe the old-fashioned bedspread that was causing the problem. She glanced at the clock and groaned when she saw that it was only seven. Sunday was usually her lay-in day as long as her charges didn't need her. She inched her way out from James's grasp, trying not to wake him too, although there didn't seem too much danger of that happening. She'd never seen him so out-cold. His face looked far younger and more relaxed than normal. She took a moment to just admire it, wondering if she'd ever get immune to his beauty.

Downstairs, Marion was pouring a cup of tea, having calculated that she had enough time to skim through the paper before people started waking up, and she'd need to start breakfast. She wondered who it was padding down the stairs so early and smiled when she saw it was Sarah, clutching her laptop. "Sorry, I didn't think anyone would be up yet. Don't let me disturb you."

"Nonsense, it's nice to have some company. Tea?"

They sipped their tea, sitting in companionable quiet at the large wooden kitchen table, which Sarah noticed had been frequently scrubbed clean in its lifetime. She opened her laptop and began checking all the forums dedicated to James, which she did every morning. "Do you get tired of looking at screens?" Marion asked as she flicked open her newspaper.

"Sometimes, but I check what's been discussed about James overnight when the Americans are all online, just in case I need to

The Fixer

intervene or steer the conversations."

Marion frowned. "It's seven o'clock on a Sunday morning."

"The Internet never sleeps," Sarah countered, before quickly typing something on her keyboard. Marion wondered what it was. "I'm currently keeping the conversations firmly on Cosmic Warriors and away from James's whereabouts this weekend. Somebody floated the idea that he could be visiting his parents, so I just claimed to have seen him in London late last night, before changing the subject to his costume glimpses that were released the day before yesterday."

Marion smiled, pleased that Sarah was supportive of James's career. She'd seen too many girls chase after him, blinded by his good looks and thirsty for his fame and fortune, only to forget that they'd have a part to play too. Sarah struck her as entirely different, a woman dedicated to protecting her man, while not seeking the limelight for herself. As she sipped her tea from her Cath Kidston cup, she sat considering if she should monitor the forums too, being the one who'd contributed the most to his fame and fortune. She also wondered if Sarah knew about the episode of James's life that she'd dubbed "the lost years," not that she'd dream of being the one to bring it up. It was down to James if he decided to tell her about it, Marion thought, although she was sorely tempted.

After breakfast, James announced that he would take Sarah on a tour of the island, show her some of the places he'd loved as a boy. "Before you go, there's something I need to ask you," Marion said. She refilled his cup from the pot and placed the milk jug in front of him. James stifled a sigh, as her "talks" either meant that she wanted to tell him how much better her friend's offspring were doing-one of them was an actor who'd gotten a gig on a trashy daytime soap last time he'd visited, or she wanted him to do something for her. He'd paid for their new conservatory the previous year. Sarah watched him as his shoulders tensed and his jaw hardened.

"Shirley Davenport was asking if you'd be a patron of her otter charity," she blurted, "It's not just otters mind, she does hedgehogs, badgers, and voles too."

"And Shirley Davenport is?" He asked.

"From my women's institute club. She's the membership secretary, so if I want to get onto the committee..." She paused. "It would just mean taking some pictures with the otters, maybe holding a vole or something."

James stifled a laugh. "It'd be quite good for your public image," Sarah chimed in. She turned to Marion, "Is it a registered charity?"

"Oh yes. Shirley did it all properly. There's a charity number and everything. She's even got a website where she shows all the sick squirrels. People sponsor them. It's about time you did something for somebody else. It's all very well gallivanting around the world, but charity should start at home."

James sniggered, prompting a daggers stare from his mother. "I'm sure it's a very worthwhile cause," he said hurriedly. "If it's just a few pictures, then we can swing by there this afternoon."

That afternoon, after a trip to James's favourite hidden cove, they drove over to Luccombe to find the Furry Friends Rescue Centre. A small notice on a rickety gate confirmed that they had the right place. The owner, Shirley, was a matronly powerhouse of a woman, with a sharply-cut dyed red bob and alarmingly white dentures. She showed them around the enclosures, telling them each animal's story as they toured the legion of one-legged and one-eyed rescues. For once, she seemed a little immune to the Morell charm, which was rare for a woman of any age.

At the end of the tour, Shirley summoned her husband to take some photos of James with the creatures. Her husband, Chris, set up his tripod and camera on the back lawn, and positioned James with a large yew hedge as a backdrop. "You're gonna want to take face pictures from my left side," James said, not really realising what a dick he sounded. Shirley handed him what she described as the "tamest" one-legged squirrel. It promptly bit him, causing him to drop it. The creature then attempted to scarper on its remaining leg, moving at quite a lick until Shirley grabbed it by its tail and shoved it back into a cat carrier. Sarah couldn't help but feel sorry for the poor thing. She wondered if Shirley, who had come across as very cold and rather cruel, had been chopping poor squirrel's legs off for profit.

They had better luck with a one-eyed vole, who posed nicely with James for promotional pictures and a video, before taking the opportunity to let loose a long stream of wee all over his hand and the leg of his trousers. Mindful of the squirrel's great escape attempt, all James could do was hold on tight and continue to try and look interested in what Shirley was saying about riverbank conservation.

The Fixer

While James was washing his hands and attempting to mop the pee off his trouser leg, Sarah asked Shirley for copies of the pictures and film that they'd taken that day.

"Of course dear, it's not a problem. Why do you want them though?" She replied.

"I can get James's fan club to distribute them. It'll raise a lot of awareness for your cause." Sarah pointed out.

"He has a fan club?" Shirley looked shocked. "Marion said he was an actor, but not that he was famous," she added.

"You don't know who he is?" Sarah asked, incredulous. She wondered if Shirley lived under a rock. "Did you not see Cosmic Warriors?"

Shirley shook her head. "I never go to the cinema."

It left Sarah wondering what on earth Marion's problem was, and how badly it had damaged James.

CHAPTER 8

Anna

Every day Anna attended Bart's gym. After a while, she ceased to notice the grimy floor and sweat-encrusted mats as she religiously pumped iron alongside the men. After a few weeks of this regime, they seemed to accept her, including her in their own training and chatting more easily around her. She'd kept detailed notes as to Mitch's workout habits in her file at home, so that she was always there just before him each day.

She discovered that he was married and had a step-child. Listening to him moaning about his wife, she wondered why he'd bothered, as he didn't seem particularly happy, often complaining about how difficult she was. Anna discovered by eavesdropping that he'd only agreed to marry her due to her father bribing him with a house and land as a wedding gift. In Anna's mind, it left him wide open to temptation.

One Thursday, when it was just Mitch and her present, she decided to test the waters and flirt a little. A touch here, a smile there. She complimented him on how strong and powerful he was. As in the parable of the crow and the cheese, Mitch most definitely dropped his cheese. It had been a while since a woman had made him feel good about himself. His wife spent most of her time just criticising how little he earned as a trainer. He hadn't even told her about the film contract at that point, although he'd wanted to, just to shut her up. He was holding that bit of information back, just in

The Fixer

case she decided to leave him before then. He didn't want her sticking around just because of his big payday. He watched Anna bench press some pretty impressive weights, noting that she had quite a rack on her.

"You're doing well," he ventured as she stood up.

"Pressing about double what I was at first," Anna told him, her voice breathless from the exertion. "Gotta keep the girls perky." She ran her hands over her breasts before cupping them. Mitch's eyes nearly fell out of his head, which made Anna smile. "Do you think they've gotten perkier since I started Match-fit?" She asked. She watched him squirm a little, which pleased her.

"You're definitely tighter and more toned than when you started here," Mitch said eventually, before grabbing two barbells to do some squats. Anna stood watching, her eyes greedily taking in all the details of his straining quads, his powerful muscles sculptured by repeated hard work.

She counted down for him, "eight, seven, six, five, four, three, come on, two, last one." He threw the weights onto the floor and indicated that it was her turn. Smiling, Anna picked out some lighter ones and positioned herself in front of him. As she began, she was hyperaware of him examining her in great detail. When she began to struggle on her seventh rep, he dragged his eyes up to meet hers and smiled.

"You can do this," he said. "I've seen you squat heavier weights than this."

At his behest, she leaned in to the final squat, before throwing her weights down and shaking out her jellied legs. "Have you been watching me?" she asked, putting on a show of fake coquettishness.

"Might have been," he said, smiling at her. "I saw you at church on Sunday. You're part of the Webb clan?"

Anna nodded. "My dad is Ricky Webb." She watched his reaction carefully, noting his surprise.

"Bart'll be interested in that bit of info," said Mitch, "he's been eyeing up a unit on your dad's industrial estate. This old place is falling to bits."

"I don't think any units are free at the moment," Anna said, puzzled. "I do know that he's just had plans approved to build some more on this side of the estate though." She unwittingly confirmed the rumour. She didn't want to talk about her dad's boring business though. "So come on, why have you been watching me?" She tilted her head down slightly and looked up at him through her lashes.

His lips stretched into a wide smile. "I might like what I see." He held her gaze. "What're you doing this weekend?"

"Hunting with my daddy," Anna said, noting with satisfaction the look of disappointment on his face. Mitch wasn't the type of man she was attracted to, being a bit of a meat-head with tribal tattoos and a severe haircut, but he seemed to be her best way "in" to the gym. She smiled sweetly at him. "I'm not busy next weekend," she said. Her dad was away for the weekend at some gun convention, so she'd have fewer awkward questions to answer.

Mitch grinned at her, relieved that it wasn't a "no," making him look a fool. "Next weekend it is then. Keep it free." He turned back to his weights and began working his biceps, seemingly absorbed in the process. For all his machismo with weights, guns, and bullets, Mitch was generally unsure around women, having grown up without a mother or siblings. As a youngster, he'd been a feeble, skinny child whom the girls ignored. It was only after marrying the only woman who had been prepared to give him the time of day, that he'd taken up bodybuilding and given himself the type of physique that appealed to females. In the years that followed, he'd had two affairs, both of which had ended when the girls had married someone else. Thankfully for him, he didn't suffer a guilty conscience from cheating on Erika. Besides, he suspected that she was just as bad. He noticed that she spent a lot of evenings comforting upset friends around their houses, never bringing them back to theirs.

Anna wrapped up her workout for the day and headed home. She wondered if Mitch would tell Bart who her daddy was. As it was, she needed to work on her father and keep him fully wrapped around her little finger, an activity at which she was well-practiced.

She logged on that evening to discover that her picture had even more likes and shares. Even more gratifying were the comments about how "hot" she looked. Someone from Utah had even called her "sex on legs" in the picture of her astride the giraffe.

CHAPTER 9

Sarah

Sarah's parents arrived at King's Cross on Friday afternoon, dressed sensibly in slacks and comfortable shoes, bearing little weekend cases on wheels, like the ones air hostesses use. Sarah was waiting on the concourse and hugged them tightly on arrival, squashing the three of them together. She missed them, despite speaking regularly on the phone. She loved having them to stay, her mum instantly resuming the mothering role and getting her house gleaming, her fridge filled, and her laundry taken care of, while her dad fixed loose screws, unblocked sinks, and changed lightbulbs in hard-to-reach places.

On the way back to her house, they chatted about the journey down, the neighbours at home and news about their offspring, with whom Sarah had attended school. It felt grounding and normal, far away from the superficial, slightly mad world that Sarah normally inhabited, where expensive designer clothes were given away free to people who could actually afford to buy them.

During the taxi ride back, her mum asked how it was going with James. "All fine thanks, you'll meet him tonight so you can check him out for yourselves," Sarah said. She wondered if her mum had Googled him.

"Where are we going tonight?" Her dad asked, wary of too much fancy foreign food, which repeated on him dreadfully.

"The Ivy. You're OK, Dad, it's English food," Sarah said,

smirking at him. "I know what you're like."

That night, the three of them got to the restaurant half an hour before James, so as not to arouse suspicion amongst the photographers who were permanently stationed outside. Bob would collect James, who would be wearing casual dark blue trousers and a dress shirt that Sarah had picked out and left hanging outside his wardrobe. He would briefly pose for photos before being ushered through to the most private part of the restaurant where they'd already be seated. Sarah had it all carefully planned out.

She watched her mum's jaw drop when James came striding over to their table. Her dad shook his hand rather forcefully, while her mum blushed pink while she took her turn, which reminded Sarah of her first sight of him. After introductions, they sat down and began to peruse the menus. "I think I'll just have the soup and the shepherd's pie tonight," said James, before snapping his shut. He turned to Tom, "The soup here is always exceptional."

"You like soup?" Chirped Linda. Small talk had never been her forte.

"I do indeed, especially homemade soup," said James before flashing her his megawatt smile. To Sarah's utter horror, her mum actually giggled. Sarah wanted to kick her. Instead, she changed the subject onto safer ground.

"What did you do this afternoon?"

"I watched the rugby, well, the second half of it."

"A rugby man?" Tom asked, pleased to talk about a subject close to his own heart.

"Sure am. I used to play at school. The studio won't let me play nowadays for obvious reasons. You?"

"Used to play fly half. Only for the county team though."

"County? You must be fast."

Sarah tuned out of the conversation and just watched the interaction between James and her dad, the easy way they chatted about nothing of consequence, in the way that men do when they're sizing each other up. Sport or roads seemed to be the universal secret codes of man-speak, she mused.

Her mother was positively bedazzled, struggling to rip her eyes away from her daughter's beau. She eventually glanced over to see Sarah narrow her eyes at her. Chastened, Linda went back to poring over the menu, relieved that it was written in English, unlike

The Fixer

the restaurant they'd visited last time they were down. When she'd chosen her meal, she cast her eyes around the room.

"Don't look now Sarah, but it's that man off Corrie," Linda whisper-squealed, "I don't know who he's with though, maybe his wife?" James stole a look over Sarah's shoulder to where the man was seated and gave him a wave. To Linda's utter delight and total mortification, he waved back. What Linda didn't appreciate was how excited the soap star was to be recognised by James Morell himself. In fact, he dined out on it for weeks afterwards.

It felt strange to James saying goodbye for the night in the restaurant, but as Sarah's parents were staying with her, and the paparazzi were stationed outside, James left first, posing briefly for the pictures, and declining to comment on who his dining companions were.

His house felt cold and too large when he walked in. He threw his jacket over the banister and wandered through to the kitchen to make a drink. He glanced at the clock. It wasn't even midnight. He had a whole ten hours before he'd see Sarah again.

He'd quite enjoyed meeting her parents for the simple fact of being in the company of people who loved Sarah too. He'd liked watching the little interactions between her and her mother, and the way her father softened as he looked at her.

He loved her.

He rolled that thought around his head.

He'd always assumed that he was too cold a man to fall in love. An empty shell who didn't experience feelings in the same way as the rest of the human race. Here he was, feeling "in love" and lonely without her. A two-for-the-price-of-one deal on emotions.

The next morning, Sarah awoke to the sound of her mum singing along to the radio in the little kitchen downstairs and the scent of bacon wafting through the house. She pulled on her dressing gown and padded down to see what was going on.

Her mum was busily wiping down her kitchen cupboards while grilling bacon and making a pot of tea. A load of laundry was humming round in the washing machine, and the bin had been emptied. Sarah smiled gratefully and sat down at the little breakfast bar that her dad had thoughtfully provided in the postage-stamp sized room. "Morning Mum, sleep well?"

She already knew the answer.

"Lot of traffic noise dear. I'm not used to it. I think your dad slept OK though. Breakfast won't be long, just crisping up your bacon."

"What did you think of James?"

Her mum placed a mug of tea in front of her. "He's better looking than I envisaged. Doesn't seem to have made him arrogant though. Well, not as arrogant as I'd have expected."

"He's quite normal, considering," said Sarah.

Linda arranged her features into her "concerned mum face." "Is he too handsome? I mean, will you worry that he'll have women flirting with him all the time? He's a catch and all that, but not if he doesn't make *you* happy." She emphasised the "you" as Sarah was all Linda really cared about.

"He makes me very happy," Sarah told her. "If anything, he's a bit clingy. He seems oblivious to other women."

"At the moment," her mum said, fixing her with a hard stare. "He's certainly in love with you, the man couldn't take his eyes off you all evening."

"But?" Sarah asked.

"But infatuation passes and while you can keep this all secret now, if it carries on, it'll come out eventually. What will your boss have to say about it? Have you thought about that?"

"My bosses know; they're quite happy. If anything, they'd like us to go public sooner. It's me that's not ready for it. James's fans are legendary for being brutal, so the longer I can fly under the radar the better. After the car kiss, I made sure I disappeared. As it stands at the moment, I'm just a rumour, nothing more."

Her mother's lips pursed. "So you need to be pretty sure that this man is worth giving up your privacy for?"

Sarah nodded. "Did Dad like him?"

"Yes, thought he was a nice fella."

"Well that's something," Sarah said, eyeing up the bacon sandwich her mother was busy cutting. Her mum noticed and placed it on a plate for her.

"It's not that I don't like him, I do... a lot," Linda said, "I'm just worried he's going to turn your life upside down, then swan off to his next job."

Sarah chewed her sandwich and thought about what her mother had said. If anything, she found James too clingy, almost needy in his desire to always be with her. When other women had flirted outrageously with him, not knowing that Sarah was more than his assistant, he'd simply not responded to them, even throwing away the phone numbers frequently slipped into his pocket. Her main concern was keeping her anonymity until she was convinced that what they had together was real. She took all the practical steps, such as keeping out of photographs and locking down her social media, but it only took a careless inclusion in a fan photo and she'd be outed.

Two weeks later they managed a whole weekend away together, driving down in a hired Mercedes convertible to a tiny cottage in Devon for two gorgeous sunny days in July. In-between lovemaking, they walked, talked, and explored nearby villages without James being hassled. It was idyllic.

On the Sunday, they packed a picnic in a hamper they'd found in the cottage, alongside a tartan blanket, and set off into the woods behind the house. The two of them held hands as they wandered along the meandering paths, enjoying the shade of the trees and the dappled sunshine dancing around them. Eventually, they came upon a small clearing and spread out the blanket on the soft grass. James opened a bottle of wine, poured them both a glass and lay back to survey the scenery. "This is heaven on Earth," he pronounced. Sarah hummed her agreement. "When I'm finished as an actor, I'd like to retire someplace like this. Somewhere rural and peaceful, with no hustling for publicity and no paparazzi." He took in the sight of Sarah laid out on the blanket like a bucolic nymph in an old master painting. It made him long for a simpler life, one not controlled by the publicity gods or the fickle demands of a fandom. He ran his finger down her arm, her soft skin proving that she was indeed real.

She propped herself up on her elbow to look at him. He had that same wistful expression that she'd come to know so well. "Is it bothering you? You know, the fame thing?"

He smiled, "Only insofar as I worry that it'll affect us, that you'll get fed up with all the scrutiny and nasty comments." He paused, gazing into her eyes, "I'm in love with you Sarah, and I worry that by loving you, I'm exposing you to the whole world tearing you apart."

Sarah reeled at his words. Although they'd become close, it was the first time he'd admitted he was in love. They'd been the words she'd desperately wanted to hear. "I'm in love with you too," she said, "and it'll take more than being told I have man hands to scare me away."

He smiled tentatively. "I couldn't bear to see you upset or hurt. I know how nasty some of my fans can be about the women I've been out with."

"Have you been in love before?" she needed to know.

"Not like this, no. I've been in lust, and I've been fond of past girlfriends, but I've never felt like this before. Have you?"

Sarah shook her head. Her previous relationships had seemed grey and bland compared to this. James loved in glorious technicolor, an all-encompassing type of love. She had no doubts about the depth of his feelings towards her; he was so passionate both in and out of the bedroom. When they weren't making love, they were making each other laugh, sharing secrets, or just able to be together in companionable silence. She'd never been so intimate with another human being.

"What do you really want in a woman?" She asked. It was a question that had been bothering her. James lay back on the blanket and thought about it for a moment.

"I want someone who will never leave me, someone I can count on," he said eventually. Sarah stayed silent. "I know lots of women would say that they could be that person, just based on how I look, but its not easy being the partner of an actor. It takes a lot of self-belief to cope with the attention, plus of course, it can be a dirty business," he paused, "as you probably already know."

He leaned over to kiss her, a fierce, passionate kiss, filled with the emotions they were both experiencing. The picnic lay forgotten as they spent a magical afternoon in the woods, just touching, caressing, and loving each other. Sarah floated back to the cottage on a cloud.

She convinced herself that what they had was unique, invincible. His fans could say what they liked, and she wouldn't care. She was too busy being loved by her wonderful, gorgeous man to be bothered about other people's opinions. They hadn't spent a night apart in weeks, and when it was time to fly to Rome for his filming, she'd cancelled the second hotel room, knowing that they wouldn't need it.

CHAPTER 10

Anna

Mitch glared silently at his wife, who was seated with her back to him in the kitchen, her laptop open in front of her. He felt nothing but disdain for her. At the start, they'd gotten along quite well even though there was little passion in their relationship, but after a few years, even their friendship had fizzled out. All Mitch was hanging on for was the big payday when her dad finally pegged it, which wouldn't be too far away. He stared at the large skull and gun tattoo on her upper arm. It always made him cringe.

"I'm spending the day at the nursing home with Dad, then visiting my friend Ellen this evening. She's so down at the moment, I thought a girly night with a bottle of wine might cheer her up. Todd's having a sleepover at his friend's house, so I might stay over at Ellen's rather than drive." Her voice irritated him almost all the time, but in spite of that, Mitch smiled. He didn't particularly need her out of the way, but it wouldn't hurt to have her busy doing whatever she had planned.

He tried to sound sincere. "OK, no problem. I guess I can keep myself busy. Say hi to your dad for me." He knew full well she wasn't going for the day. Her dad had end-stage dementia and had no idea who any of them were. At best, she'd poke her head around his door and say "hi" to the drugged-up figure laying unseeing in his hospital-style bed. Erika hated it at the nursing home and spent as little time as possible there.

Mitch turned on the TV and flicked through the channels until he found a sports one showing a baseball game. He turned the sound up loud and set about making a protein shake, ignoring Erika's sigh as she closed her laptop and slid off the barstool. He fixed himself some scrambled eggs and took them into the lounge, slumping onto the chair before flicking on the TV in there to carry on watching the game.

As Erika snapped shut her laptop and stormed off, Mitch ruminated on the fact that she appeared to dislike even being in the same room as him. It made what he was planning to do that day even more delicious.

Anna had kissed her daddy goodbye the previous evening, sending him off happily to his convention. She used to have to stay at either her uncle's or her aunt's houses when he went away, but since turning eighteen, he allowed her to stay home alone.

She'd spent the evening reading up on James Morell, his habits, his preferences. Gleaning snippets of information from various interviews he'd done, plus she watched at least twenty YouTube videos of him. Her friends on IMDB still seemed to think that he had a girlfriend, but nobody could say for sure as she hadn't been featured in any of the numerous fan pictures that were regularly posted online. It was a rumour that Anna took seriously though. Along with many of his fans, she'd pored over the picture of James and Sarah outside the Ivy, forensically examining it for clues as to their relationship. Her reasoning was that if he was indeed hiding her, he was ashamed of how she looked. If he wasn't hiding her, then they were no longer seeing each other. Either way, it made him ripe for the picking. She just wanted the next couple of months to go quickly and without any more new women coming onto the scene.

Early that evening, she drove over to the bar that Mitch had suggested they meet at. It was twenty miles from their town, but the distance meant fewer tongues would wag. What Anna didn't know was that the roadhouse also had rooms to rent as well as a bar and grill. She grimaced as she pulled into the parking lot. A huge neon sign announced that rooms were available by the hour in confirmation of the seediness of the establishment.

She made her way to the doorman rather gingerly, wondering if she'd get ID'ed. thankfully, he didn't bother and nodded her through. The bar was short of women that evening. Mitch was

The Fixer

already there, having arrived way too early in his excitement. He appraised Anna as she walked through the door. In her short, tight dress she looked like a toy, a Barbie doll. He noticed other men eyeing her up too as she scanned the room, searching the sea of faces for him. He waved to her and was gratified by her obvious relief to see him. She tottered over in her stupidly high heels.

"Drink?" He asked brusquely, the embarrassment of being on a first date making him abrupt.

Anna smiled at his obvious discomfort. "I'll just have a beer please." She paused. "Have you been here before?" She asked as he waited for the barman, a twenty grasped in his hand. He nodded, wary of her response. His answer just confirmed what Anna had suspected, Mitch was a player. He was the type of man to cheat on his wife. He'd be easy to blackmail into doing what she wanted, as in Anna's mind, he'd already shown his weakness.

Less than an hour later, they were ensconced in a rather shabby room containing a double bed bearing a waterproof mattress cover and an extremely dubious, splotch-patterned bedspread. Anna was kneeling on the worryingly sticky carpet, sucking greedily on Mitch's cock. She stopped him, just as the sheen of sweat was forming on his upper lip and he was begging her to let him fuck her. "I'd really like to work at the gym, learn to be a Match-fit trainer. What do you think?" she asked breathily as she stared at Mitch's dick, which she had her hand delicately wrapped around.

"Let me talk to Bart," Mitch gasped. He wondered why Anna was asking him rather than asking Bart herself. The thought flicked briefly through his mind before it was replaced by other, more erotic ones as Anna slid her knickers down her legs. He stared unashamedly at her tight, young flesh, fashionably shaved bare of hair and reached silently for a condom.

CHAPTER 11

Sarah

The first sight of the hotel was amazing. It was built in the style of a palazzo with pretty arched windows sheathed by shutters and a vast marble and gilt entrance. The concierge recognised James and greeted him warmly before personally taking them up to the penthouse. Sarah gazed around the enormous suite in awe. She was used to hotel rooms; her charges often stayed in them, but this was a whole other level. Large windows presented exquisite views over Rome from three sides of the suite. She was mesmerised by the perfectly-lit domes rising up above the rooftops.

"It'll be even better in daylight," James said, wrapping an arm around her. He planted a brief kiss on her cheek then began to fish around in his wallet for a note to tip the concierge.

Once alone, they pored over the room service menu, having not eaten on the flight. James ordered while Sarah began to unpack their cases, hanging everything carefully in the large wardrobes.

"Drink?" asked James after placing their order. He opened the minibar and examined the contents carefully before choosing a bottle of champagne, which he opened adeptly and poured them each a glass. "To Rome!" James raised his flute in a toast. "The most romantic city on Earth." Sarah clinked her glass with his. Part of what she loved about James was that he liked to celebrate everything. Most people would become jaded by luxury travel, yet

The Fixer

James still treated it like an adventure. He felt as though he'd never get used to the Hollywood lifestyle, so wanted to make the most of every moment.

They'd barely sipped their champagne when James's phone began to ring. Scowling, he pulled it from his pocket and answered it without checking the screen. "Hey you, I need your help. I'm in Rome right now, can we meet up?"

James recognised the voice straight away. His ex's nasal Brooklyn accent was irredeemably etched into his brain. She didn't need to introduce herself. His stomach began to churn.

Sarah watched his face go a little pale, and he flicked his eyes away from hers. "What are you doing in Rome?" He asked the caller.

"I'm here shooting some stills. The studio is screaming at me to get publicity and it's not happening in this god-forsaken backwater. Then I heard that you arrived here…"

Sarah could make out a woman's voice.

"I don't care if you need the publicity, I'm here with my girlfriend. You told me to get lost and meet someone else, so I did."

"You owe me for all the publicity I gave you when you were a nobody, or have you forgotten all that? I don't give a shit about your bit of fluff, what I care about is my movie tanking."

The caller sounded angry to Sarah. James saw her watching him, her face concerned. "I'll talk to her. Maybe she'll understand." he said before walking out onto the terrace for some privacy. Sarah's blood ran cold. After all the openness and sharing of secrets, she knew that she was being shut out. Her mind raced with all the possibilities. She debated trying to listen, but felt rooted to the spot, unable to move, not able to think clearly as to what to do. A loud knock heralded the arrival of their food. She let the waiter in and found James's wallet to find some cash for a tip.

James, meanwhile was trying to reason with his ex, Sophia. The last thing he wanted to do was meet up and re-open that particular can of worms. It'd been a messy break up between them, especially given her habit of sharing the details on social media in an attempt to maintain her voracious need to be at the forefront of the public eye. As it was, once James was out of her life, her fame had withered. Enraged, she tried every trick in the manipulator's book to guilt James into doing what she wanted. Under her threat of her giving the Inquirer a lurid and detailed kiss-and-tell article, he caved in and agreed to her plan.

Eventually, James went back into the suite. He looked sheepish, embarrassed. "Who was that?" Sarah asked, unsure as to whether she was keeping her voice even.

"It was my ex," he said without emotion. "She wants to meet me for dinner tomorrow night. She needs some publicity, and she knows if we're pictured together we'll be on the front pages of all the gossip rags. You know exactly how the game works." He couldn't look at her. Instead he tried to wrap his arms around her rather rigid shoulders.

"I heard you saying that it was at her command that you found someone else," Sarah challenged. He rolled his eyes.

"I didn't mean that I just do everything she tells me to. She gave me an ultimatum, and I chose my career. Her parting words were that I was a selfish idiot, and that I should go find someone else, which I did." he tried to nuzzle her. Sarah pulled away.

"I know that I'm gonna be either the girl getting in the way of a reconciliation, or the poor, clueless sap you're stringing along. The fans will crucify me, and you, if we ever go public, that is." Sarah's PR training kicked in. It was a no-win situation, and she really didn't want him walking headfirst into a trap.

"Its just a bit of publicity," he'd bleated, clearly not willing to understand why she'd have an issue with Sophia's plan.

"But your PR people haven't asked you to do this," she pointed out. "You're just jumping to her tune, nobody else's."

"We're friends, and as a friend, I can help her out. Would you prefer it if I was a selfish, callous bastard who only thought of myself?" he asked. The thought of having to call Sophia and say no to her was far worse than putting up with a strop from Sarah for a night.

"Yes I would," Sarah countered. "This has every chance of backfiring spectacularly, with you coming out as the bad guy. She's your ex for a reason, and she doesn't get to call the shots." She was losing her temper with him.

"She's not calling shots," he spat. "She's just asking for a favour."

"A favour that could end up costing you dear." Sarah paused. "Does she have some sort of hold over you?"

"Don't be so ridiculous," he snarled. "You're making a

mountain out of a molehill." He stomped off to sit out on the terrace and finish his champagne, the mood soured. Sarah sighed and carried on hanging up their clothes. When it appeared he wasn't coming in, she got into bed and tried to sleep, hearing him pad back into the room ten minutes later and slip into bed quietly. Their food lay untouched.

It was the first time they'd gone to bed on an argument, both angry and neither giving way. James managed to doze off quite quickly, but Sarah lay awake turning the evening's events over in her mind. The serious downside of being involved with her charge was laid out directly in front of her. She just couldn't understand why James would ignore her advice, even if it was purely from a professional perspective.

As Sarah lay on the furthest edge of the enormous bed, a wide gulf between them, she pondered him spending the evening with his ex. *'One click of the fingers and he goes running'* she thought, despondency settling over her. In the slow, lonely hours of the night, Sarah let all her old insecurities run unchecked around her mind. She listened to the little voice whispering that she wasn't beautiful enough, talented enough, or interesting enough for her gorgeous man.

At the first hurdle, he'd fallen, dancing to the tune of another woman, one who embodied everything that Sarah felt that she wasn't. As the little travel alarm clock that Sarah had packed for James ticked loudly in the silence, she ruminated on how fake it had all been. She allowed the hurt to wash over her, letting tears fall in silence, fearful of waking him and having to discuss it. Indeed, the last thing Sarah wanted to admit was how insecure she felt, as though it would alert him to her ordinariness, a fact that he might not have otherwise noticed.

By the time the first glimmers of dawn licked across the sky, she'd decided to book another room, and place some distance between them. She slipped out of bed at five, pulled on some clothes, and tiptoed out. James didn't even stir. As she sped down in the lift, she felt a surge of relief flood through her at being away from him. The whole night had been torture.

"Is there anywhere to get a coffee this early?" Sarah asked the concierge at the main desk.

"Certainly Madam. Would you like it served in the breakfast room or the lounge?" he eyed her curiously.

"The lounge will be fine," she replied. She waited while he phoned her order through to the kitchen. "Can I enquire if you have any rooms available please?"

"I can check for you, although we are pretty full at the moment. How long will you need it for?"

"Till the third of September."

He glanced up at her, before turning back to his screen. "I only have one room available. It's on the first floor. It's a basic room though, not a suite."

"That's fine," she said. She handed over her credit card. Sarah knew James would be on set by eight that morning, so it would be easy to move her stuff out of his room and into her new one without there being a scene. She signed the chit, took her new key, and made her way into the lounge in search of her coffee.

James reached out in search of Sarah's warm little body while his mind was still mostly asleep. It took a moment to process the cool patch beside him in the emperor-sized bed. Eventually his eyes opened and he scanned the room, expecting to see her working on her laptop.

It took a further couple of minutes to check the rest of the suite, calling out in case she was tucked away on the balcony before he realised that she wasn't there. Sarah wasn't an early riser by nature, so it was very definitely unusual for her not to be present. A loud knock made him jump. He opened the door, half-expecting to see Sarah back from an early walk. Instead, a waiter stood behind another large silver trolley full of food.

As James sat alone, chewing absently on toasted ciabatta, it finally occurred to him that Sarah may have gone off in a huff. He'd expected her to understand that sometimes stuff had to be done for publicity purposes alone. She had a PR background and had probably engineered more than a few fake "dates" in her time, just to get column inches. She *knew* it wasn't real life. He wondered if she'd forgotten that their breakfasts would be served in the suite each day. Sarah was always a bit ratty when she was hungry.

His day didn't improve when he arrived on set, still none the wiser as to Sarah's whereabouts and with his phone about to die for lack of charge. The director, the renowned Rizzi Di'Alba, seemed to expect him to know which trailer was his, which costume he was meant to be wearing, and the exact American accent that his character in the film would use. James began to lose his temper at every line he delivered being picked apart.

Sarah hid in her new room until she was certain that James was out of the way and busy on set. It took just an hour to move all her clothes and stuff from the spacious penthouse suite and down to her little bedroom. The bathroom in the penthouse had been bigger than the entire room she was going to be occupying for the next month or so. It all felt so terribly disappointing.

As she sat on the bed, she contemplated what she was doing. *'Would James be upset? Or would he be relieved I was out of the way?'* She wondered whether he'd use the opportunity to get back with his ex, the thought of which she found surprisingly painful. She let out a sob. All the emotions she'd held back came flooding out as she sat on her new bed, one in which she'd sleep alone, without his strong arms wrapped around her. She sobbed like a baby, letting out the frustration of not being good enough for the man she loved.

She was interrupted by her phone ringing. She glanced at the screen to see it was Bob. "Hi," Sarah croaked.

"Sarah, where on Earth are you? And why is His Nibs in such a foul mood? Is there trouble in paradise?"

"I'm in the hotel," she told him. "We had a row..." she sniffed loudly.

"Well, I guessed that much. He's like a bear with a sore head. Mr Di'Alba's getting quite fed up with him. His head's not in the game this morning, blowing apart his 'one take James' persona. At this rate, the director is gonna send him back to the hotel and get on with some of Harry's scenes."

"I'm not sure what you expect me to do about it," Sarah snapped. "I'm not the one having dinner with my ex tonight, for publicity only, of course." She sounded scathing, even to her own ears.

"I see," said Bob, understanding dawning. "Shall I drive them tonight? Make sure you find out where they both end up and all that?"

"It's beside the point. Even if they sleep apart, he's still happy to be seen with her, and it's not his PR ordering it either." Sarah didn't normally talk much to Bob, but with nobody else around, she had to unload to someone.

"Hmm, that's not good. He'd be pretty upset if the boot was on the other foot," Bob pointed out.

An hour later, James walked into the suite, slamming the door loudly behind him and throwing his dead phone onto the bed. "Sarah? Are you back yet?" he called out, hearing the annoyed edge in his own voice.

Silence.

He sighed loudly. It had been a disastrous morning. He'd forgotten his lines, struggled to get the accent right, and tripped over a prop, tearing a hole in the trousers of an extremely expensive bespoke suit, which had been made on Savile row out of fabric originally woven in the sixties. The director had put it down to jet-lag and given him the afternoon off to acclimate to the searing heat.

He pulled a bottle of water out of the minibar fridge and took several large gulps while he scanned the room, searching for his phone charger. It took him a little while to realise that Sarah's things were no longer there, but when he finally opened the wardrobe and discovered that only his clothes hung in the large expanse, a pernicious prickling sensation began to work its way up his spine. He ran to the bathroom and saw instantly that her toothbrush and face creams had gone.

'*No. Fucking. Way.*' He threw the half-drunk bottle at the wall where the blue glass shattered loudly, the noise piercing his anger.

He paced as he waited impatiently for his phone to charge enough to switch on. She couldn't leave. She was contracted to stay in Rome. She wouldn't leave him… The thoughts raced around his head as he watched the stupid red bar on the screen of his phone, waiting for it to turn into a stylised apple, indicating that he could access her number. By the time it was ready, he'd worked himself into a rage. His heart raced as he jabbed at the screen to dial her number.

No answer.

He tried again.

Still no answer. He left a voicemail, speaking through gritted teeth. "Can you call me the moment you get this message." He stood on the terrace to stare absently at the view.

Sarah, meanwhile, had listened to his message and deemed it too rude to answer.

James decided to text her. At least he'd be able to ascertain whether or not she'd read a text.

For god's sake Sarah, answer your phone. How am I meant to fix this if you won't even speak to me?

He was gratified to see that it had been read, but after staring at his phone for ten minutes, plus switching it off, then on again, he realised that she was ignoring him. *How dare she?*

Then as the afternoon went on:

Stop being so juvenile. You won't dictate who my friends are, or who I see.

Still no answer. By this time, James was furious. Angry at being ignored, worried that something had happened to her, and bemused because her job was to answer his calls. People just didn't pretend not to notice his texts.

Finally he sent:

Fine, have it your way. Do what you like.

After that, Sarah switched off her phone. The temptation to call him was getting pretty strong and she didn't want to become either a madly possessive girlfriend, or alternatively a doormat who allowed him to behave exactly as he wanted. Sarah cursed him for putting both of them in that position to start with.

The meal out with Sophia was a nightmare from start to finish. James didn't want to be there and was pre-occupied with Sarah's silence. Sophia was pissed that James hadn't worn anything designed to impress. In truth, he'd pulled on the first T-shirt in the pile, and his cheaper, everyday watch rather than anything ostentatious. He had a bit of a headache and really couldn't be bothered to make nice small talk once the paparazzi had got all their pictures. He was starving hungry though, and the food was fantastic. He eyed up Sophia's uneaten food hungrily. She always ordered a normal meal, ate two bites, and left the remainder untouched. "Mind if I?" He asked, gesturing towards the plate, his winsome smile plastered on his face purely for her benefit. She was scowling after he'd spent the entire meal telling her how wonderful Sarah was.

"Go ahead. I take it you don't need to be low body fat at the moment then?"

"Nope, not till the next shoot."

"Lucky Sarah then," Sophia said moodily, "I got the starving ratbag, while she gets you full of pasta."

"I wasn't that bad," James huffed, before stuffing another forkful of spaghetti into his mouth. He wondered if Sophia had ordered it in the hope of recreating the "Lady and the Tramp" moment for the photographer that she had hidden in a bar across the street. He resisted the urge to wave as he caught the glint of the lens. He did, however, put on his best smile, knowing it would be beamed around the world.

"Yes, you were that bad," she whined. "I put up with hell when you had to diet last time. It was you that forced me into Chad Hilton's arms."

James began to laugh. "I *forced* you, did I? OK. Stick with that story Soph, it doesn't make you sound passive-aggressive at all. Anyway, I'd love to stay and chat, but I truly can't be arsed, so I'm off back to the hotel. Have a nice life babe, and I hope your movie goes OK." He pulled some notes from his wallet and handed them to the waiter before striding out onto the street to find Bob.

Sarah sat in her room that evening, pretending to watch the tiny TV in the room and sulking, helped by a bottle of wine. She contemplated heading down to the bar to get rip-roaring drunk, but worried that the two of them would spot her there when they arrived back. With the cast and crew present, her humiliation would be complete. The combination of a night without sleep and a day of high emotion caught up with her, and she practically passed out on the bed.

Sarah woke early the next morning and blinked at the sunlight streaming in through the window. She checked her phone to see if James had called. Nothing. Groggily, she sat up and took a swig of water, before opening her laptop to check her emails. Straightaway, she spotted one from Clive.

"OMG Sarah, what on Earth is going on out there? Saw this late last night. Internet has gone crazy over it. Is it your doing? Because if it was, then it backfired spectacularly."

She clicked on the link, and was faced with picture after picture of James and his ex, Sophia, having what looked like an intimate dinner at a nearby bistro. They were both holding aloft goblets of wine, drinking a toast to each other. James looked quite happy and relaxed. His ex was grinning like a cheshire cat. Sarah zoomed in to examine the grainy paparazzi pictures more closely. There was one in particular that looked as though they had been aware of the presence of a photographer, and had positioned themselves for the best shot. James was gazing at her with a look Sarah knew well. It was a look she thought he reserved for her alone. Lust, love, and longing, all rolled into one, expressed perfectly on his beautiful face.

She closed the laptop, pulled the sheet back over herself, and sobbed her heart out. She was certain she'd been played. *'Maybe James used me to make Sophia jealous, or I'd been a convenient and available rebound girlfriend to salve the ego she'd shattered.'* Either way, she felt unbearably stupid.

Clive called her five minutes later to find out what was going on, breaking up her pity party. "Have you seen the gossip blogs this morning? The fans are ripping him apart. What on Earth is going on out there?"

She sighed, "I don't know Clive. I didn't want him to meet up with her, for lots of reasons. He refused my advice on it, on both a personal and professional level." She paused. "We're not speaking right now." She considered asking Clive if she could be replaced in Rome and go home to lick her wounds. Sarah just didn't want to have to face the task of damage limitation caused by his reconciliation with Sophia, who hadn't been popular in the fandom.

"Speaking or not, you need to get your fixer's head on and sort this out. Pull in favours, get onto Lainey, see if you can swing her round to cheer this on. If she comes out in favour of them getting back together on her blog, maybe his fans will calm down."

Sarah's blood ran cold. Clive knew that James and she were a couple, yet he only cared about the PR perspective. He didn't give a toss that she was broken hearted and hiding in a stuffy, airless hotel room. "Clive, I'm a bit upset about this, and I'm not sure that steering the gossip is an option for me right now." She was upfront.

"Sarah," Clive sighed. "I don't give a toss whether he was the father of your babies or not. We have a job to do, and we need to do it. It's not personal, but if he goes back to his ex, we need to present it in a certain way, regardless of our personal feelings. Anyway, I seem to recall you thinking that Mr Affleck was a complete tosser, yet you presented him in a favourable light every time regardless."

"I know," she said in a small voice, past the lump in her throat. It was her job. How she felt didn't play a part in it. She sniffed.

"I know you're upset. Hell, I'm upset for you, but we need to do this, Sarah. I'll kick him in the balls for you later. Is that fair?" Clive's voice was softer.

Sarah ordered room service and spent the next hour checking out the gossip sites to see what had been written. Where she could, she steered the conversation away from the dismay his supporters felt and tried to put a positive spin on events. Her heart really wasn't in it, but it was her job, and she took professional pride in being able to do it well, using multiple identities online to make it seem as though lots of his diehard fans supported his relationship with Sophia. She also emailed all her contacts in the blogging world to ask them to put a positive spin on things. As most of them were aware that James and her had been together, albeit discretely, it raised a few sympathetic emails in response. There were also a hell of a lot of questions which needed to be answered.

By eleven, she'd covered all the bases that needed covering, but Sarah knew that she had to answer the blogger's burning question; were the two of them back together? The only person who could tell her definitively was James himself. Taking a deep breath, she picked up her phone and dialled his number. She knew he was on set, so half-expected him not to answer, but call her back between takes. It rang twice before it was picked up. A woman's voice said; "Hi, James's phone," in a strong, American accent.

"Is, is he available… to speak?" Sarah stammered, caught off guard. She wondered why sophia was with him on set.

"No, he's filming right now. It's Sarah isn't it? His PA?"

She was floored. Surely Sophia knew she wasn't just his PA? He'd obviously not told her the truth. "Yes, it's Sarah. Can you ask him to call me back when he's free please?"

"Sure," she drawled, "saw the spin this morning. Was that your doing?"

"Yeah. The bosses were going crazy over all the comments. I had a hell of a clean-up job to do." Sarah wanted her to know that people hadn't been happy, and she'd been ordered to fix it.

"Great publicity though. The gossips just can't get enough of mine and James's story. The two of us are front page everywhere. It's great."

Sarah took a deep breath. "I'm being asked if you're back together. What would you like me to tell them?" She braced herself for the answer.

"Tell them that after a night of passionate making up, we are most definitely back together. You can even hint at a proposal if you like. Something along the lines of us realising we're made for each other." She sounded almost giddy with triumph.

Sarah's blood ran cold.

The Fixer

"OK, leave it with me," she told her through gritted teeth before prodding her phone to end the call without even saying goodbye. She sat back and debated what to do. She had a choice between doing her job properly, which meant spinning events in a positive light, or behaving like a woman scorned, and unleashing the flying monkeys.

The flying monkeys won.

Sarah sat and crafted a press release, detailing how James had dropped her the moment his ex had clicked her fingers. She wrote a heart-wringing piece about being stranded in Rome, relegated to a tiny box room so that James could entertain *her* in the suite they'd shared. She detailed the conversation she'd had with her, and how the Titanium Rod hadn't even had the balls to tell her himself. In short, Sarah aimed a giant wrecking ball at his nice guy image.

She read it through several times, before pressing send to her entire contact list. She figured she was pretty much kissing her career goodbye, but felt sick at the deceit she'd found in the world of celebrity, and she was ready to quit. Sarah knew full well she could get a job at any of the gossip magazines as a journalist.

As she waited for the furore to begin, she packed her case, ready to go home. She didn't have to wait long for the phone to start ringing. Clive was first. "Have you gone mad?" He barked.

"Something like that, yeah," she admitted. "I'm coming home. Sack me if you want, I don't really care."

"Sarah," he pleaded. "They'll all go nuts over this! I really need you to stay and help fix this. Besides, it's all very well throwing a tantrum, but how do you think you'll survive without a job? You're being way too hasty."

"Hasty? Me? I've been cheated on in public, Clive. I'm not putting one more single bit of 'positive spin' on that callous git's behaviour. Stuff him, stuff the studio, and stuff everyone." She jabbed at her phone to cut him off. It rang again straightaway. Greg O'Brien wanted to do a hatchet job. "Do your worst," she told him.

"Will do," he replied cheerfully, pleased to be sticking it to James, especially with Sarah's blessing.

The rest of the afternoon was jammed with phone calls and emails. Sarah just about found a few minutes to sort out a flight, which would mean leaving at six. She glanced at the clock. It was nearly three, which gave her plenty of time to shower, dress, and check out.

Sarah ordered a coffee and sandwich from room service and was just checking the furore on IMDB, when there was a knock on the door. She tied her robe tightly and opened it, fully expecting to see a waiter. Instead, she came face to face with a white faced, livid James.

He stalked into the room, clearly struggling to keep a lid on his fury. "Do you want to tell me exactly what all this is about?" He snarled.

She saw red. Her own fury bubbled up, eclipsing the part of her brain which controlled tact and reason. "You went back to her. What did you expect, a pat on the back and a cheery 'good luck' wish?" She went back to her packing, breaking eye contact. Just looking at his familiar, beautiful face was destroying her.

"I joined her for dinner Sarah, she needed to get her name mentioned in a few places. What exactly is wrong with that? Even the gossips were cool with the pictures this morning, until you sent them all that little essay of yours. Why'd you do that to me?"

She decided to be honest and tell him the truth. "I was steering the gossips this morning, spinning it, you know. While I was cleaning up the mess, I was being asked whether the two of you were back together. I didn't know what to say, so I called you to ask."

"I didn't get a call from you, so don't lie," he butted in.

"Yeah, you did, only it wasn't you that answered it. Your girlfriend did. Told me all about your night of passion, and that you were back together. She even told me to put it out there that you were about to propose." Stupid tears began to leak out of her eyes, rolling their way, unwanted, down her cheeks. She watched as James pulled out his phone and checked his call history. When he saw that Sarah had indeed called him, his spine began to prickle.

"She was only there for ten minutes. She just came to say goodbye. She's on her way to L'Aquila to start filming her next movie. I was only away from my phone for five minutes."

"Yeah, whatever," Sarah sneered nastily, as though she didn't believe a word of it. "So why'd she know I was your PA? Is that what you told her because you're ashamed of shagging your fixer?"

He didn't answer, as he was too busy prodding his phone. She watched as he held it to his face. "Did you answer my phone to Sarah?" He asked as soon as Sophia picked up. "Why did you tell her we spent the night together when we didn't? Were you just being a bitch?"

"I was only joking. God you people are so sensitive." She replied.

Sarah could hear her voice raised through the handset, but couldn't make out what she was saying. "I told you how much she means to me. Why did you try to sabotage that?" He listened intently. "I don't give a toss that my name is front page on TMZ. It's not on there for the right reasons, and right now it seems that you're doing your best to wreck my life." Another load of squeaky sounding shouting poured down his phone.

They were interrupted by Sarah's lunch arriving, and after taking it from the waiter and tipping him, she only caught James shouting: "Don't ever call me, speak about me, or contact me in any way ever again. There'll be no more favours or help. Do. You. Understand?" He listened for a moment, then jabbed at the screen to end the call. He turned to her, "does that reassure you?"

He clearly wanted her to declare that everything was alright and throw herself into his arms, forgetting about the events of the previous night. In a typical blokeish way, she figured that he thought that they'd get back to normal, and it would all be swept under the carpet. As much as Sarah wanted him, she just couldn't set herself up for the heartbreak that she thought was going to come eventually

"I'm not coming back to you," she stated. "I just can't deal with being the mousey girlfriend hidden in the shadows. I'm sorry."

He sat down on the bed. "You're not a mousey girlfriend. If I'd known what she was going to do to us, I'd have never agreed to it. I just thought you were being a bit juvenile about it." He scrubbed his hands over his face.

"Oh, come off it," she yelled. "you knew full well I didn't want you to meet her. I told you, plus I moved out of our room. I might not be a famous actress, but I'm also not a doormat either. You went out with her knowing that I advised you not to, both personally and professionally. You're just angry that I'm not falling into line with what you want. Now, I've decided to go home. You'll be a couple of days without a fixer, so just try not to get into any more trouble."

"You can't just leave. It's your job to be here, despite what's happened between us." James was incredulous.

"I told Clive to sack me. I've had enough. I just can't live in your world, with all the fakery and secrets. I'm sick of constantly worrying about the gossip sites, and whether they approve of stuff or not. I'm going back to London to change jobs and find a nice, uncomplicated man who doesn't let TMZ dictate whether he upsets his girlfriend or not."

He scrubbed at his face again. "I really don't want you to go. I thought what we have," he gestured between them, "was something special, something I've never had before. I thought you felt the same." He looked defeated. The spine prickling had been replaced by a sick feeling in his stomach.

"It was," she agreed. "But then you left me to have dinner with another woman, one that you've had sex with before. I saw the pictures of you gazing lovingly at her. I just can't compete, and I know at some point you'll want the whole 'Hollywood actress power couple' package. I can't fulfil that, so it's better to do this now."

"I'm an actor. Of course I can gaze lovingly at a lady's face when I knew there'd be paps around. It'd be more worrying if I couldn't," he asserted. "It doesn't mean anything."

"It meant something to me," She shouted. "It was the same expression as when you look at me. I recognised it. Tell me, were you acting then as well?"

"Don't be ridiculous," he snapped. "How I feel about you is real." He watched as her nose turned red.

Sarah felt the tears bubbling up. She just didn't know what to do. Torn between desperately wanting to believe him, but at the same time, she couldn't just forget how hurt she was. If she stayed, she'd have to repair all the damage she'd done to his public persona, plus she'd be going through the same thing every time the PR people wanted him linked to other actresses. It was just too much. She let out a sob.

Instantly, she felt his strong arms wrap around her as she gave way to the tumult inside. "We can get through this," he murmured. "You and I can get through anything."

"I don't want to 'get through' stuff. This is gonna keep happening," she managed to say through her sobs.

"No it won't. I'll make sure. I'll tell them I'm not prepared to have fake relationships any more. From now on, it'll only be you." He wiped his thumbs under her eyes, sweeping away the tears. Inside, James was praying. Praying that she wouldn't leave him. He knew for certain, at that moment, that he needed her beyond anything he'd ever experienced before. The little voice in his head that taunted him for not being good enough for her had to be silenced before it drove him mental. He knew he didn't deserve her. If she stayed, he'd try and become the man she deserved.

Sarah sniffed. "I'll cancel my flight, but you need to promise me that you'll never jump to her demands again."

"I promise I'll never even speak to her again, is that better?" He offered. She nodded. He wrapped his strong arms around her and pressed his lips to hers. His kiss was needy, urgent, as his tongue found hers. He felt her undoing his trousers, slipping them down over his hips before grasping his cock, making him hers again. He undid her robe, dropping the tie onto the floor. She was entirely naked beneath the rough waffle material. She'd discovered that the fluffy, luxurious ones were reserved for the penthouse suite inhabitants.

Both desperate to reconnect, Sarah shucked off the robe and hopped onto the dressing table, which was the perfect height for James to plunge straight into her. As he slid in and out, she heard herself cry out at the sensations. When he placed his thumb onto her clit and rubbed, she felt as though she'd explode. As he poured himself into her, James offered up a silent prayer. They clung together through their orgasms, truly joined at the hip.

Afterwards, James ate her lunch while she cancelled the flight. "Are you back on set this afternoon?" She asked. He shook his head.

"I thought I'd help move your stuff back upstairs."

Sarah had to do some serious spinning to get things back on track online. Some of the bloggers weren't happy with her, and there was an undercurrent of annoyance that she'd used them to "punish" James for agreeing to a PR exercise. She had to just shrug it off and grovel to Clive, who was most definitely rather angry with her.

James made an enormous effort to reassure her that they'd get over their hiccup. He moved her things back into the suite before taking her out to dinner in a cute little bistro on a quiet back street. She sipped her Chianti and broached the subject of his ex. "So what is she like?"

"Sarah, do you really want to discuss her after the day we've both had?"

"I need to know," she countered. She wanted to find out if she could compete with Sophia. She was a film star in her own right, while Sarah felt invisible.

"She's alright, if you like that sort of thing," he said warily, clearly worried where the conversation was going. "I didn't see that much of her to be honest, as both our schedules were pretty mad. I suppose it's why the relationship lasted as long as it did."

"She's very pretty," Sarah blurted. She looked down into her glass, not meeting his eyes.

"With her makeup on, yes she is. Not as pretty as you though."

"I'm sorry. I'm being a bit pathetic and needy, aren't I?"

He looked sympathetic. "I see you as so together, so strong. It was a shock watching you fall apart like that. I thought you'd just see it for what it was, me doing an old friend a favour. She needed the attention."

"It was lazy PR. They could've used hundreds of other techniques for getting her name mentioned. I mean, is she planning to piggyback your profile forever?" Sarah was scathing.

"I doubt it, but she just got dropped from one franchise. This new one is pretty important; it's probably her last chance."

It was news to her, and she felt a smirk of satisfaction try and creep its way across her face. She attempted to suppress it. "A bit of fake PR I can live with," mused James, ignoring her smug look. "What I can't forgive was the deliberate attempt to sabotage our relationship, and the disrespect she showed you. I told her all about you, so her thinking you were my PA was all an act."

"She's still in love with you?"

He shook his head. "She was never in love with me, and I wasn't in love with her. We just… got along. It was convenient, us both being in the same game, but she was what you would call an 'asshole' actor. Someone who scrapes into the "B" list, yet tries to demand all the perks and advantages that the "A" listers get. I gather Angelina Jolie has a shorter rider."

Sarah snorted with laughter. There was nothing worse than "nobodies" in the film world who had delusions about their own importance. She'd babysat actresses like that many times. Desperate women who tried to hold onto fame and the trappings of it, long after their moment in the sun had passed. They tended to take their frustrations out on the people around them.

"I still think you should've listened to me and not gone along with it. Your reputation is trashed, and it nearly broke us up. No friend is worth that, no matter how much she needs the fame."

He stared into his glass. "You think I haven't realised that? I felt sick when I walked into our room and realised you'd gone. My reputation can be repaired. I'd even be happy to do a hatchet job on her, you know, set the record straight. Would it make you feel better?"

She shook her head. "Just oxygen to a fame-whore. Best thing to do is ignore her. I'll do some spinning, put it out there that you discovered she just wanted publicity. Just you keep quiet and don't give her the satisfaction of feeling that her little ruse worked." A plan was forming in her mind. She could simply tell the bloggers the truth, that James had been used for publicity and in his naivety, he'd trusted her. He'd been an idiot, but she'd been the liar.

He snapped Sarah out of her trance. "I think we should go public."

"No! I'm not prepared to get ripped apart again just yet." They were accepted as a couple by the crew, friends, and family, the people who mattered. Sarah found the thought of being scrutinised by the public horrifying. She'd read all the comments about his ex on the fan sites. The vast majority had declared her "not good enough" for him. No woman would ever be deemed good enough for their god. When Sarah had been outed before, she'd found it pretty harsh reading that she had man hands, and that she wasn't considered attractive enough.

"At some point, we need to declare to the world that we're together," he pressed. "Now is as good a time as any. We can say that my meeting with her made me realise how much I'm in love with you. The gossips'd lap it up, especially as I never normally discuss my private life."

"They'll just think I'm second best," she warned. "They'll assume she didn't want you, so you settled for me, Miss Average."

He banged his hand on the table, making her jump. "Don't talk about yourself like that," he hissed angrily. "It drives me mad. You want to know what I see when I look at you?" He was getting mad. "I see a gorgeous, sexy, intelligent woman. One I want to jump on at every opportunity. One whose mind and body drive me wild with desire. Don't ever think that I'd rather have a vapid actress over you. I just wish you'd drop this 'Miss Average' rubbish and take a look in the mirror."

"That's easy for you to say, being the most beautiful man in the world— physical perfection. You've never had to worry about me running off with someone more handsome," Sarah countered, getting cross at his cluelessness.

"True, but you could run off with someone wealthier, more intelligent, less restricted, or simply someone not in the public eye. Looks aren't everything you know. Mine will fade in time, and I'd like to think there was more to me than just a pretty face." He looked annoyed, which only served to make him ruggedly handsome. Sarah wondered if he cried prettily too.

"True, but you've got a rockin' body too," she quipped, mainly to diffuse the atmosphere brewing between them. It worked. A smile tugged at the corners of his mouth.

"Not as sexy as yours though. I've missed you," he admitted.

"Missed you too."

"I'll get the bill. I have the urge to take you straight back to the hotel and teach you how to view yourself through my eyes." He licked his lips. She shivered.

They sped back to their hotel, barely able to keep their hands off each other. As soon as they were in the room, James ordered her to strip. She undressed slowly, as he lay on the bed, watching her intently. His red-hot gaze made her feel wanton; his evident appreciation left her in no doubt as to how much he desired her.

As she slid her knickers down her legs, finally nude, he moved off the bed, throwing off his T-shirt and shorts, revealing his arousal. He was Adonis himself, every plane of his body perfected, every inch of skin perfectly buffed. Sarah instantly felt unworthy.

He must've sensed her hesitation, as he took her over to the mirror and stood behind her. "Look how beautiful you are," he whispered as he ran his hands over her. "Look how delicate and soft your skin is, how full and sexy your breasts are." He cupped them gently, kneading them while he pressed kisses down her neck. She stared at the two of them in the mirror, entranced by the sight of him worshipping her body.

His hands slid lower, "and this," he murmured, "drives me wild, beyond wild. I'd walk over hot coals just to see this, taste it. Have you any idea what just the scent of it does to me?" He glanced at her face in the mirror. She shook her head. "It turns me into a wild, insatiable caveman, unable to ever get enough of you." His fingers probed her gently. "Don't you think that you have the most beautiful pussy in the world?"

"It's just ordinary." It was actually something she'd never really thought about before.

"Oh no," he murmured. "It's most definitely not ordinary. There's nothing ordinary about you, any part of you. You were made to drive me crazy with desire."

Sarah stared at the image of the two of them in the mirror. She could see he was telling the truth. He was running his hands over her, a look of pure reverence on his beautiful face. This man was both perfect and imperfect at the same time, and he desired her above all others. There was no shyness between them, as she knew he loved every part of her. She turned to face him, and kissed him deeply, grateful for his reassurance.

"Let me love you," he implored, his voice husky with need.

"I'm yours," she told him.

CHAPTER 12

Anna

"Mitch told me you'd like to teach Match-fit, is that right?" Bart boomed. Anna beamed a smile at him. She liked Bart a lot. For all his beardy gruffness, he was at heart a nice man.

"I would. It'd be great to get more girls working out. We could maybe even form a team to compete in the Match-fit league if there were enough of us." She knew that Bart wanted more new members.

"It's hard, you know, without nice changing rooms and all that fancy-schmantzy stuff," he said. "Attracting more ladies would be great 'n all, but don't you think it'd be easier if we were in a better box? This one's OK for men, but we ain't got no room to expand."

"If I worked here, I'm sure I could talk to my daddy about a new place in that swanky new complex he's building. I don't know if I could get you more than a fifty percent discount on the rent, but I could try..." She dangled an enormous carrot in front of Bart.

Her father was delighted when she announced that she had a new job at the local gym. He knew her boss from church and approved of him. Bart was a good, solid, soldier of the Pentecost in Ricky's opinion. Plus, he was glad that Anna had finally made use of all the courses he'd paid for over the years.

When she'd sounded him out about expanding Bart's gym into one of the buildings he'd just erected on the edge of his industrial estate, he was all in favour. Not only did he get a good tenant, it also meant he could keep an eye on Anna. At nearly twenty it was inevitable that she'd find herself a husband soon. If anything, she was leaving it a bit late. The church elders had tried to introduce her to some suitable boys, but nothing had come of it. Ricky regarded Anna as a total daddy's girl, which pleased him enormously.

He made the decision years previously that he would remain true to Anna until she married. When that happened and he lost his girl, he would find himself a nice young woman and marry again. He quite liked the idea of an oriental mail-order wife, somebody quiet and submissive who would tend to his needs in Anna's place. The only fly in that particular ointment was that he preferred blondes.

On the day that Bart signed the contract for his new premises, Mitch had managed to steal a quickie with Anna in his truck down at the end of the dirt track that led to the creek. As she bounced up and down on his dick, he gazed, transfixed, at her breasts bouncing in time to the Queen song playing on the radio. "I want to break free" struck him as entirely apt as a soundtrack for his life. Erika was still spending as much time as possible around her "friends," her father was still hanging on, eluding the grim reaper, and the training that the film crew had booked was moving ever closer.

In an ideal world, if Erika's father would peg it, the money from him would then have to be shared between the two of them when he divorced her. He would get to keep his new earnings a secret from her as they would be outside of the marriage. He would then be free to shag Anna or other girls whenever he pleased, rather than having to sneak around and screw in his truck. Thankfully, Anna hadn't complained about it. If anything, she'd proven to be the most easy-going girl he'd dated, never complaining about his lack of chivalry or the fact that he never took her anywhere.

He'd expected her to be a princess type, so he'd been pleasantly surprised when she just accepted that he'd call her for a shag, then drop her home or at the gym afterwards. The only time they didn't shag was when they were working out together.

Two weeks later, they both helped Bart move into the new "box," as gyms of that type are generally called. The ladies' changing room was still being fitted out, but the rest was good to go. It was significantly larger than the previous place, so Bart had spent a lot of time planning where everything would go, and the move went smoothly.

CHAPTER 13

The two of them seemed to take a while to get back into their previous intensity. James was working on set a lot of the time and spare moments were used for prepping and learning lines. Sarah tried to stay off the subject of Sophia, and thankfully, the fans online seemed to want to forget about her too. James kept pressing the subject of going public though. One evening, they were sitting in the bath, an enormous, marble, double-ended one, which he'd filled with silky, hot, oil-scented water. James was sipping a glass of wine and laying back, soaking away the stresses of the day. Sarah was massaging his feet, which he liked.

"What's gonna happen when I have to go back to America? You could come with me."

She paused the massage. "I can't just up and leave, you know that. I have my job, my house. My whole life is in London." She'd been trying to avoid thinking about the situation. Everything which made her the person she was, was in London, except for James, whose life was mainly in LA.

"You were able to come to Rome for six weeks with no problems," he countered.

"I'm technically working," she reminded him, slithering her hand up his leg playfully. "I'm still getting paid. It's a hard job, but somebody has to do it." Her hand reached its destination and she gave him a gentle squeeze, which made him laugh.

"Naughty girl," he chided. "Are you trying to distract me?"

"Is it working?" She asked coquettishly. He smiled.

"Yeah." He pulled her towards him, the oily water making her slippery enough to slide right up his taut, firm body, until she was in the position he was clearly aiming for. As she sank down onto him, the conversation was forgotten.

The next day, an invitation arrived for the BAFTAs. James was asked to present an award, which was quite an honour. It would be a widely-publicised affair, on live television, and attended by the top tier of British celebrities. It would be terrific for raising his profile, particularly with a UK-based film in production. Sarah checked his schedule to discover that he'd still be in London that evening and was available. James seemed happy to do it, so she emailed his acceptance and sat in his trailer to organise a designer to dress him.

Half an hour later, James arrived for his lunch. As he tucked into his linguine, she outlined what he'd have to do for the BAFTA ceremony. "Tom Ford put his hand up to dress you," she told him.

"Good. Are you gonna accompany me?"

Sarah shook her head. "PR will probably want you to accompany a starlet." She was startled when he thumped his hand down on the table.

"No bloody way," he exclaimed. "This is the perfect opportunity to show the world that we're together. I said before, I'm not doing any more fake PR stuff. I'm taking you, so get onto Tom Ford and see if they'll dress you too."

"I'm not famous, so they won't be interested," she said weakly. "Isn't it rather… public? You know, to have our first night out together?"

"Well then, tip off the paps and I'll take you out tonight," he snapped. "Sarah, you have to stop letting fans, trolls, etcetera dictate how we are as a couple. We have to do what's right for us, nobody else. I want you on my arm at the BAFTAs, done up to show what a beautiful lady you are. I can't think of anything worse than having some trampy starlet hanging off me, dressed like a slut to get attention." His eyes flashed his annoyance. Even angry, James was delicious.

Sarah stayed silent. She could understand his reticence about the PR, especially after the last disaster, but she felt awkward about having to ask for a free dress. It was one thing doing it for clients, but asking for herself was totally another matter.

"What is it?" He asked. "I can tell something's bothering you."

The Fixer

"It's just…" She began. She stopped, unsure how to put her fears into words.

"It's just what?" He demanded, his voice softer, less angry, more concerned. He never stayed angry for long, especially in front of her.

"Asking for a free dress… I'm not famous. What if they say no?" She stuttered.

"Then I'll buy you one."

That was it, the subject was closed. She decided not to mention all the other issues racing around her head, namely that she'd be publicly ripped apart, her man-hands brought up again, and two days afterwards, James would be disappearing from her life back to America for the best part of a year.

"Don't get hung up about it," he interrupted her musings. "It's only a dress. We can look for one here if you like. There's some boutiques in the main boulevard area."

Sarah debated telling him what she was really worried about, but dismissed the idea as he had to be back on set within ten minutes. There was just enough time to clean his teeth and change his shirt. She shoved her worries to the back of her mind as she checked him over and bagged up that morning's shirt for the laundry.

When he'd gone back on set, she emailed all the designers again to request that they dress her, informing them that she'd be James's date for the awards. She cringed slightly as she pressed "send." Ten minutes later, her heart sank as several emails came back declining. Only Tom Ford accepted, albeit offering to let her choose something from their ready-to-wear collection. It ran the risk of someone else wearing the same outfit, which would be a disaster. She decided to look in some of the Rome boutiques instead.

James was livid when she told him. "Email Tom Ford back, and tell him I'm declining his offer of a suit. If he won't accommodate you, then he's not getting his clothes on my back. I'm not filming tomorrow afternoon, so we can go shopping then."

"Isn't that a bit childish? You said yourself that you love his suits." Personally, she thought it was a wrong move, but he was adamant.

"I'll go to Mayfair Tailors. I'm damn sure Alessandro would jump at the opportunity. We met at a party last year, and he said he'd like to dress me. Can you dig out his number, please?"

Sarah did as he asked, and as predicted, the owner of Mayfair Tailors was delighted. James fixed an appointment, and she emailed over his measurements. The first problem was solved. An hour later, her second problem was sorted when Alessandro called back to tell her that an up-and-coming couturier friend of his would be more than happy to loan her a dress for the evening, in return for a mention.

It left the problem of handling Tom Ford, who was understandably pretty cheesed off. Sarah spoke to the head of PR, who informed her that it had been an underling who'd acted without authority, offering Sarah their cheaper, less-exclusive collection.

"Oh, that's such a shame," she said, "but I couldn't run the risk of two of us wearing the same dress. It's such a huge event. I'm sure you understand." She was being a little snarky, given that she had a plan B, but the excuses were hogwash, only given because they wanted to claim credit for James's tuxedo. She didn't warn to burn bridges, so she soothed the PR man, vowing to get in touch for the next large event.

With that issue solved, Sarah kept busy the rest of the afternoon getting her hair done and ensuring a photographer would be present that evening at Il Convivio di Troianai, where she'd booked a table for their first, very public date.

She'd taken some advice from Clive, as he was the expert. He advised her to take up James's offer to go public sooner, rather than at the BAFTAs. "Get used to it on a small scale first. After the BAFTAs, the world and his dog'll have an opinion, so let the fans get in first with their views. Your skin'll be a bit thicker by then."

"Oh great, you think they're gonna be hateful, don't you?"

"Sarah, you could be a Victoria's Secret model who'd won the Nobel Peace Prize, and they'd still claim that you weren't good enough for the object of their devotion. Get used to it, and whatever you do, don't take it to heart. This is terrific PR for James, so don't worry, we're all covering your back."

With her hair freshly done, a new outfit on, and a fake smile plastered on her face to cover up the hideous nerves churning her stomach, James and Sarah sped over to the restaurant in a taxi. He, of course, looked his usual calm self, used to the vast amounts of attention he got whenever he stepped out of their hotel. He squeezed her hand. "You OK? You look tense." Her brows were furrowed and her jaw clenched.

"I'm scared," she admitted. "I'm not usually on this side of the gossip columns."

"It'll be fine," he reassured her. "It'll just be a flurry of opinions, then it'll all calm down."

Their "date" was delightful. James was in good form, smiling a lot, giving his best "smitten kitten" expression when he thought they were being observed or snapped. He'd advised her against choosing anything difficult or messy to eat, reminding her that getting papped with sauce round her gob wouldn't seem so funny in the morning.

For the first time, Sarah experienced hostility from one of his fans, who asked for a photo. She practically shoved her out of the way. "Just James," she'd barked at the bemused waiter who was taking the picture. She'd practically draped herself over him as he stood quietly in his usual good-natured way.

They hadn't discussed his impending return to the States, which James was glad about. It seemed such an intractable problem that he was trying not to think about it. They kept the conversation light, James regaling her with funny stories from his school days, making her laugh. She suspected he was making sure the paps got photos of the pair of them clearly having a good time.

As they left, the paparazzi went crazy, sticking their lenses in their faces. "Guys, if you just calm down, you can have some proper pictures of us," he told them. They stood and posed, James holding her firmly round her shoulder, pulling her in close.

"So how long have you been together?" One of the crowd asked.

"Not long," James replied, his voice confident and self-assured.

"What happened to the last one?" Asked another.

"We were never back together," he answered. "It was just dinner. You guys read far too much into it. Sarah and I are together now."

A hundred further questions were yelled at them. James ignored them and lifted his hand to wave goodbye. "Ciao everyone. We're off now." They hopped into the waiting car and drove off.

"That seemed to go OK," Sarah said, relieved it was all over.

"Yep. Think they got some good shots. It'll be round all the fan sites within the hour."

Back at the hotel, James opened a bottle of champagne. "We

should drink a toast to your coming out," he said as he poured two glasses.

"That sounds wrong on so many levels," she laughed.

"Well you're public property now. We need to enjoy your last night of anonymity. He handed her a glass of bubbly. "To being publicly together." He raised it in a toast. She clinked with his and drank, the bubbles tickling the back of her nose.

"To being together," she agreed.

"And now I think we should consummate our decision," he purred, taking her glass and placing it on the table. He fixed her with a look so scorching it would burn the sun.

Her body responded immediately, "What would you like?" She asked playfully.

"You," he breathed. "Naked and ready on that bed."

She squealed as he grabbed her and kissed her hard. His sculptured lips seemed to need to kiss every inch of her lips, face, and neck. As she gave in to the intense pleasure, the pesky seed of doubt wormed its way back to the front of her mind. Not only would the whole world know they were together until he left to go home, but Sarah knew she'd never again meet a man like him. She would be ruined for anyone else.

The next morning, she was up at the same time as James, which was unusual. He was still having to train hard every day before going on set, so he was generally up with the lark. Sarah was the lazy one who liked to roll out of bed at nine.

She sat up in bed drinking her coffee, checking out all the comments from the pictures which had been released overnight. Some of his more eagle-eyed fans had spotted that she was the same girl as the London pics.

The comments were fairly tame. James sat on the bed while she read some out. "See, told you it'd be fine," he said, kissing her wetly on the cheek.

"They all seem to be more interested in discussing someone called Superwoman," she told him, frowning at the screen. She read through some more threads. "Apparently she claims that she's your best friend."

"Never heard of her," he laughed and added, "just another fantasist." He took the laptop off her and pulled her into a hug. "I'll see you on set. Be good."

After he'd gone, Sarah carried on checking all the various sites.

The Fixer

Initial reception had been OK, so she turned her attention back to the weird girl claiming to be his best friend. It didn't take long to get onto her Twitter feed. She obviously wasn't aware of Sarah's name. She read through streams of Tweets listing out how she was the best friend of many celebrities, James included. Sarah smiled as she read her Tweets that morning claiming to be flying first class to Florence for a lunch date with James, clearly unaware that he would be in Rome having lunch with her. Feeling rather mean for laughing at her along with other James fans, she clicked off her Twitter feed and concentrated on her emails.

Clive had been delighted with the pictures, remarking that Sarah "hadn't let the side down." She huffed a bit, but composed a nice reply, thanking him for his support. She hadn't spotted any PR steering going on, but that wasn't to say it wasn't being done. To be honest, she just figured everyone was relieved that she was female. Gay rumours had dogged poor James for years, with every girlfriend dismissed as a "beard."

Her own Twitter feed had exploded, messages of support and advice from friends and colleagues mingled with Tweets full of questions and curiosity from his fan base. One jumped out at her though: *keep your hands off James or you die bitch* It was Superwoman.

She shuddered. She'd known that sort of thing would happen, but it was still shocking. She took a screenshot of the message before blocking the sender, wondering why anyone would behave like that.

By the time Sarah met James on set, she'd forgotten all about it.

It was a bit of a shock to her system, suddenly becoming semi-famous. All her life she'd been able to walk around with no make-up on, or her hair in a ponytail. Overnight, she was thrust into a world where she was constantly judged. James was used to it, and his extraordinary good looks were entirely natural. He woke up looking like a movie star. Sarah woke up with mad hair and a face that resembled a ghost. It astonished her just how quickly his fans were able to find out her personal details. She cringed as they gleefully posted snippets online, broadcasting where she lived, worked, and who some of her exes were. Someone even discovered an old school photo and put it on Instagram. Sarah wasn't amused, as she'd wrongly thought that her social media had been locked down better than that.

Everywhere they went together, paparazzi followed. Sarah wondered aloud whether they'd get bored trailing around after the pair of them as they shopped for souvenirs before leaving Rome and moving on to the next location in Florence. "I doubt it," laughed James. "They're all set on getting pictures of you."

"God knows why," she muttered as they walked along the main shopping street. They stopped outside a jewellers which sold Omegas, as James needed a new strap for his watch. After perusing the new models in the window for a while, they went inside.

The interior was beautifully cool after the blazing sun outside. James's grasp of Italian was far better than Sarah's, so he was able to ask for a new watch strap with only a minimum of sign language. They showed them into a private room and brought out a selection for him to look at. He chose a plain black leather one and slipped off his watch for them to change the strap over. It took a little while, but pleased to be in the cool, they sat and waited.

"Is there anything else you'd like to look at while you're waiting?" enquired the assistant, a small, wiry man who spoke pretty reasonable English.

Sarah shook her head, but James had other ideas. "We need a souvenir for you," he said. "Would you prefer a necklace or a watch?"

"I don't need anything," she protested. It was clearly an expensive place. To her, a suitable souvenir was a tea-towel. James wasn't having any of it.

"Could I see a selection of necklaces please? I think the lady prefers gold."

"I didn't expect anything," she spluttered.

"I know. It's why I want to treat you," he said, before leaning over to kiss the tip of her nose. "You deserve nice things, especially after going public for me. I know how much your privacy meant to you."

Before she could object, the assistant arrived carrying three trays containing various necklaces. She watched as James looked through them. "Which one do you like?" he asked. He followed her eyes to a cute little stylised heart pendant. "This one?" he asked, before pulling it gently from its mount.

"It's beautiful," she murmured. He placed it around her neck and did up the little catch. The assistant brought over a mirror for her to look. The necklace caught the light, glimmering against her bare skin. It was subtle, yet incredibly stylish, which epitomised James.

"You look beautiful," he told her, unembarrassed by the presence of the assistant. "We'll take it please."

"Thank you. I love it," she said softly. It was the nicest gift she'd ever been given. She had no idea how much it cost and neither did he. She just hoped he wouldn't get a shock at the till and change his mind. The assistant unclipped her new pendant and took it to be boxed up. James trotted over to pay for it and pick up his watch while Sarah nosed around the rest of the store, gazing in awe at the massive diamonds on display in a glass case.

"One day," said James, making her jump. She hadn't heard him approach.

"Not sure about that," she quipped. "I think they're too big. That bracelet would weigh a ton," she laughed, pointing at a heavily-encrusted bangle. It had crossed the line from bling to gaudy.

"That's not what I meant," he said quietly, his voice was serious. Her tummy flipped.

Sarah still had a stupid, goofy grin on her face as they left the jewellers. They'd planned to visit the Trevi Fountain that afternoon as tourists after a spot of lunch. As they walked out of the door, away from the air-conditioned quiet, they were besieged by photographers yelling James's name. Even though they posed for a few minutes to allow them to get their shots, they wouldn't leave them alone, following them down the street as they headed for the fountain.

"Sod this," James barked as they jostled the two of them along, yelling stuff in Italian that he didn't understand. "I think we may have to abandon and get back to the hotel. These idiots aren't gonna give up." By that time, a small crowd had grown, people wanting to see what all the fuss was about. James managed to flag down a taxi and get them both in. People had been pulling them back, shoving cameras in their faces. It was terrifying. Even as the cab pulled away, they were trying to open the doors. Sarah prayed that he hadn't dropped her new necklace in the mêlée.

As soon as they were clear, she saw that he was still clutching the little bag. "Is my pendant safe?"

He turned to her, regret and fear clouding his lovely face. "Yes, but you aren't. You've got a cut above your eyebrow." She touched it, instantly feeling wetness. Sarah swiped at it with her hand. It didn't feel as though she was bleeding heavily.

He examined the cut, wiping it with a tissue from her bag. "How did it happen?"

"It must have been when that pap shoved his camera in my face," she replied. She was a bit shaken up, her hands were trembling, and she was fighting the urge to cry.

"Hey now," said James, scooping her onto his lap. "C'mon tough girl. Don't let them get to you. We won't go out without security again, I promise."

"Sorry," she sniffed. "It was just a bit of a shock, that's all."

He held her tight all the way back to the hotel. She loved how protective he was. Being in his arms always felt like her safe place.

Sarah's poor, battered face looked puffy and bruised. She stared at it in the bathroom mirror, horrified at what they'd done. The cut was small and superficial. It wouldn't need stitches. The events of the afternoon had been a huge wake-up call for both of them. James always said he was used to the attention. He saw no problem with posing for pictures or taking the time to chat with fans and sign autographs, as he enjoyed the fuss. Sarah, on the other hand, wasn't famous and didn't want to be. She'd been terrified by the photographers grabbing at her and the people who just wanted to stare as though she was some kind of freak. For the first time, she understood why previous women had run for it.

Instead, she flexed her steel backbone, washed her face, and set about organising some extra security. She was damned if she'd let anyone drive her away from the man she loved. James was out on the terrace, brooding, she suspected. He tended to internalise problems and had a bit of a habit of sulking.

With her face all cleaned up, she went to find him. He was seated at the little iron patio set, so she slid onto his lap and gave him a kiss. "You OK?" He asked when they came up for air.

"I'm fine. It'll take more than a few rabid photographers to upset me." She felt as though she needed to reassure him, make him realise that she'd stick with him, no matter what. "I've upped our security detail though. We have budget for far more than we were using, so I've ordered the full whack."

"Good, well done." He seemed pre-occupied and a little distant. "Shall we test them out tonight? We could go out to dinner, celebrate our last night here."

The Fixer

Sarah beamed at him. "I'd love that. I'll book us somewhere nice. Do you want to invite any of the others?"

He shook his head. "Harry and his wife left today. They're having a couple of days' holiday before he's needed in Florence. Rizzi already has plans tonight, he was telling me about it earlier today."

Protected by security, they had a wonderful last night in Rome. Sarah booked an upmarket, Michelin-starred restaurant, and they were pretty much left alone. James loved the food and ate with gusto, no doubt enjoying the last few weeks of freedom before he once again began his training for the next Cosmic Warriors role, which would entail a tightly-controlled diet and exercise routine.

That night, after making love, James lay gazing at her. His face was so beautiful, so perfect, that Sarah was transfixed. "What?" She asked, smiling at him.

"Nothing, just looking," he replied. "You're just so perfect. Sometimes I can't believe you're real."

She laughed. "That? Coming from you? The man with the most perfect face in Hollywood?"

"Not as perfect as yours. I couldn't love you any more than I do already. I never thought I'd find you, find this." He gestured between them, "It just feels so right."

She knew what he meant. They had an intimacy between them. Before she'd met James, when friends described their boyfriends as their soulmate or their best friend, she'd been skeptical, dismissive even. She only fully understood it after experiencing her relationship with James. They were two halves of the whole.

"It does," she agreed, "but I'm worried about you going back to the States. You'll get busy and forget me." It was her fear, that they'd try and keep a long-distance relationship going, but it would just fizzle out.

"We'll work it out," he said, before nuzzling into her, his talented hands distracting her. Again.

Sarah woke up to an empty bed. Glancing at the clock, she could see that James was probably at the gym. He'd left a little note by the bed, just saying "I love you," which made her smile. She made a coffee, ordered some breakfast, and opened her laptop to get on with some work.

Her smile soon faded when she discovered she had four hundred emails waiting. She clicked on one from Clive that simply asked her to call him ASAP. Susie had sent her a link, followed by a load of ????, and a request that she call her too. Sarah clicked on the link, which took her to a well-known gossip site.

James and his girlfriend Sarah go shopping for an engagement ring today

The pictures showed them going into and leaving the jeweller's. There was also a grainy shot of them both staring into the diamond cabinet in the shop. *'No wonder the Paps had gone mental at us.'* Sarah thought.

Still smiling at the misunderstanding, she clicked through all her social pages. IMDB had gone into meltdown, while the Facebook pages were being more sensible, urging their readers to wait for an official announcement.

The smile was wiped off her face when she checked Twitter. Someone with a new account calling themselves @Hat2465 had Tweeted: **I told you to leave him alone. Now you must die bitch. He's mine.**

CHAPTER 14

Anna

Fury. White hot, incandescent fury. As she stared at the screen, Anna had the almost overwhelming urge to put her fist straight through it. The sight of her man, James Morell, looking at diamond rings with that, that... tranny bitch with the big hands. It was just too much for her to process. Who did that... whore think she was? She slammed her fist down on the desk, making the keyboard jump.

Anna went onto IMDB, where the consensus was that James had been brainwashed by an obviously-pregnant witch. They'd already worked out the timeline and declared that it couldn't possibly be James's child, and she was attempting to dupe him into marrying her. Some of the more unhinged posters urged everyone to email his agent to call his mother and try and "save him" from her.

Anna, of course, joined in with the condemnation, offering her own theory that she had isolated him from his family and brainwashed him, all the time hoping and praying that Sarah would be gone by the time he came to film in Illinois. In fact, she decided to help things along in that department. Sarah had blocked her on Twitter, but it was easy to make a new account and warn her off. It would be doing her a favour really, as she wasn't really suitable for James and would only end up hurt, Anna reasoned, as she composed her Tweet. It would be better all round if James came to Illinois alone.

Her little town was getting excited about the prospect of the film crew arriving. Nothing as big as this had happened in years, certainly not in Anna's lifetime. Even the church elders had thrown their considerable influence in favour of the cast and crew being made welcome in the area and by the church, if they needed somewhere to worship. In truth, gaining a celebrity endorsement was the holy grail of niche churches. The elders were secretly hoping that James Morell could be persuaded to join the Illinois Pentecost, as they'd seen what Tom Cruise had done for the Scientologists.

Her uncle and his family were all packed and ready to stay with them for the duration, which both Anna and Ricky were dreading. The boys were noisy, messy, and constantly hungry. The last time they'd stayed, when his brother and sister-in-law, Jen, had decided to have a new extension built, the fridge had been emptied on an almost daily basis, with gallons of milk necked and a constant supply of snacks being prepared and eaten. Both Anna and Ricky, who was a surprisingly good cook, were used to their kitchen being pristine and fridge well stocked. The perpetual mess and emptied cupboards grated on both of them enormously.

Jen tossed the letter Matt had received from the production company aside. It demanded that she shell out for contract cleaners and a yard maintenance company to ensure that the house and garden was "fit" for its employees. She glanced at the pile of boxes in the corner of the room. With all their belongings out of the way, she could easily give the house a once over herself to save a few hundred bucks, she thought, oblivious to the dust-streaked furniture and scuffed floors. As she slowly pushed the Hoover around, she ruminated on spending six months at Ricky's place. Her tummy flipped at the thought of being in close proximity to him every day, sharing his space. He was a fine specimen of a man, she thought as she remembered the times he'd taken her over her kitchen table back when they were both younger, when their kids were all small. He'd lost interest in recent years, and she wondered why.

It had been around the time all their children had hit adolescence. Prior to that, Ricky had been a beast, an insatiable man with an unusually high sex drive and a kinky bent. He'd loved to spank her hard, calling her a naughty girl, then take her hard and fast. Matt had been boring and staid in comparison.

Then one day he'd lost interest in her. It had been as simple and sudden as that. At first, Jen had thought he'd got himself another woman, but no girlfriend ever appeared. When she'd tried to find out what was wrong, he'd blown her off with a dumb excuse, saying his sex drive had waned. She hoped it had come back, at least a little bit.

CHAPTER 15

Sarah

It promised to be a frantic day. Not only did Sarah have to pack them both up and move them to Florence for the next leg of filming, she also had to deal with the fallout from the misunderstanding in the jeweller's. Even her mum got wind of it and called her to see if it was true. She packed their cases with her phone permanently tucked under her chin.

Clive advised against issuing a statement denying the engagement. Ever the PR man, he knew that the mystery and conjecture would keep the public talking for a while. All Sarah could say to the various journalists and bloggers was that she could confirm it was indeed them in the shop, but no official statements would be made.

James seemed to find the whole thing funny. He read a couple of the articles when he got back from the gym, and apart from calls to his mum and one of his brothers, let her get on with dealing with the press.

The journey took around three hours. They both sat quietly, watching the scenery, each lost in their own thoughts. They would be in Florence for two weeks, then London for another few days. After that, James would be flying to Illinois, the setting for his next film, for pre-production training. Sarah knew she had him for less than three weeks before he'd fly out of her life. She'd go back to being a gofer for spoilt actors while he'd be immersed in a nine month filming commitment in Illinois.

"You're not still brooding over that death threat are you?" James interrupted her thoughts. "Whoever it is was, firstly has to find us, second, get past our security, and lastly actually carry out his threat. It won't happen, it's just a nutter."

"No, I'm not worried about it," she told him. She'd actually put it to the back of her mind. Sarah had far more pressing things to worry about. James's hand found hers, he squeezed it gently in an act of reassurance. She scooted across the seat to snuggle into him, painfully aware that she had to make the most of his physical presence while she could.

Florence was delightful, although poor James barely saw it. The crew were cramming in as much filming as possible into a short window of time, as both James and Harry had other commitments elsewhere. His days were full of costume changes and endless takes. During the long, boring days, Sarah busied herself organising stuff for their return to the UK. Their evenings were spent eating out, seeing tourist stuff, or staying in their hotel room making love.

Sarah could sense a new urgency to their lovemaking during that time, as though they were both trying to get even closer, if that was possible. James seemed even more insatiable than usual, needing to be inside her at every opportunity. It was as though he wanted to constantly remind her how great they were together, as if she needed reminding. Sarah tried to give him all the attention he could possibly want. She worked in his trailer during the day, so if he had a break, she'd be there, ready and willing.

Florence was genuinely a happy time for them both. They existed in a bubble of unreality, just the two of them, totally wrapped up in each other. Sarah was still getting online threats, mainly from the "Hat" person. She hadn't blocked him or her, instead choosing to just read, screenshot, and ignore. There were plenty of nutters online, so someone describing themselves as a world traveller who sent nasty messages was, in her mind, not to be taken seriously. She put them in the same category as the obviously gay fellow on Twitter who regularly begged her for a photo of James's dick.

As their return to London came ever closer, she sensed a despondency in James. It was the elephant in the room they'd both been ignoring. During the few days they had at home before he flew back to the States, he was booked back to back with interviews, appearances, and photo-shoots. They both began to hate his job. Even devoting an evening to the BAFTAs turned into a chore.

It all came to a head on the plane going home. Sarah was running through his schedule with him, explaining the various commitments. "So when do we get some alone time?" He asked. "You've booked me up until I step on the plane." She could see he wasn't happy.

"All of these were deemed imperative by both the studio and your agent. If you want someone to moan at, talk to Alan. I only do the scheduling. I'm not exactly happy about it either. Your bloody job strikes again." She turned back to her iPad in a huff.

"My job strikes again? I think that's a bit rich coming from you. You knew exactly what my job was and what it entailed when you met me. You're the one who won't come to the US with me. You're the one putting your job first, ahead of us." He was keeping his voice low, but she could hear the anger and frustration.

"It's not just my job," Sarah hissed. "It's my life. My house, my salary, and my friends are all in London. I'd be homeless, jobless, and penniless in America, or is it only about you and your precious career?"

"Don't be so stupid," he huffed. "You'd live with me, and we have plenty of cash. You make it sound as though I'd dump you on the streets and let you starve. Rent out your house. That way you can build up some savings in the UK."

"You make it sound so easy. Unlike you, I can't work in the US. I'd be totally dependent on you for everything, and unlike you, I don't have a few million in the bank to soften the blow of giving up a career I've worked my arse off to get."

"Oh, there's an easy solution to all that," he said, flashing her his heart-melting smile.

"Really?" She said sarcastically. "If there is, I can't wait to hear it."

"Marry me," he whispered. He held his breath. It was the first, the only time he'd ever uttered those words. He'd run through scenarios in his head, trying to plan the right moment, the perfect, romantic proposal that Sarah deserved. Instead, he'd ended up muttering it on an aircraft. He felt as though he'd short-changed her somewhat.

Sarah's world stood still. She tried to process his words, but he was staring at her with intense blue eyes, as though he was trying to read her thoughts, which were a jumbled mess. She opened her mouth to speak, then closed it again, lost for words.

"Say something," he said. She saw a flicker of fear cross his beautiful face.

"Was that a proposal?" She asked, concerned that she'd either misheard him, or that he'd just said it in the heat of the moment because he didn't want an argument.

"I've been trying to ask you for ages," he said, sheepishly, "but the moment was never right, and I kind of bottled it. I don't want to be without you."

"You won't be away forever," she reminded him.

"Sarah, I fell apart when you moved out of our room for a day. I really don't want to be without you for nine months out there. We know we're good together and that we'll end up growing old together in our country cottage, so why not just accept the inevitable?"

He was unyielding, determined not to be apart. James might be a nice guy, but he had a quiet determination. She knew from his bio that he wasn't the type to give up easily. He'd attacked Hollywood over and over again until they'd let him in. If he really wanted something, he wouldn't stop until he'd won. "That was a crappy proposal," she pointed out. He flashed a grin.

"It was a bit. I'm sorry."

"I expected better from you, maybe something stylish and romantic." She was prevaricating and they both knew it. It wasn't that she didn't want to marry him-- she did. It was more that she wanted it to be right.

"I'll go and get you a stylish and romantic ring as soon as we land," he pressed. "So apart from a crappy proposal, will you marry me?" She could see he was shaking slightly. Her supremely confidant man was actually nervous. He grasped her hand. She wondered if he could feel her pulse racing as she processed her thoughts. She knew she wanted him, wanted the togetherness they'd built. She loved what they had together, the intimacy, the sense of completion. She knew she didn't want to wave him off at Heathrow and have a long distance relationship.

"Yes, I'll marry you." She heard the words come out of her mouth, as though her lips were a disconnected part of her, perfectly capable of making decisions on their own. James let out the breath he'd been holding, before leaning over to kiss her, not giving a damn who saw them.

When they came up for air, he ordered some champagne from the stewardess. The two of them toasted their engagement at forty thousand feet, giggling together at the enormity of what they'd just done. "You know there's gonna be thousands of hearts broken all round the world," she teased. He shrugged.

"As long as your heart's intact, that's all that matters," he pronounced. He seemed lost in thought as he played with her fingers. Eventually he spoke. "I can't wait to put a ring on this." He waggled her ring finger playfully. "I can't wait for the world to know that you're the special one."

It was frustrating being in the air, and as such, not being able to tell anyone. Sarah couldn't wait to land; she needed to call her parents and James needed to call his. The flight seemed interminably long after that.

"I've proposed to Sarah and she's accepted," James blurted down the phone as soon as his father answered.

"Ooh, I'd best go and get your mother," his dad said, leaving James feeling strangely deflated. He heard his dad calling "Marion, phone," in the distance. "It's James, he's got some news." His mum picked up the phone a few moments later.

"Hello?"

"Hi Mum, just thought I'd let you know that I've proposed to Sarah and she's accepted." He liked saying the words.

"Super. Shirley Davenport nominated me for the committee last week. It's good news isn't it? Said that Sarah organised people off the Internet to donate, not sure how much mind, but Shirley seems very pleased. She's put me forward for Diary Secretary."

"Good, I'm pleased for you." He tried to keep the disappointment out of his voice. Alan, whom he called next, was far more celebratory, yelling loud congratulations down the phone so that Sarah could hear too and promising champagne the next time he saw them.

Sarah was beaming after the call to her parents, who had congratulated them both and promised a visit soon. Even the normally surly Bob grinned at them as he loaded their luggage into the car. "Can we stop off at Cartier?" James asked. He planned to buy a decent ring to make up for his clumsy, unromantic proposal. Sarah spluttered.

The Fixer

"I don't expect an expensive ring," she protested.

"You deserve it, indulge me," he told her, enjoying her reaction. While he loved her normality, it was fun to remind her that he was a man who could buy her anything her heart desired. Plus, if the ring was going to be scrutinised around the world, he'd make sure it was suitably extravagant.

The jewellers had an air of luxury, with pristine cabinets that were home to rare and fabulous diamonds. The assistant recognised him straightaway and took them through to a private room, where trays of rings were placed in front of them. "Does Madam have anything in particular in mind?" He asked, smiling benevolently.

Sarah shook her head. The rings in front of her were all stunning. She wondered how she'd possibly choose between them. They were also devoid of prices, which bothered her.

"This one stands out," said James, pointing to a large, square diamond set in a platinum band which was encrusted with smaller diamonds. It was ostentatious but beautifully crafted. The assistant removed it from the tray and handed it to Sarah to try on.

It felt heavy on her finger, its weight would be a constant reminder of its existence. James held her hand up to see the light bouncing off the diamonds, glittering perfectly. "I like it, but it's your choice," he told her.

"It's beautiful, but I didn't expect anything this... big," she said.

"In which case, we'll take it." James was decisive. Sarah slipped it off to allow the assistant to check it over, then he placed it back on her finger. "She can wear it home," he said, before handing the man his card.

Stepping outside, James half-expected to see photographers waiting to capture such a momentous occasion, but he was disappointed to find the world just carrying on its business as usual. The ring had been eye-wateringly expensive, so he desperately wanted to show it off to the world. Instead, he had to make do with snapping a picture of it on his phone in the car and sending it to his mum, who ignored him.

They made their way back to James's house to dump their bags and get showered and ready for a meeting with the studio regarding his next movie. There wasn't even time for a celebratory drink. Thankfully, Sarah had arranged for his house to be cleaned and stocked, so they decided it would be better for her to stay there while she organised her house to be packed up and cleaned prior to being put up for rent. It promised to be a mad busy five days. There was also the BAFTAs to attend.

Sarah also had to face Clive and hand in her notice.

He wasn't happy. She didn't know if it was the prospect of her leaving, or the problem of James no longer being seen as available to his fans. It may even have been a combination of the two. "Why don't you just transfer to the US and carry on as his handler out there?" He'd barked.

"I didn't think that'd be an option," she said.

"Of course it's an option," he told her, rolling his eyes. "You're one of the best in the business Sarah; the studio won't want to lose you, and James is yet to be assigned to anyone in Illinois. Truth is, they're all LA based, and nobody wanted to spend nine months on location, especially there. This may well just solve a problem all round. Still got the issue of every woman in the western world wanting to claw out your eyes, but I'm sure you can deal with that one." He tore up her resignation letter and dropped the contents in his waste paper bin. "Now shoo, sort out what you need to and be ready to leave by Friday. I'll sort your work permit."

"Thanks Clive," she said. "I owe you big time for this." She blew him a kiss and headed into her office to clear out her stuff and say goodbye to everyone.

The following five days were challenging. Sarah was accompanying James to engagements from ten till ten each day, as well as clearing out both their homes and putting their personal stuff into storage so that both properties could be rented out. In the middle of that, she had to deal with her phone ringing constantly as news of their engagement broke due to her flashing her ring on the red carpet. It was a whirlwind of constant activity, culminating in the pair of them finally getting on the flight to America together late on the Friday night. Sarah was just grateful to have got through it all and could travel knowing that everything was sorted. Even the BAFTAs had gone well, despite her being so nervous that she'd been unable to speak as they'd walked down the red carpet together, James's hand firmly grasping hers. He loved the adulation, the cheers, and the flashbulbs popping. Sarah had fought the urge to look at her feet, keep her head down, or race into the venue. She was more used to being one of those black-clad behind-the-scenes people who scurried about bearing a clipboard and herding the stars to where they needed to be. She found the scrutiny of being in the line of fire, so to speak, exhausting.

She eyed the airplane chair-bed, delighted that she'd be able to sleep, having managed the previous five days with just little cat naps. They were both drained but happy. One glass of champagne later, she could feel James placing a duvet over her. The last words she heard were: "Sleep well, future Mrs Morell."

CHAPTER 16

Anna

Quinsville was buzzing with excitement at the prospect of the next Cosmic Warriors movie being filmed there. The studio had rented a huge tract of land and had shipped in a large workforce who were busy building the sets required. It meant that an air of prosperity filtered around, although the chippies and builders lived in portacabins near the set. The bars and restaurants began to fill up every night with handsome men spending their considerable salaries.

Rumours flew around the area as to who would be there, how long they'd be staying, and whether they'd be hiring locals as extras. Erika, unfortunately for Mitch, discovered he would be training James Morell and quizzed him about the contract she found stuffed into his desk drawer, detailing that he'd be paid sixty thousand dollars for the nine months he'd be needed. Knowing it would be paid in stages, she decided to keep any extra-curricular activities with the film set crew a little more discreet.

Matt, Jen, and the boys moved into Ricky and Anna's place a few days before the arrival of the cast. Everyone was intrigued as to who would be staying at the house and who would be ensconced at the Hubbard's. There were rumours that James Morell himself would be renting the place, which excited Anna beyond belief as it meant they'd be practically neighbours.

The Fixer

Jen was intensely irritating, Anna decided, due to her constant questioning, plus the annoying way she'd decided to play pseudo-mom. She didn't need anyone fussing around, asking if she'd done laundry that day. She snapped at Jen to just look after her own men, Anna would take care of her father, which resulted in a deep sigh and a lecture on wasteful use of the washing machine.

At the gym, Bart was putting up posters advertising the new ladies Match-fit team that Anna had organised. A large photo of Anna holding dumb-bells and wearing tight Lycra shorts and a crop-top beamed out across the reception desk. James couldn't miss it, she thought, as she checked out the list of girls who'd signed up. "Two more just this morning," Bart called out.

"For Match-fit, or just gym memberships?" She asked him.

"Both. Sure is getting popular with the ladies," he stated, unaware of the possibility it was the rumour of Mr Morell using the gym that had prompted such a large surge in membership. He congratulated himself on taking on Anna, which to him had been a total success, especially given the great deal he'd got on the new premises. "The church want to put some posters up too, what do you think?"

She glanced over at him. "Why not? Maybe some of the new people'll need somewhere to worship on a Sunday. They're always looking for more members too." She unrolled the poster Bart handed her. It contained a picture of a happy, smiling, all-American family standing outside their church, shaking hands with Pastor White. It painted a picture of wholesome apple-pie country life, which made Anna wonder why there was no mention of the Reptilian overlords.

That evening, after her sneaky shag with Mitch in his truck, Anna walked up the path to hear screaming and shouting so loud she could hear it from outside. Jen and Matt were clearly having a disagreement about something. Anna walked round to the back of the house to find her father sitting on the back porch, a glass of whisky in his hand. "Hey there sweetheart. You had a good day?" He asked.

"Good thanks. They're arguing?" She cocked her head towards the back door. Ricky nodded.

"Nothing new according to Matt. He said they fought a lot this past year."

"So how are we meant to get our dinner ready?" Anna asked.

She was starving after taking two Match-fit sessions back to back.

He shrugged. "Jen said she'd take over the cooking while she's around. I wasn't sure how you'd feel about that, so I didn't say yes."

"Did you tell her no though?" She prayed he had.

"Not as such, no. I just didn't say anything."

"Oh great. Lentil and roadkill stew every night it is then," she wailed, "with a miniature portion for me because Jen thinks I eat dolly-sized amounts." She'd refused to allow Jen to serve her food after cottoning on to the fact that she always gave Anna the gristle while serving the better meat to her sons. One meal in particular, Anna had ended up just eating carrots and gravy, served on the smallest plate Jen possessed, leaving the pile of fat and gristle on the side. That had caused a row too, with Jen accusing Anna of being fussy and wasteful and refusing to let her eat anything else. Anna had been about seven at the time.

"Shall we go over to the Blofield's place for a steak?" Ricky suggested. "Get out of their hair for the evening and get you fed properly?" He noted how quickly her face broke into a smile. Leaving his whisky, he took her arm and led her to his truck.

"Shouldn't we tell the others?" Anna asked. He shook his head.

"They've got some hideous baked thing that smelled revolting while Jen was making it. If they know we're getting steak, they'll want to come with us. I'd rather have you to myself."

Anna hopped into the passenger seat of Ricky's large truck and clipped her seatbelt into place, relieved to be out of there. "I'm not eating her rotten food for six months," she muttered, "and I'm not putting up with her sticking her nose into our business. We managed just fine by ourselves, hell, our house is cleaner than hers."

Ricky pulled out of the drive and down the track towards the town. "They can't afford a cleaner three times a week like us," he said eventually. "Try and be a little accommodating, Jen's used to mothering everyone."

"She's just so... so... nosy," Anna replied, "I can't have her going through my room or my stuff."

"Why? What secrets have you got?"

"Well there's a very obvious one for a start." Men could be so obtuse at times and her father was no different.

"Hide all the things you don't want her to see in my room, or in the bunker."

It was actually a great idea, Anna thought. The bunker was a large series of rooms underneath their yard. It was built to withstand any sort of attack that the church warned the Reptilians might try. It had air filtration, supplies, and a well-equipped armoury. It was only accessible via a solid steel door, protected by a code that only Ricky and Anna were privy to. If Jen was going to keep snooping, it was the only place that would be safe.

Once their steaks and fries were ordered, Anna's medium rare, Ricky's rare, he took a sip of his beer and looked at her expectantly. "You've been out a lot, how's it going at the gym?"

"Good thanks. Membership is growing at the fastest rate ever."

"Bart must be pleased?"

Anna wondered where her father was going with his line of questioning. "Yeah, I think he's stoked."

"I know he's single. Is there something going on between the two of you?" Although Ricky felt that maybe Bart was a little old for her, he was a good soldier of the Pentecost and would make a solid husband. Anna shook her head.

"Nope. Don't go getting any ideas about trying to pair me off with him. Bart's a nice man but... no."

"You could do worse."

I could do better, like James Morell better,' thought Anna, although she didn't say it. She was puzzled by her dad though, as she'd expected him to be possessive, to try and scare off any suitors. The way he was talking, he was positively encouraging her to get a husband. Maybe he wasn't so keen on her as she got older, she mused. "Anyone would think you were trying to marry me off."

He patted her hand. "Wouldn't want to see you getting left behind honey."

"What if I met someone who wasn't in the church?" She asked. It was a question she'd asked as a young girl, and Ricky hadn't answered. He'd just blown her off with a non-answer and changed the subject. She had him pinned to the spot now.

"We'd bring him into the church," he replied airily as if it was no big deal.

"What if he didn't want to join?"

"Mixed marriages don't really work. You've only got to look at me and your mother to see the results. It's always best to keep to your own kind."

"Do you ever hear from my mum?" If Ricky was in the mood

to talk, she wanted to make the most of the opportunity. Ricky was generally all about the doing. He liked activities, hobbies, and action. Sitting and talking just wasn't his thing. Anna knew that if she hadn't been there, he'd have eaten his steak sitting at the bar, watching the game on the TV positioned on the wall opposite. Either that, or he'd have picked up a burger and scoffed it in his truck.

He shook his head. "No, not since the day she left us."

"Were you heartbroken?"

"I still had you honey, so no, I had what was important." His eyes crinkled at the corners as he smiled at her. She truly was the female version of himself, an alter-ego to be proud of.

Meanwhile, on the other side of town, Erika dished up Mitch's favourite meal, roasted chicken with mashed potatoes and fresh greens.

Mitch was big news, almost a local celebrity. It was all around town that he'd been contracted to train James. She'd never thought he'd get as big a gig, just on the back of a course he'd done a few years back, thanks to her daddy's money. She resolved to get their marriage back on track. Besides, it would be exciting to meet a real life Hollywood star, maybe hang out with the cast. Mitch had finally admitted that he'd gotten the contract. Well, he couldn't deny it given that everyone was talking about it. She'd even started training at his gym, which was far better than the old place Bart had started off with. She wasn't keen on his work mate, Anna, though. Erika thought she was stuck up and sly, but she kept her thoughts to herself as Mitch seemed to be quite friendly with her. Erika had even added her as a friend on Facebook.

CHAPTER 17

James and Sarah arrived in Quinsville, which they'd been told was one of the more upmarket districts in Illinois, late that evening. The studio had rented a large, fully-furnished house for James. That was where their resident fixers had stopped. There was no food or drink in the place, and it was patently obvious that nobody had been in to clean prior to their arrival. Sarah had been so tied up sorting out the stuff in London that she'd left it to the LA lot to get everything ready for them. She tutted at how sloppy they'd been, unaware that Jen had simply pocketed the money they'd sent for cleaning services and provisions.

"They did know we were coming, right?" James said as he checked out the empty fridge. They'd both slept their way through the flight, so neither of them had eaten. It was ten at night and even if Sarah found an open grocery store, she didn't fancy venturing out till she'd got her bearings in daylight. She searched around for a listings magazine or some takeaway leaflets to no avail.

In the end, she had to Google. She found a pizza delivery place and ordered some food and drink. It wasn't ideal, as James was starting intensive training and needed to limit his carb intake, but it was either that or nothing. With their food on the way, she began to explore the house.

James was already unpacking their cases in the master bedroom, a large, imposing room with a decent-sized ensuite. Sarah ran her finger along the fireplace, dislodging a covering of dust. It hadn't been cleaned in weeks. She decided organising a cleaning team would be first on her agenda. "This place is alright, isn't it?" James said cheerily.

"Once it's been cleaned, yes."

"They don't all have your organisational standards Sarah. This is better than most of the accommodations I've been put in over the years," he told her. "There was one place in Ireland where I stayed that was riddled with fleas. Never itched so much in my life. It took the production assistant a fortnight to get an infestation crew in." He shuddered at the memory. She laughed. After scoffing their pizza and hanging their clothes in the wardrobe, they fell into bed.

"You need to sleep?" He murmured, as his hand travelled up her thigh. She rolled over to face him.

"No," she paused. "We'll be OK here won't we?"

"Of course we will." He sounded confident as he stroked between her legs, his fingers probing her, arousing her. In the soft light of the bedside lamp, she looked delightfully mussed up, just how he loved her. His mouth found her nipple, which lengthened in response to the flicks of his tongue. She groaned loudly, a familiar sound in such an unfamiliar place, and her hands roamed over his skin, igniting every nerve ending as they went. He was already as hard as a rock by the time her little hands had worked their way over his abs and wrapped around his cock.

James fought the urge to just lay back and let her do the work. He threw off the covers and exposed her naked body. In the half light, she looked magnificently juicy and tempting. He crawled down the bed to settle himself between her legs and thrust his tongue between her folds, lapping gently at her clit.

Just the sight of her gorgeous man pleasuring her was enough to take Sarah to that place on the edge of her orgasm, where her entire body centred itself in the clit. She writhed, trying to control the pleasure as he licked and sucked her mercilessly. "Stop," she gasped, "please fuck me... please," she begged, desperate to have him inside her, filling her. He liked hearing her beg.

He slammed into her, his body rearing up to push as deep as possible. "Oh God, yes," she shouted as he slammed into her again and again, each thrust pushing her further and further towards that fantastic release. Other times, he would have slowed down, or even stopped a while to prolong their pleasure, but relieved that she was there with him, he fucked her hard and fast until she screamed her orgasm.

He let go a moment after she did, pouring himself into her, gasping for air as he felt her shuddering beneath him. It was normal sex, no toys, no inventive positions, but it was what he needed.

The next day, after sending a stroppy email to the administrative team at the LA studios, Sarah was sent a care pack listing local services, a map, and a rather insincere apology. They'd assumed that she'd be organising everything from the UK, so hadn't bothered to check up on cleanliness.

James was picked up fairly early for a meeting with Martin, the director, to discuss their shooting schedule and other requirements, so Sarah was free to get their place organised. She discovered rather quickly, that as soon as she mentioned the words "Cosmic Warriors," every company in Illinois bent over backwards to accommodate them. In almost no time, she had a cleaning squad beavering their way through the house, a grocery delivery on its way, and the back yard being tidied up. Unfortunately, word quickly got back to Jen that the "Happy Maids" were in her home, which she took as a personal affront, especially as half the town had spotted the vans parked outside emblazoned with their logo. She was sure people were sniggering behind her back as she bought the groceries that afternoon.

James, meanwhile, had been to see the set, a vast endeavour considering how much CGI would be used in the movie. Temporary buildings sprawled over several acres, with whole streets of storefronts constructed to appear like a small town. It saved having to try and film in Quinsville itself, which would've been tricky and disruptive for the locals. "Is your place OK?" Martin had asked.

"Bit grubby, but Sarah'll sort that out. Where are you staying?"

"Local hotel. Maria, my wife, said there was no way on earth she was coming out here for nine months. Besides, we have two kids in school, so it's not that easy. Originally, we were going to rent the house, but apparently Sarah said you weren't keen on a hotel?"

"Not for that long, no. We like a bit of privacy."

They walked through the set and into an area full of portacabins and trailers, where James had his dressing cabin. He had the same trailer as he'd used for the first Cosmic Warriors film. This time it all felt familiar, much less nerve-wracking than the first time he'd played Titanium Rod. As he checked out the facilities, he felt a growing excitement. It was all suitably luxurious, from the butter-soft sofas to the well-stocked drinks cabinet, it was a reminder that he was the star of this movie. He needed the validation after that weekend with his mother, the way she belittled his achievements, compared him unfavourably to her friend's offspring. He was back in his own habitat where people deferred to him. He grinned at Martin.

"You're meeting your new trainer in a minute. The gym is local, but he's affiliated with our LA one." Martin told him. He liked working with James, as he was diligent and easy going, which were attributes that were unfortunately rare in actors at that level.

Mitch was waiting in the site office, a temporary building constructed solely as a hub for the administrative duties of the shoot. He was sweating as though it were ninety degrees and jumped when the door swung open to reveal Martin and James.

"Mitch Johnson, meet James Morell," said Martin. They shook hands.

"Great to meet you," Mitch said.

"You too. I gather you're training me for the duration? Did Sarah email my training schedule over?"

"Yep. Seemed pretty straightforward, a little tedious, but easy enough to stick to if that's what you require."

"I must admit, I found it pretty boring," James admitted, "What would you suggest?"

"It's all about bulking up, which isn't always that good for the body. If we could achieve the bulk you need, but mix it up with some general fitness and strength, it'd be much healthier long term. I teach Match-fit, which advocates total mind and body fitness, like athletes use." He glanced at Martin, worried that he'd overstepped the mark in wanting to change things.

"That sounds great. I might have a go at that myself," Martin said.

"OK, we'll give it a go," James said, feeling cheerful that it wouldn't be endless bench press and bicep curls like his previous training.

They spent the following hour going through his diet, adding more protein and upping the calorie intake to allow for more cardio training. James warmed to Mitch, who seemed to know what he was talking about. He assured James that the gym would be closed to clients while he was present, and all of the staff had signed NDAs which had been sent back to Laker Brothers. "Was there a camera phone clause?" James asked. Mitch nodded. The last thing the gym needed was a security leak of photos of James in training. He also wanted to keep Erika away, given how excited she'd been at the prospect of meeting all the stars. She was so fame-thirsty it had the potential to be embarrassing. She was also getting in the way of his fun with Anna, always hanging around and chatting with Bart.

"So are you local?" James asked, mainly to make conversation after Martin had left to greet his co-star, who had just arrived at the main entrance.

"Yep, born and bred here," Mitch replied. He was proud of Illinois and considered it the best state in America. "I can show you around a bit if you like. There are some terrific hiking trails through the forests."

"That'd be great, thanks," James said, a little absently as he'd spotted Jemima, his co-star arm-in-arm with Martin walking towards the trailers. It had never failed to amaze him how ordinary she looked in real life compared to how she appeared on screen. She was definitely one of those actresses that the camera loved.

James was in a great mood when he arrived home that evening. He'd met with Jemima, been to meet everyone at his new gym, and checked out a few of the various sets they'd be using for filming. "My new personal trainer is a great guy," he told Sarah, "does Match-fit competitions for fun, and wants to introduce me to the other people doing them. He suggested that rather than just bulking up for the part, I should use the opportunity to get super fit as well."

"You're already super fit," she said, frowning slightly. "What does Martin think about it?"

"He's quite happy," James told her, "as long as I bulk up enough for the part."

It took Sarah quite a while to settle into life in Illinois. In London, she was sure-footed, knowledgeable about the best places. She knew lots of people, had lots of friends, and had tried and tested contacts. In Illinois she had nothing and nobody but James. She waited eagerly for him to come home each day as there seemed little for her to do and no-one for her to talk to. Even the gossip boards were quiet. She figured that he lost a lot of fans when they announced their engagement.

Sarah spent her days pacing around the house, bored silly. James was busy with his training and all the pre-production stuff that goes on before a shoot. It felt like a massive waste of her organisational talents, but with no public appearances, no social engagements, and very little hassle, she was at a loose end. She missed her life in London, and how relevant she'd felt. It made it even worse when James had delivered the bad news that one of his co-stars had delayed the project due to a scheduling clash, so they'd be in Illinois an extra month. It felt like a life sentence to Sarah as it was. She began ticking off days in her calendar app and counting down the days until she'd be back in London.

James was quite enjoying himself during the hiatus. He got to know all the crew on the set, and had been taken out sightseeing by Mitch. Illinois had some fantastic trails and Mitch and Erika were pretty expert hikers. It had made a change from endless hours in the gym. They'd introduced him to a few of their friends from their church, who'd made James feel extremely welcome. He'd given up his one and only dabble in religion when he'd had a bit of a bad experience, but there was something about churches that he'd always liked, whether it was the serenity or the friendliness of them, he wasn't sure, but he'd liked everyone he'd met from the Illinois Pentecost. They'd made sure of that.

Anna had almost passed out when she'd been introduced. She'd rehearsed the meeting in her mind many times over, but when faced with him... wow. The pictures hadn't done him justice. He took her breath away. When he'd shaken her hand, she'd smiled on autopilot and got a hit of his delicious scent. All she'd managed to say was "hi," when Mitch had brought him to meet the staff.

She began to come in early every morning to man the desk while Mitch and James were training. James always said hello, goodbye, and remembered her name. He really was daydream material, which was just as well because Erika was always around, hanging around Mitch, not letting him out of her sight. If Anna had been bothered about Mitch, she would have been a nuisance. Instead, Anna chatted to her about Match-fit and accepted her friend request on Facebook.

She watched James as much as she thought she could get away with, her eyes straying to the bulge in the front of his sweatpants when she knew he couldn't see her. It made her tummy do that delicious squeezing thing, just at the thought of what treasure lay there. By the time she managed to sneak off in Mitch's truck, she'd be wet and desperate for some relief. Twenty-four-seven fantasising could drive a girl crazy, she thought. She'd never actually wanted a man so bad. Mitch just thought it was his muscles that were driving Anna crazy as she held onto his biceps and closed her eyes as she bounced furiously on his cock, to all intent and purposes masturbating using him as a human dildo, all the while fantasising about how James would feel inside her, how he'd smell and taste.

It drove her crazy.

CHAPTER 18

When filming eventually started, James began working long hours as well as training hard. Sarah barely saw him. He could see that she was unhappy, but was at a bit of a loss as to what to do. Between his new friends and his co-stars, he was happily occupied and enjoying the social side of working on a movie again.

When he walked in one night to find Sarah in tears, he suggested that she join him at his new gym to try and introduce her to new people. Anna was horrified at James introducing the object of her vitriol, but instead of showing her disdain, she made sure that Sarah couldn't keep up and was made a bit of a fool of by some of the other women, who were all super-fit. There were sly remarks about "slowing them down." Sarah swore never to go again, especially as she'd felt so unwelcome and awkward.

James was training a huge amount at that point, so she felt it was better to let him get on with it. Sarah spent her days monitoring his online presence and steering the gossip sites. It was around that time that things began to go wrong between them and the arguments started. James began to avoid sex, and was spending longer and longer hours out of the house, far more than he needed to. When he wasn't working, he was hanging out with Mitch, Erika, and the others from the gym, who were all thrilled to be part of his circle, especially Anna. They gave him a free set of sweats with Bart's logo emblazoned on them, which James began to wear every day, to Sarah's horror.

They began to mention their church and how great it was. Bart even told James that it gave him a sense of family after his parents had disowned him for being a drug user. "All in the past now of course," Bart assured him.

"How long did it take you to get to the point of not craving?" James asked him, genuinely interested in his story. They were all in the local bar, enjoying a beer and a game of pool.

"You never 'not crave' as such," Bart said. He was candid about his past. In a small town, everybody had known about it anyway. "I just follow what Pastor White says and put my trust in a higher power." He gauged James's reaction carefully.

James looked interested. Bart wondered if he'd been fighting similar demons at some point. "So your church helps addicts?" James asked.

"Course. It's not just the perfect people that need love and support. Pastor White embraces the whole of humanity. He's a very compassionate man," Bart replied. He thought it best not to mention the Reptilians. The pastor explained it all so much better, he thought.

"What does he say about you all drinking?" James asked, nodding at the bottles lined up on the table. As fitness enthusiasts, none of them were particularly big drinkers and nobody drank liquor.

"Nothing," Anna piped up. "The pastor is a true man of the people. He knows that people enjoy alcohol, and he says he's partial too. I think he's more disapproving if it's drunk to excess, but not the odd beer after work."

That night, James wandered back to the house, thinking deeply about his struggle with addiction. Cocaine had eaten up most of the money he'd earned from one of the movies before Cosmic Warriors. His father had stepped in at that point and taken over his finances before he'd been forced to sell his house to pay off a tax bill. It had been humiliating having to ask his dad for cash, as though he was a child again. Worse than that was having to deal with his mum's triumphant "I told you so" lectures. He hated the way she expected him to fail at everything. It'd taken every ounce of resolve to wrestle his money away from them again and place it in the hands of an accountant, who'd wondered why James's father had kept so much of it for himself. At least coke made him feel like king of the world, if only for a short while.

At least it made him feel... something.

James knew from the therapy he'd had in rehab that his mother was a classic narcissist. To the outside world, she appeared jolly, normal even, yet she'd terrorised her children, played them off against each other, bullied them into submission. He'd always been the scapegoat child. He had no idea why she'd chosen him for that particular role, but she did. The upshot was her refusal to admit that he was a successful Hollywood star, and the knowledge that she would never be able to bring herself to say "well done." His father was just like her, backed her up with everything she said. His older brother, Miles, could do no wrong, despite having a love life like a train wreck and constantly sponging money off everyone to pay gambling debts. Marion had hated the fact that James was more successful financially than Miles and had often badgered James to help his brother more.

His therapist had told him to go "no contact," but he couldn't bring himself to go that far. He kept his visits infrequent and short, protecting his rather fragile ego from the worst of her bile. Having Sarah there had helped enormously, as his parents were rarely nasty in front of anyone else. They presented a united front of a happy family if anyone was watching. It was all a facade of course. The tensions would be bubbling below the surface, the need to scratch at James's self-esteem to keep him in his place.

His mother had taught him to worship her, provide her with all that she felt she was due. Unfortunately, a narcissist is never satisfied and nothing was ever enough. The constant criticism had rendered him unable to understand self-love as a concept of self-care. James could feel love for Sarah, feel compassion for others, just not himself. The idea that a pastor could reach out and show care and nurturing without an agenda was alluring.

Sarah wasn't invited on these nights out, not because James didn't want her there, but because they were often last-minute decisions or happened organically. He'd finish his workout with Mitch, only to see Bart and Anna close up for the night. Someone would suggest a beer and that would be that. A couple of new bars had opened in Quinsville, due to the large cast and crew staying around the town. Evenings were buzzing with activity.

Fan pics started popping up showing James and his trainer out and about. Sarah resented the fact that he wasn't home with her, and began to get depressed and needy. It became a vicious circle; the more depressed she got, the less he came home. It wasn't that

The Fixer

he wasn't sympathetic, he was, it was more that he didn't know how to handle the situation, so withdrew from it. Each night became a war of attrition, with him staying out late, Sarah staying up, then culminating with a row. Another night perched on the edge of the bed, the gap between them as wide as could be.

For her own sanity, she made a decision.

"I'm going back to London," she told him. "I'm lonely and this isn't working."

He looked like she'd slapped him. "Sarah, just go out and make some friends," was his response. He knew he'd been a bit of a dick, but he'd been having a good time and it'd only been a couple of weeks. She had to go and spoil his fun.

"I don't want friends, I want you," she said. Tears pricked at her eyes. This cold, harsh man wasn't the James she'd fallen in love with. He was an asshole star.

"I come home to you every night," he snapped, as though he was doing her some great favour by not staying out all night. He'd gotten home at midnight the previous night, '*he might as well as stayed out*,' she thought.

"I just think it might be better for me to get out of your way," she said. He didn't reply. "Come on, why not just admit that this isn't making either of us happy," she shouted. She was losing her temper. She wanted him to react, to be scared of losing her. Instead, he just seemed annoyed that she was having a go at him.

The confrontation immediately made him freeze. She sounded like... no, she couldn't sound like... her. He needed her to just... go away, leave him alone.

Stop shouting at him. He couldn't deal with her shouting at him.

"There's no pleasing you," he said eventually. "You wanted to come to Illinois, knowing I'd be working. What did you expect? Did you think I'd be at your beck and call? Maybe if you got up off your arse and started doing your job, making contacts, you'd be a bit happier."

His words stung. In a lot of ways Sarah could see that he was right. She'd shut herself away and ignored her job. She had irate emails from various people, namely his PR and Alan, his agent, asking her why he'd been seen in clothes branded to his gym, as opposed to his sponsor. It was the sort of thing she was supposed to prevent, but whenever she'd broached the subject of his involvement with his trainer, she'd gotten her head bitten off.

"You're not letting me do my job," she said quietly. She felt defeated. "Nor are you letting PR do their jobs, or Alan do his. I don't know what you're playing at, but this can't go on. Your sponsors are going nuts over the clothes you're being photographed in, the studio isn't happy with all the photos of you with a drink in your hand, and Alan's grumbling about all the work you're turning down."

He didn't answer, just glared at her and stomped off up to bed. Sarah sat with her head in her hands for a while, debating what to do. By three a.m., she'd made a decision. She emailed both the studio and Alan and told them that she was no longer prepared to work for James. She then emailed her friend Rosie in London to let her know she'd be over and needed a place to stay.

Then Sarah booked her ticket home. By that point, she had tears rolling down her face. She was walking away from the most beautiful man in the world and nobody would care. She dreaded the jubilation that would follow, vowing not to read the social networks for a few weeks. She would need some privacy and time to lick her wounds.

James left the house early that morning, after grunting his annoyance that Sarah hadn't been to bed. As soon as he'd left, she packed her case and took a cab to the airport. She doubted very much that he'd be bothered that she'd gone. In her own mind, she figured he'd be relieved not to have her clinging on the whole time, spoiling his fun. She didn't even leave a note. She did, however, leave her ring on the dressing table.

By the time Sarah reached Rosie's place, she was an exhausted wreck. Rosie took one look at her and pulled her into a hug before making Sarah some tea and toast and showing her up to her spare room where she slept for twelve hours straight.

She woke up at noon the next day and shuffled downstairs. Rosie was sitting at the kitchen table, working on her laptop. She was a writer and worked from home. She made a tea and placed it in front of her. "So do you want to tell me what happened out there?"

The whole sorry story came flooding out. Sarah told her how James had been out almost every night with his new friends, how lonely she'd been, and how he'd made it impossible for her to do her job. "Well, you can stay here as long as you need to. How long is your house rented out for?"

"Another two months," Sarah told her. She'd been in Illinois for four months at that point. She couldn't have done a fifth. She knew she'd made the right decision.

After a long, hot shower, Sarah felt human enough to check her messages. Sure enough, there were a whole load of texts, calls, and emails from James. Her hands shook slightly as she opened them. She'd fully expected either a rant or a plea and wasn't prepared for how devastated he clearly was. She checked the rest of her emails. Alan had expressed his sorrow at the situation, and the studio just ranted a bit. Nobody else knew.

James knew Sarah had left him the moment he walked into the house. It had a desolate, empty air. He stood silently for a moment, trying to work out how he felt about it. A part of him was relieved there wouldn't be another argument that night, the other part of him was busily constructing an iron box to stuff the inevitable feelings of loneliness and failure into. It wasn't till he spotted her engagement ring on the dresser that it truly hit him.

She'd run.

He was a failure.

Just like his mother had always told him.

He made himself a coffee in a daze. Taking it into the lounge, he sat down on the sofa and tried to process his thoughts. He'd truly believed she'd never leave him. He'd been so caught up in the shoot, his training, and his friends, that he'd forgotten about Sarah, and what she'd given up to be with him. He'd forgotten how wonderful it'd been to walk into the house filled with her presence, the smell of cooking, the lights on. Her perfume.

Pulling his phone out of his pocket, he texted her; ***Where are you?***

James couldn't remember how long he'd sat there waiting for a reply. It seemed like hours. Eventually he realised she wasn't answering. Knowing that she hadn't gone far the previous time she left him, he went to bed. It was four in the morning. He had to be up at six. He fell into a restless sleep.

Sarah stayed quiet all that week, hiding herself away. James's fans had got used to her not being visible, so nothing was said online. She hadn't replied to any emails from either the studio or Clive. She knew her career was in tatters. Instead, she read, cried, and watched telly. Rosie was a terrific friend, filling the freezer with copious amounts of Ben and Jerry's and making endless cups of tea. James was still messaging her constantly, begging to speak to her. She just didn't feel up to it.

He'd confided in Mitch that Sarah had gone, and he had told Anna. She refrained from pumping her fist into the air in triumph, mainly because she was impaled on Mitch's cock at the time, having sneaked off in his truck for a quickie, half an hour before Erika arrived at the gym.

She was hanging around a lot, which was annoying Mitch. Even James had noticed that something was wrong. "I've got a thing going with Anna," Mitch admitted to him one evening. "It's just difficult with Erika around the whole time."

"I thought she and Anna were friends?" James asked.

"On Facebook, mainly so that Erika doesn't suspect anything," Mitch replied.

"Maybe she does suspect, and that's why she's here every day. Women aren't stupid, you know."

"I was worried about that."

"This thing with Anna, is it serious?"

Mitch shook his head. "She's great... you know, in the sack, but I'm married and it's not a good time for Erika, what with her dad being so ill."

"She's gonna catch you eventually. Women aren't stupid, they're on high alert when single women hang around their husbands." Personally, James thought Anna was OK, if a little immature.

"You know what we should do, kill two birds with one stone," said Mitch. "Pretend you're seeing Anna. It'd make Sarah jealous, flush her out of wherever she's hiding, plus it'll throw Erika off the scent."

"Dunno about that mate," James said, unsure as to Sarah's reaction.

He'd had no contact for a week. A whole fucking week with no texts, emails, or calls. He'd ignored everyone else, just scanning his phone for signs that she might be softening. He suspected that she might have hightailed it back to London. He thought about her constantly.

"Best way to get her running back, you know, if she thinks she's got competition."

"I thought I might fly to London after my gig on Sunday, see if I can find her." James had a charity run that weekend with

The Fixer

Jonathan, one of his brothers. It'd been planned for several months.

"Really not a good idea bro," Mitch warned. "She'll just think you're a stalker. You gotta let her come to you. Maybe I should go with you, save you from yourself."

Anna was delighted at Mitch's plan.

It was one step closer, she thought, as she walked into the bar that night tucked under his arm. She was even more delighted when a fan took a photo of the two of them. "Are you his girlfriend?" The woman asked.

"Sure am, just call me Lady Titanium," she chirped.

James cringed.

Sarah knew James was doing a charity event in Tenerife that weekend with his younger brother, and wondered if he'd fly to London afterwards. She missed him dreadfully, but as she hadn't been in touch, felt as though there was a deep chasm between them that she couldn't breach. By that point, she was in a deep depression, regretting her actions, but too low to do anything about it.

She watched his Tenerife run online, but was horrified to see his trainer, Mitch, with him, edging his brother out of the way. The event had been planned months in advance, and there hadn't been any need to include a personal trainer. James seemed happy though and must've posed with every resident of the island as well as every competitor. He certainly didn't look heartbroken or upset.

Rosie placed another tub of ice cream in front of her, probably as a precaution. She watched as Mitch ran between James and his brother, taking centre stage. She also noticed that they were both wearing shorts branded to his gym. Rosie just shook her head when Sarah pointed it out.

"I did a bit of reading up on this Match-fit thing," she said. "It seems they treat it like a little cult, call themselves the Match-fit family, that sort of thing, probably because all the bona-fide trainers sneer at it, or don't agree with it. Why was James booked to train there?"

"Laker Brothers booked it direct, and I didn't know enough to change that. I thought a gym was a gym. Seems this place is wringing maximum publicity out of James while they can." The thought of him being used saddened her. People around him had worked hard to build his career, and some hangers-on had just jumped on his coat tails.

He didn't call or stop off in London. It felt as though he'd forgotten her completely. Cue more crying and another tub of chocolate chip.

Back in Illinois, Anna's father invited James for Thanksgiving at his house. With the whole family in attendance, all excited about meeting Titanium Rod, it was a raucous affair. "Hey, Titanium Rod, let's have a picture," Matt shouted as they all squeezed round Ricky's large dining table.

"I've only just sat down," said Anna, as she plonked herself down on the chair next to James. They all cheered as Matt snapped some photos.

James didn't cheer. He was wondering how on Earth he'd got there. He was also in shock from attending their church that morning.

Reptilians.

What. The. Fuck.

These people believe in Reptilians,' he thought as he sat at the table.

All the love-bombing, all the warm welcome he'd received; now he knew exactly what they wanted. James was a lot of things, but he wasn't stupid. They wanted his fame. He often thought that celebrity had a habit of distorting the way people viewed him. It was just one of the myriad reasons why he'd fallen for Sarah, she was unaffected by it. The people around the table were dazzled by it and wanted to use it.

During the meal, he discovered they were all members of the batshit crazy church he'd attended that morning. He'd only gone along at Mitch and Bart's request. They thought it would, in their words, be good for him in his current depression. He'd sat through the service expecting some answers to his very human problems, instead he'd been urged to prepare for a war with aliens who were supposedly running the American government.

Bat. Shit. Crazy.

And what was worse, he was surrounded by people who believed it all. He'd thought his mother was the nutty one. These people made her look positively benevolent.

He didn't spot Matt hand the camera to Nat, or Nat disappear for half an hour. As James sat through post-prandial brandies, pictures which had been sent to a couple of James's Facebook pages were starting to be shared around the world.

The Fixer

Sarah felt it was her own stupid fault she saw it. She was reading Datalounge, checking out some of the outrageous James threads on there, when she saw a post claiming that he had a new girlfriend and that he'd met her at his gym. She went cold. She found out more at IMDB. Anna was tweeting about their relationship from yet another Twitter account. Sarah cringed at her Tweets about her "A" list boyfriend, egged on by Mitch's wife, Erika, who was clearly trying to get publicity. The gossip sites lit up with it all, mostly because she seemed oblivious to the damage she was doing.

As Sarah watched it all play out, someone unearthed some photos of Anna out hunting. She'd killed a giraffe and was posing with the dead body almost as though she was riding it. It was revolting. What made it even worse was whoever posted those pictures tagged James's wildlife charity. *'James is in so much trouble,'* she thought, plus of course, he didn't have a fixer.

James was shown one of the photos by one of his co-stars, who was getting concerned by his pale, depressed appearance and had wondered what was up. He felt sick when he saw the fan picture of him and Anna. He felt even worse when he saw the photos of Anna that his fans had unearthed. He needed a fixer. Fast. He needed Sarah.

Sarah debated what to do. As heartbroken as she was, she still loved James and cared desperately for him. While she was debating how best to handle the situation, her phone rang.

It was James. She took a deep breath before answering it.

"Sarah, I'm so sorry," he began. "I'm sorry I was too self-absorbed to see what was happening to you, to us."

"You're in trouble aren't you?" She said.

He paused. "A bit, yes. Lots of rumours, pictures being manipulated, things aren't what they seem."

"I guessed that much. Maybe it's that person who was tweeting death threats. They stopped as soon as I left."

"Are you sure?" He sounded panicky, unsure of himself.

"I'm fairly certain. Are you seeing someone else?"

"I'm heartbroken over you, of course not. I'm barely holding it together out here. I miss you."

"It didn't look like it." She knew she was being snarky, but he had been an idiot.

"I'm an actor, in case you'd forgotten. I can do a happy face no matter what. Truth is I'm in pieces and I miss you. Where are you staying?"

"With Rosie. She's been looking after me."

"Thank her for me. I've been beside myself with worry. I hate it when you do the disappearing thing. I know I wasn't listening though," he paused. "I know it was my fault, and I want you to know that I'm sorry and I love you." The relief he felt at just hearing her voice was immense.

Her voice cracked as she told him; "I miss you."

"I miss you too. Come back? Please?"

It broke her heart to hear James was in so much trouble, but she recognised that it was a problem of his own making. Sarah knew that if she just gave in and skipped back to Illinois, nothing would change. She'd be alone, while James would effectively have a free pass to behave however he wanted. "I don't want to come back to Illinois," she said in a small voice, "I was lonely and bored there while you were out with your friends."

"I need you here, with me."

"You need a fixer, James, not a girlfriend," she reminded him. It sounded as though he just wanted her back in order to make the rumours stop.

"I need you."

"I'm staying in London. I'll wait for you here."

"Saraaahh," he whined, "It'll be ages. I miss you. I want you here. I don't know what else I can say."

"That you'd ditch the Match-fit crowd?" It was his last chance.

"Why? There's nothing wrong with them. We're tight. They're a great bunch of people. You should give them a chance." He really didn't want to confess about the creepy church thing, besides, Mitch was OK, and he liked Bart too. The only other gym in the area was at least five miles away.

Sarah suppressed a sob. "This girl you're seeing, allegedly, she's part of that crowd isn't she?"

"Well, yes, but it wasn't her fault."

"Her family have been posting on social networks that you're her "A" list boyfriend, and that they're certain you'll marry her."

Silence. He felt sick, his stomach lurching into his chest. He hadn't seen that bit.

"No way," he breathed. "You must be mistaken. They're nice people, even invited me round for a family dinner."

"Pale wood dining table and you sat at the head next to Anna, is that correct?"

"How the hell did you know?"

"It was posted yesterday. They claimed you joined them for Thanksgiving as their prospective son-in-law."

More silence.

"Oh God, Sarah, I had no idea." He was genuinely horrified. He hadn't been told about that one.

"So as far as your fans and charity are concerned, the ambassador for a wildlife charity is marrying into a family of sadistic hunters. Are you really trying to tell me you had no idea about this? Did nobody call you and tell you?"

"I've been avoiding Alan, not taking his calls, or anyone else's. I've just been working out and filming. I did wonder why Martin asked me if I had checked IMDB though. Nobody at the gym said anything."

"Well they wouldn't would they? You're their free publicity. They'll have every young girl for a ten-mile radius signing up, plus of course, all the young men following behind. This was a huge coup for them and you walked right into it." She was angry at his naivety.

"I'm sorry you had to see all that, read all those lies."

Sarah reflected for a moment. "James, why did those people believe you were seeing their daughter? Invite you to their home, brag about you? Did you lead this girl on knowing I'd see it all?"

Silence.

"Well?" Sarah demanded.

More silence. She was right and she knew it.

"We were just friends. Maybe her family saw things differently."

"Did you sleep with her?" To Sarah, it was the defining difference whether someone was "just a friend" or something more. It would account for her family thinking he was serious about her.

Silence. Her heart sank.

When the silence stretched a few more moments, Sarah glanced at her screen to find it had gone blank.

'*What a time to run out of battery,*' she thought. She wanted to hurl the phone across the room in fury. Instead, she lunged for Rosie's landline, and called him back. "What happened?" He asked.

"Ran out of charge. So, back to the question, have you slept with her?"

"No, I haven't," he said. "Sarah, it's you and only you. Surely you know that by now?" His voice was soft, earnest. He sounded like her James again. She let out a breath that she didn't even know she was holding. "Please Sarah, I just can't be without you. Hearing your voice..." He trailed off.

"I miss you too," she said softly, "but I hit rock bottom out there."

"I know you did, and I didn't take care of you as I should have. I know that. I just sort of avoided it."

"This girl," she said. "She thinks you're her boyfriend. It's all over the networks. Her family have been telling your fans that you're gonna marry her."

"Oh Jesus," he breathed. "I just trained with her, she's a Cosmic Warriors fan." He paused. "I stupidly thought if you saw me with a girl you'd be jealous enough to come back. Mitch introduced us."

"Was it his idea to make me jealous?" She asked. Sarah needed James to figure out for himself how much he'd been played.

"Yeah," he admitted. "Listen, I need to make some calls. Can I call you back in a little while?"

"Sure. I'll charge my phone."

"I love you Sarah. It's only ever you, don't forget that." He sounded choked up. The phone went dead.

CHAPTER 19

Sarah busied herself making a drink and tidying up. It gave her time to think. She wanted desperately to run back into his arms, but she'd hated being so far away from her own life. In a moment of clarity, she realised that she'd done nothing and seen nobody but Rosie since she'd been in London. Her life wasn't in a place; it was with a person, and that person was James. She prayed that he'd understand how he'd been used and walk away from the malign influences around him.

Sarah thought about how it would feel to go back to him, to be back in his strong arms, kissing his beautiful mouth. She'd seen similar scenarios destroy seemingly happy couples, people in love who'd fallen victim to the users and coat-tail riders that hung around celebrities. She'd always believed it to be a travesty when those people won.

She logged on and viewed the photos of Anna with the dead giraffe. The triumph on her face, the lack of remorse for having taken a beautiful animal's life, for no material reason whatsoever. Sarah could see that Anna was being ripped apart online, with a petition started to have her prosecuted for "Gerald the Giraffe's" (As he was now known), murder. In the court of Internet opinion, Anna was a monster who deserved jail.

She even had an email from Shirley Davenport from Furry Friends, asking her why random people were sending her pictures of a dead giraffe.

It was a mess, a giant, unholy mess of massive PR proportions.

Sarah sipped her tea and set about composing a reassuring email to Shirley.

She loved a challenge.

An hour later the phone rang.

"Hiya," she said.

"I've been had, haven't I?" He said without preamble. He'd spent the previous hour shouting at various people. He'd sacked Mitch, let rip at a rather traumatised Anna, and told Bart where to get off. He'd also had to listen while Alan told him in no uncertain terms what the ramifications of all the bad publicity could be.

"I think so. It's certainly how it looks to me. Have you spoken to Alan?"

"He's just torn me a new one. Apparently my charity is on the verge of dropping me, the studio is looking around for a new leading man, and the investors for my next movie are extremely nervous. Alan's having kittens; he thought I'd been on drugs or something. I just didn't realise how isolated I'd been." He sounded despondent.

"You need to publicly cut them off. Have you spoken to the gym about changing your trainer?" Sarah's neck prickled with fear at the thought of him losing his place in the franchise. She knew how much it meant to him to complete the whole series of movies. He had to complete them to keep hold of his merchandising rights.

"Yes. I just don't know how to fix this. I looked at the gossip sites. You know they're hashtagging #careerender, don't you?"

"I do. I've been watching it unfold."

"And you didn't think to tell me?" He sounded annoyed, which Sarah thought was a bit rich given it was all his own fault.

"I thought you were happy with her. It's how it looked. I never joined in with the online slating and speculation. I didn't drive it, nor did I try and stop it. I just read it."

"Did you see what they wrote about you?"

She gave a hollow laugh. "Of course." She'd actually been quite gratified that the fans had done a turnaround and agreed that she was far better than the "huntin', shootin' animal killer" that appeared to be James's new girlfriend. They'd shut up about her man hands and wondered aloud how James could go straight from "a lady" like her to a redneck like Anna. They concluded that he'd lost his mind.

"They'd welcome you back with open arms, almost as much as I would," he told her.

"Sack your trainer and change gyms. I'll come back."

"Already done." She could almost hear the smile in his voice.

"I'd better go book a flight then. Do you have a fixer out there yet?"

"No." He paused. "Did you lose your job?"

"No, I took a leave of absence. Clive was very understanding."

"I'm sorry I forgot to ask earlier. I know I'm a selfish bastard. I just got so caught up in all this, they used love-bombing techniques. I've seen it before. I didn't twig until it was nearly too late."

"Your lost years?" It was the first time Sarah had brought the subject up. She'd suspected an addiction problem and rehab, although she hadn't wanted to pry. She figured he'd tell her when he was ready.

"Not quite. We can talk about that when you're here. I'm a bit paranoid about talking on the phone. How quick can you get here? I truly can't wait to wrap my arms around you and hold you tight."

"Then I'll tip off the paps that I'll be arriving and you'll be meeting me at the airport. They'll all want the reunion pictures."

"Let's give them some pictures worth printing eh? God, I've missed you. Have you missed me? Even a little bit?" He felt elated at the prospect of seeing her again.

"Of course I have."

The paparazzi were waiting to pounce as she disembarked. They'd been told to expect a first meeting between James and Sarah, and probably weren't sure whether she'd kiss him or slap his face. Either way, they wanted to see it. The story had made the Nationals, so the photographers were out in force.

Sarah had butterflies in her tummy at the prospect of seeing him again, of being back in his arms. She wondered if he'd still have the same effect on her, or whether their spell had been broken and they'd have to work hard at re-building what they'd lost. She turned the corner, past immigration, and was confronted by the melee of photographers, standing behind an extremely nervous-looking James.

Her heart lurched. He still had the same effect on her. The moment he spotted Sarah, his beautiful face lit up. He pretty much sprinted towards her and pulled her into a fierce hug, lifting her off her feet. "I can't believe you're finally here," he murmured before kissing her hard. Flash bulbs were going off all around them, but she didn't care, she was too caught up in their personal moment to worry about onlookers. All Sarah cared about was her beautiful man, who by some quirk, wanted her as much as she wanted him.

Breathless, she pulled back. "I've missed you so much," she admitted.

"Missed you more," he murmured before kissing her again.

The press called out myriad questions, mainly about the scandal with Anna. James just ignored them, muttering "no comment" every now and then as he led Sarah out of the airport and into the waiting car.

They sat in the back. Well, Sarah sat on James's lap as they sped through downtown Chicago. She needed to feel him, to reconnect with him. She knew he felt the same as he wrapped his arms around her and held her tight all the way home, almost as though he worried she might run away.

She rested her head on his shoulder. "Am I walking into Beirut?" She asked. James wasn't the tidiest of people and could create a mess just sitting still. She figured that what with his schedule and no fixer on hand, the house would be a tip and the fridge empty. He beamed his movie star smile.

"Are you kidding? I've been so excited about you coming home that I've got everything ready. I've made us some lunch, I thought you'd be hungry after the flight. I've also had that cleaning company in that you found."

"That's so thoughtful," she said. It was true that she was famished. James knew she never ate airplane food. He ran his hand gently over her face.

"I just want to care for you. I know I made mistakes, but being without you, it's been hell." Sarah looked closely at him. He was still movie-star handsome, but his eyes betrayed his tiredness.

"This girl, truly, did you sleep with her?" It was a question she needed to ask face to face. She could always tell when James was evasive or outright lying. He shook his head.

"She's having an affair with one of the married trainers. I was pretty much the cover story for the pair of them, so his wife wouldn't be suspicious of her tagging along with us everywhere. It was more a favour to him really." He saw the disapproval on her face. "It's a guy code thing," he said with a sigh. "He could knob her whenever he wanted without raising suspicion and he thought it would make you jealous."

"Well that backfired spectacularly," she said ruefully.

"Not really. Well, at least the fans will be delighted I'm back with my 'lady.' I think they'll change their tune about you."

"True. At least I didn't shoot Gerald Giraffe," she said, a little bitchily. James just laughed.

"I'll be honest. She was a total pain in the arse. It was like babysitting a twelve-year-old, plus both her family and she only called me Titanium Rod. It was really creepy. The family would he horrified that she's shagging her way around the gym. I'm sure they think she's an innocent virgin."

"Anyway, as long as you didn't touch her..." Sarah said before planting a kiss on the corner of his mouth.

"Never," he confirmed. "My heart and dick belong only to you."

Back at the house, they couldn't keep their hands off each other and spent the entire afternoon and evening in bed, only getting up to fetch the food that James had prepared, which they ate naked, in bed. It was heaven.

After they'd eaten, James sat back and pondered whether he should broach the subject of his "lost years" as his mother had dubbed them. He decided he needed to be honest, especially after she'd given him another chance. "I need to tell you about the reason I didn't work in 2011 and 2012," he said. He fixed her with his clear, blue eyes.

"I'd kind of assumed a drug problem and rehab," she replied.

"Not quite. I was targeted by a cult, got quite involved. They got me into cocaine, reliant on them, you know."

"But you're not now?" She was puzzled by his admission. He'd never struck her as the type.

He shook his head. "I was looking for something, I guess. I felt I was lacking, you know, empty inside. I'm not explaining it too well." He stared at his fingers, picking a bit of imaginary fluff off the sheet.

"What did you feel you lacked?" She asked.

"I don't know. I suppose it's that feeling of never being good enough, or being substandard. My rational head told me it wasn't true, but inside, I was an empty shell. They promised I'd be fulfilled, whole, if I joined them."

"And it didn't work?" She probed gently. It wasn't the first time she'd heard of it within the film industry. Cults all wanted a famous figurehead, knowing that their fans would follow.

He shook his head. "I had a bit of a breakdown, ended up handing financial control to my dad for a while and checked into the Priory. They were great-- they understood straight away and set me on a de-programming therapy as well as weaning me off the Charlie."

"It's not in your file. Does anyone else know about it?"

He shook his head. "It was all done very discreetly. The worst bit was wrestling control back off my parents. I think they'd been creaming off a bit too much each month and got used to it."

"Thank you for telling me," she said. His honesty meant a lot to her. She kissed him, hard, which was his cue to stop talking and start making love... again.

Morning came all too quickly. Sarah was so warm and comfortable in James's arms that they both woke a little late, which meant James had to run to make the start of filming. She sat up in bed watching as he pulled on a track suit, smiling at her mussed up hair. "You look like you had a good night," he said.

"I did," she replied. "I feel thoroughly ravished by some film star. Think he might have been some sort of Titanium Rod the way he performed last night."

His grin got wider, "You think so? I wonder who that could have been. I must ask him for some tips." He paused, "Seriously, will you be OK here on your own? I've got quite a long day ahead."

"Go, I'll be fine. I might even get some work done, see if I can rehabilitate your image."

He planted a firm, wet kiss on her lips, and disappeared out to the waiting car. Sarah decided to make some coffee and have a look at the effect of their kiss at the airport.

Nothing could've prepared her for the online outpouring of relief she saw. Very few fans had anything negative to say at all. It was immensely satisfying reading how much they all thought she was a good match for James and how happy their reconciliation had made his fandom. On IMDB, there were at least five threads on the subject, two of them read-only due to the sheer number of posts that had been made overnight. Facebook was full of it too. It felt as though they had the whole world cheering them on.

Sarah made the mistake of checking Twitter. Old "Hat" had been silent when they'd split up. Now the person was back with a vengeance. ***You should've stayed away, now you'll pay the***

price.*

She shuddered and made a mental note to report it to Twitter, before shoving it to the back of her mind to allow herself to bask in the happiness she felt at being back in James's arms.

Anna, meanwhile, was hiding in her room crying. Not only had she lost James Morell before she'd even really had him, but it was all public. Plus, that horrible Sarah woman was back on the scene.

She'd had to turn off her Facebook after seeing that her photo had been shared over two hundred thousand times. People were calling for her to be deported to Africa and sent to prison just for shooting it. Her daddy had assured her that big game hunting was perfectly legal, and told her not to worry, but it was still scary how the Internet could turn.

Bart had sacked her after the gym had been daubed with paint proclaiming it employed animal murderers, and Mitch had been no help. She'd found out from Erika's Twitter that he'd been sacked as James's trainer due to his involvement. She hoped Erika didn't leave him, and he came sniffing around again. Mitch was OK, but no great catch. Erika was welcome to him. Besides, he'd told her he didn't want to see her any more, not that she thought he meant it.

Jen knocked on her bedroom door. Anna unlocked it and took the tray of food from her. She placed it on the dresser and went to shut the door again. Jen thrust her foot in the way. "Not so fast missy," she hissed. "Thanks to you, Quinsville is a laughing stock. Did you know there are reporters asking about the church? I don't know what you thought you were playing at, throwing yourself at that film star. You should've known he wouldn't look twice at someone like you."

"He wasn't like that," she said weakly, thinking back to how kind and gentlemanly James had been with his proper manners and lovely English accent.

"Your father is furious about the whole thing," Jen told her. "He said you can marry your cousin Jake as soon as possible and put this whole sorry affair behind you."

"There's no way I'm going anywhere near Jake," Anna wailed. "He's not all there, and he's creepy. There was that rumour about him and that girl who disappeared down at the lake, remember?"

Jen huffed, secretly delighted that Anna had been taken down a peg or two. "Your dad said to tell you to go see him in the bunker. He wants words with you." A shiver of fear ran down Anna's spine.

She knew exactly what that meant.

Sarah and James soon settled into a new routine. She worked while James was filming, managing to settle his fans. She also encouraged his charity work, which had fallen by the wayside a little in the wake of the "hunter girl" scandal. James was training a lot less, as all the shirtless scenes had finished being filmed and his physique wasn't quite so critical. They spent their time off exploring Illinois, making new friends, and rebuilding their relationship. Outside of Quinsville was some beautiful countryside, and Chicago had a great restaurant scene.

The only blot on the horizon was the "Hat" person on twitter. Every day Sarah would get a new death threat, which she pretty much ignored, but one particular day, the Tweets listed out where she'd been that day. Sarah went cold and her spine prickled, she realised that she was clearly being followed.

After telling James about it, she arranged some more security for them both, then informed the police. She thought they'd laugh it off as just a social media prank, but to her surprise they took it extremely seriously. A rather star-struck cop arrived that evening to quiz James and her about who it could possibly be. she pointed out that James had fans all around the world.

"The person followed you," James pointed out, "so it's someone in Illinois."

"Or someone who's travelled here to stalk you both," the cop said. "We'll trace the IP address and see what we can do. I spoke to someone at the Twitter headquarters. They were surprisingly helpful and have promised to email me the information in the morning." He smiled at them both.

"What if it's a mobile phone?" Sarah said. "We'll never find them."

"We can trace the signal," the cop said. He seemed pretty switched on. When he'd gone, they sat and discussed it.

"I think it's a fan who thinks that the only thing standing in her way is me," Sarah said ruefully. "Given that a stalker fan seemed to get lucky with you last time, they probably all think they're in with a shout."

James ran his hands through his hair, a gesture she recognised as one of exasperation. "This is one nightmare after another... if anything happened to you..." He tailed off. "I just can't bear to think of someone wanting to harm you."

The Fixer

"I think it goes with the territory." He pulled her into his arms and squeezed her tight. Nestling his face into her neck, she heard him sigh loudly.

"I just want to protect you."

"And you do," she reassured him. Sarah didn't hold him responsible, even though it was clearly a batshit crazy fan of his. She recognised that such problems went with the territory.

Their snuggle was interrupted by her iPad chirping with an incoming Tweet. Gingerly, she swiped her finger across to switch it on. James read the message over her shoulder.

I can see you right now. I could shoot you through the window. Leave him.

As quick as a flash, James jumped up and dragged her out of the room. He pulled her into the downstairs bathroom, as it was the only windowless room in the house. After locking the door, he pulled out his phone and called first the police, then their security. "The fucker is here, outside the house," he hissed into the phone before ending the call and switching it onto video to record anything that happened. In the darkness and the silence, he strained his ears listening for any sounds that could indicate where the stalker was. Their security were only a few minutes away, supposedly patrolling the boundary of the property.

Sarah just stood mute and shaking with fear. James moved her into the corner of the small room, behind the door, and pressed his body over her. He knew that she was the target, so in a split second, figured that the intruder wouldn't want to harm him, if he discovered where they were hidden.

Anna crept round the back of the house. She knew every inch of the yard and the side passage, thanks to years of being dumped there while her daddy went out. She knew that even if the back door was locked, the spare key would be hidden under the first stone of the nearby rockery. The thrill of the chase coursed through her veins. She would shoot Sarah, then slip off into the woods behind the property. Nobody would ever know it was her. She blamed Sarah for that picture going viral, for getting her the sack, for stealing James just as she had him in her grasp.

It'd been thrilling, introducing him as her boyfriend, seeing how envious Jen had been, how intimidated her normally cocky cousins had behaved. She'd loved basking in the glow of James's fame, which would've been her ticket out of Quinsville. All her dreams had been blown apart by that... that... bitch with her superior air and sense of entitlement. She wanted Sarah to feel fear, to suffer, just as she'd suffered that afternoon at the hands of her daddy. He was brutal when he was angry, and he'd been angry with her ever since it'd all blown up.

Anna peeped through the patio doors, there was no sign of them in the lounge. She figured they were probably hiding upstairs. Silently, she tried the back door. Open.

Her heart was pounding as she held the high-powered rifle in position, having checked that the safety was off and it was ready to fire. She'd be careful not to fire on James though. She didn't want to hurt him. She just had to take her time, go through the house silently and methodically until she found her prey. She'd enjoy the kill, more than she loved taking the life of a dumb animal. This was killing for a reason, she decided, for a purpose.

James and Sarah stood silently as they waited for help to come, their ears straining for sounds, clues as to whether or not their stalker had gotten into the house. Sarah prayed that she'd remembered to lock the back door. They were both careful to stay silent and not give away where they were hiding. She could feel James's heart thumping as he pressed his body against her, protecting her with his life if need be. For the first time in his life, James felt genuine fear. It wasn't for himself, it was for Sarah.

Then they heard gunshots.

Three gunshots to be precise, followed by a strangled scream. Sarah gasped.

Then silence.

A few moments later they heard male voices, they sounded like their security guards, followed by the sound of sirens. Sarah clung to James, terrified at what they were about to see. "James, Sarah, are you OK?" A voice called out. With his arm around her shoulder, James opened the bathroom door. They stepped out as one. Sarah could tell by his pale face and shaking hands that James was as scared as she was. Then they saw her. Sarah let out the sob that had been suppressed. It came out as a deep yelp, followed by smaller, panting sounds, as though she'd run a marathon. She couldn't control it as she clung to him.

The stalker was laying in a pool of blood in the kitchen, only ten feet away from where they'd been hiding in the loo. They could tell from her size and figure that it was a female. A large hunting

The Fixer

rifle lay beside her lifeless body, she'd clearly meant business. "Was anyone else hurt?" Asked James. Their bodyguard, Ryan, shook his head.

"No, we were a lot quicker than her, besides, a few more seconds and she'd have got to you, so we shot to kill." He pulled off the black balaclava covering her head.

Sarah looked a little more closely. She had long, blonde hair, which was partly covering her blood-covered face, but she looked familiar. "Do you know who it is?" Ryan asked. James peered at her face. Sarah watched him go even more pale.

"Yes, I know who it is. It's Anna."

"Oh Jesus," Sarah breathed. They were interrupted by the arrival of the police, who quickly taped up the area and took charge. Given the recording, the Tweets, and the testimony of Ryan and his team, the facts were recorded quickly, and James and Sarah were taken to the Hubbard's hotel to allow the police to do the forensics and remove the body.

Ricky sat in shock as the cop relayed the events of that night. As they took him to formally identify the body, he refused to believe it was HIS Anna they were talking about. When the cop peeled back the sheet covering her body, his delusions flew out of the window and a deep fear set in. "Will you need to do an autopsy?" He asked nervously.

"Of course. We'll let you know when the body will be released for burial." The cop knew Ricky from their schooldays and wasn't a fan.

"What will they look for in an autopsy? I mean, it's obvious that fucker shot her isn't it?" A sheen of sweat covered his top lip. The cop wondered what he was hiding and resolved to dig a little.

"The post-mortem will be comprehensive, despite her being killed as an act of self-defence," he said.

"You believe that?" Ricky shouted. "Look at her, she's just a little girl. I bet it was a fella that shot her. You need to investigate that properly. Anna could've been there for other reasons." He was grasping at straws.

"Dressed in black with a hunting rifle primed to fire after sending abusive Tweets... right. I'll pass your thoughts on to the investigating officer."

"I want her body back. I don't want her being cut up," Ricky demanded. He saw the cop's expression and realised he needed to change tack. "How much will it cost me to pull her out of the autopsy? C'mon, name your price. I know you've got one."

"Can I warn you that you're currently being recorded on CCTV?" The cop told him, a little smirk playing with the corners of his mouth. "Attempting to bribe an officer is an offence, which I'm sure you don't need me to remind you, so let's pretend you never said that, eh?"

He led Ricky down the corridor and into an interview room, his interest piqued.

James and Sarah lay in bed at the hotel. Sarah had fallen asleep from sheer exhaustion in James's arms. He lay stroking her hair, mulling over the events of that evening. He glanced at the clock. It was three a.m. He'd need to be up at six. He wondered if it would throw the schedule off too much if he took a day off. He needed a break, and he wanted to make sure that Sarah was OK. She'd gone into shock afterwards. He'd had half a mind to take her to the emergency room to get her checked over.

But she was OK. They'd survived. He stroked her hair again, just to make sure.

If anything had happened to her... scenarios raced around his mind. Sarah being shot, himself being shot, and not being able to protect her. It could drive a man mental, he thought, twisting a lock of her hair around his finger. There was no way he'd let himself sleep.

As he was driven past the house on his way to the location, he saw press outside, dozens of them, some talking to camera, others filming the police as they stepped out of the front door. They were at the entrance to the set too, and swarmed towards the car as they neared the gate.

"Wasn't expecting you in today," Martin said. "Gather you had quite a night last night."

"You could say that," he replied, wondering who'd told him. "Does this mean you can change the sequence to let me off today? Only Sarah's in a bit of a state."

"Course," Martin said. "Go look after your missus."

Back at the hotel, Sarah had woken up with a start. She realised straight away that James wasn't there. It took her a moment to process her thoughts and glance at the clock. Half six. He was probably on his way to set. She flopped back onto the pillow. She felt like shit, having only had a few hours sleep. She was about to switch on the TV when the door opened and James walked in bearing two cups of coffee.

"Hey you," he said gently. "I wasn't sure if you'd be awake yet. It's only instant coffee, but it's better than nothing." He wondered how Martin had coped being at the hotel for months. He placed the mugs down on the bedside table. Sarah struggled up onto her elbows and took a sip, pulling a face as it hit her tastebuds.

"Shouldn't you be on set?"

"Martin gave me the day off. I've not slept a wink." She peered at his beautiful face. He did look a little red around the eyes, which was the only evidence that all was not well.

The fallout from the stalker incident was immense. Quinsville had press swarming around for days, there was a meltdown in the fandom, and Sarah's parents begged them to get out of there and go home to the safety of London. It was stifling. The police took numerous statements, clearly trying to make amends for not catching her sooner, although nobody blamed them in the slightest. James's trainer, Mitch, had been "let go" by both the studio and Bart's gym, who were both appalled at the incident and probably a little delighted at the publicity. Sarah and James were featured on every news channel around the world.

The whole of Quinsville, and indeed, the wider world, learned that Anna's postmortem showed traces of her father's semen inside her vagina. Ricky was charged with incest and assault, until, incensed by the whole thing, Jen came forward with her theory about his missing wife.

Ground-penetrating radar was brought in to scan the land beneath all the factories he'd built. It didn't take long before bones were discovered; two sets of bones, which triggered an investigation of the church.

A few weeks later, having moved back in, James and Sarah sat in the lounge while the investigating officer updated them on the findings of the case. "The theory we came up with was that she knew her affair with Mitch wouldn't go anywhere. Besides, she'd only got it on with him to get close access to James, who was the real object of her devotion, judging by all the material we found in her bedroom and on her computer. Mitch's wife, Erika, had befriended her and found out that James hadn't slept with her."

Sarah glanced over at James and smiled. She'd never asked him for proof, but it was quite gratifying to get it.

"She'd then discovered other evidence that there'd been an affair too, as we found a stash of receipts and notes that she'd gathered, and hidden at their house. As a result, Mitch had dumped Anna, unwilling to let her come between him and his wife. We don't know if it contributed to her state of mind or not," the cop, whose name was Todd, told them.

"So were you aware she fancied you?" Todd had asked James earlier in the meeting. He'd shrugged his shoulders.

"Most women react to me in a certain way, she was no different." It may have been the truth, but Sarah saw the disapproving envy written all over the cop's face. James's looks and charisma were just his normal, other men would have sacrificed a testicle for just a tiny percentage of it. "I just thought she was friendly and a little star struck," he sighed. "She was masculine and trashy, as well as being delusional that I'd ever go for someone like her," he added. Sarah knew he liked women who were ladylike and understated. His ex had appalled him at times with her boisterous antics.

"So you never gave her any come on, or inkling, that you'd be interested?" Todd asked. James shifted in his seat. He'd used Anna to make Sarah jealous, stringing her along without caring what he did to her, although to be fair, he'd thought it was Mitch that Anna had wanted.

"She knew I was heartbroken over Sarah when she left. I think Mitch told her. I'll admit I felt uncomfortable about her befriending his wife, I thought it was a step too far."

"Has he now repaired his relationship with her?" Sarah asked. She was curious.

James shook his head. "Mitch was never serious about Anna, he just regarded it as a bit of fun on the side. Now that it's all come out, Erika's walked out on him and filed for divorce. Everyone in their town knows what he's done, which in a highly religious Illinois town, is regarded as heresy. My guess is that he'll move away to escape the scandal."

"Serves him right; he shouldn't play with other women," she said. The whole lot of them had behaved badly and Sarah was glad that they were out of their lives. Even on a professional level, both the trainer and the gym had used James to promote their own business interests. Sarah had taken great delight in donating all the crappy "BartWear" to the local charity shop and finding James a new, more professional trainer and gym.

CHAPTER 20

Eventually the fuss died down and life returned to normal. Sarah never quite got over her fear of incoming Tweets and remained jumpy in the house. After witnessing her starting at every noise, James made the decision that they should move, despite her protests that the studio had leased the property for the full year for them and wouldn't pay for another one. "I don't care, I'll pay for it. I'm sick of the entire world knowing where we live, thanks to the rolling news, and I'm sick of how fans can walk right up to the windows and scare us half to death." It was true, she'd nearly had a heart attack when a fan had tapped on the lounge window trying to photograph them watching telly one evening. The boundary was just too large and too open to be fully secured.

Sarah found them a penthouse apartment in Aurora, high above the city, with plenty of security and a killer ensuite, which was the only thing important to James. She organised the move while James was at work, so that it didn't interfere with a rare weekend he had off. As he walked past the concierge, it felt as though a weight fell off his shoulders despite the hour-long drive each morning to get to the set.

Up in the penthouse, Sarah had unpacked their belongings and prepared a candlelit dinner. The apartment was open plan, with fabulous views across the city, visible from almost every corner. With sleek, steel appliances and acres of granite, it felt like a world away from the slightly shabby, country pile they'd been putting up with. She smiled as she surveyed the fashionable grey sectional sofas and the heavy, glass coffee table. It actually felt, for the first time, that she was indeed dating a movie star.

"This is more like it, eh?" He made her jump as he wandered into the large space. He'd taken his shoes off at the door and was padding around in his socks. "Great views here. Is everything alright?"

"Perfect," she replied, smiling at him. "Makes a hell of a change from that scabby old house. I've not had a chance to work out all the gadgets yet though."

"They can wait," he murmured before pulling her into his arms and kissing her hard. He loved seeing her happy and relaxed. He felt her entire body soften as he pressed up against her, his hands roaming over her back, down to the soft swell of her bottom. He squeezed her gently, letting her feel how aroused he was. Just being near her, that was all it took.

She nibbled gently on his bottom lip, relaxing for the first time in what had felt like forever. "I want you. Now." He said, his hands cupping her breasts. Without a word, she switched off the hob, the pans falling silent. James could hear her breathing become erratic, which in the silence was incredibly erotic.

He lifted the skirt of her dress, his thumbs caressing her thighs as it went higher. She loved his touch, the deftness of his talented hands as he hooked his fingers into her thong before sliding it down, uncovering her sensitive, heated flesh. He let it fall to the floor and lifted her onto the kitchen island, before burying his head between her thighs and licking her mercilessly.

The granite beneath her felt cool in contrast to the heat emanating from her core as he worked her towards an orgasm. He lapped at her growing arousal, enjoying the effect he was having on her. He loved watching her lose control, loved making her come loudly, feeling the flood of wetness as she climaxed.

Sarah threw her head back and surrendered, letting him do as he pleased, giving her body over to pleasure. There was something so very sexy about letting him take control, safe in the knowledge that he was a man who truly loved women.

She'd barely recovered from her orgasm when he thrust into her, pausing a moment to enjoy the sensation of being inside her. She made him feel complete, like a god. Sarah alone could fill the emptiness inside that had spurred him on to take on the whole of Hollywood and succeed. Fame and fortune hadn't been necessary, only Sarah. He pressed in deeper, before starting to move. Each thrust brought him closer and closer to his personal nirvana, the moment he could pour himself into her. It was his way of marking her, of making her his alone.

He could see that she was as in the moment as himself, the rest of the world suspended while she took the pleasure only he could give her. He could feel his own climax building, building, before he let go, pressing in deep at the exact moment that she screamed out her own orgasm. He felt her rippling inside, a velvet hug that heightened his own release.

He came so hard it almost hurt.

He heard her panting, exhausted by two orgasms, sounding like she'd run a race. He marvelled again at the sheer effect he had on her. As she pulled herself up into a sitting position, he wrapped his arms around her and kissed her again, a grateful kiss.

Half an hour later, they sat at the large, glass dining table, eating a slightly overdone pasta Al Forno accompanied by a bottle of Prosecco. "Have we got any plans this weekend?" He asked. Sarah shook her head.

"You asked that weekends be kept as clear as possible, so I turned down the 'Comic Book Heroes' awards, especially after finding out you weren't gonna win, and a Sunday brunch at that mental church cult your mates all joined."

"Good. And they're not my mates." He didn't want an argument. "So it's just you and me?"

"Yup."

"Naked weekend then. Your clothes are out of bounds till Monday morning."

"Only mine?" She had a wicked glint in her eye. He grinned at her, took the final swig of his wine, and stood up. He smouldered as he undid each button on his shirt, slowly working his way down. If it had been a shirt that he'd liked a little less, he'd had yanked it off quickly, as he'd done for a movie once, but it was one of his favourites, so he took his time.

Sarah was entranced by the show he was putting on for her. He had an intense physicality teamed with a showman's eye for the theatrical. He popped the top button of his jeans, glancing up at her to make sure she was watching. Satisfied that she was suitably mesmerised, he slid his jeans and underwear down as one, revealing his nakedness.

The Fixer

"Alan should put you forward for Magic Mike next time," said Sarah, "You're a natural stripper." He laughed.

"Your turn," he told her, rubbing his hands together at the prospect of Sarah walking around entirely nude all weekend. His favourite thing was to see her unashamed of her body, like those times he'd caught candid glimpses of her when she thought nobody was watching. His breath hitched as she peeled off her dress, revealing that she'd failed to restore her knickers from their earlier tryst. He glanced over to the island to see them curled into a little heap below where he'd made love to her. Knowing that she'd eaten knickerless was surprisingly sexy. His cock twitched, then hardened.

"Ready for round two?" She asked, looking pointedly at his dick, which was back to full strength.

It felt wonderful to get back to normal, James thought, as he ran a deep, luxurious bath in the outrageously large, egg-shaped tub, adding lots of scented oil for them. Sarah slid into the hot water gratefully. She watched as James prepared towels and lit perfumed candles, admiring his sculpted body and silky skin. He saw her staring, so turned it into an erotic show, teasing her with glimpses of his perfect bum, before revealing his thick, large dick in all its glory. She was horny beyond belief.

He slid in opposite and pinned her legs open with his before sliding his hand up to play with her, teasing and flicking her clit. Sarah sank back and closed her eyes, lost in the sensations he was inflicting. She needed him to return to being an attentive lover. With all that had been going on, their lovemaking had become a little mundane, another job to be squeezed in at bedtime due to the myriad demands on James's time and energy. It felt fantastic to be the sole focus of his attention again.

He took his time, being gentle at first, using a featherlight touch, increasing both the speed and pressure as she became more and more turned on. He knew her body well and understood precisely how to make her come, and also how to keep her on the edge with teasing strokes. She opened her eyes to see him watching her intently, his gaze almost as penetrating as his fingers. She gasped as he found the exact spot, and with a gentle flick of his thumb, caused her to fall into a deep, intense orgasm.

It set the tone for the rest of the weekend, which they spent making love, watching old films, and picnicking in the huge master bed. James was an inventive, imaginative lover, and they celebrated the shedding of stress by fucking with total abandon, safe in the knowledge that nobody could see them up high in their penthouse.

Sunday morning dawned a bright, sunny day, full of promise. With no alarm to wake her, Sarah slowly came to, with the scent of fresh coffee wafting in, mingling with the smell of bacon. A glass of orange juice sat on the bedside table in anticipation. She smiled as she pulled herself up onto her elbows, testing her body for soreness. She felt a little stiff. She swung her legs out of the bed and sipped her orange juice. He'd squeezed it fresh for her.

Sarah padded out to the kitchen to see James, naked except for an apron, frying sausages and scrambling some eggs. "I was just about to come and give you a prod," he said, turning his attention to pouring two coffees from the terrifyingly complicated coffee maker. "Full English this morning. Gotta keep our strength up." He was interrupted by the toaster popping.

"Do you want some help?" Sarah asked as he efficiently buttered the toast, spooned on some egg and flipped a couple of sausages and a rasher of bacon onto a plate.

"I think I've got it all under control," he said as he put the plate in front of her, along with salt and pepper and her coffee.

"Is there anything you can't do?" Sarah asked before slicing a piece of sausage and savouring its porky, English flavour.

"According to my mum, there's lots I'm pretty rubbish at."

"Oh yes, your mum. The woman who knows nothing." Sarah was as scathing as she dared. It was another unwritten rule that a person could moan and bitch about their own family, but not criticise another's. For some strange reason, it could prompt a heated defence of even the most psychopathic relative. It was an area Sarah had researched in depth for her thesis. "Well, you do a pretty mean breakfast, which I shall add to the increasingly long list of your talents and accomplishments."

"And you thought to provide all the ingredients," he pointed out.

"Team Morell," she said, smiling at him.

He was starving. He hadn't liked to admit it, but the breakfast had been more for him than just doing a nice gesture. They'd had a bottle of champagne the previous night, which he'd drunk most of, so he'd craved a salty, greasy fry-up almost as a hangover cure. He watched her tuck in, not complaining about calories or diets. He

The Fixer

loved the way she was "with" him in whatever they did. Most actress types would be having a heart attack at just the prospect of yolky eggs and fried sausage. He'd had enough egg-white omelettes to last a lifetime. Even just one more would most likely make him retch.

"So what's your plan for today?" Sarah interrupted his musings. He took a sip of his coffee and pondered for a moment.

"The plan is that there is no plan," he said finally, "although I'm thinking a nice, hot shower fuck should be first in the order of the day." He went back to his bacon and eggs, nonchalant in the safe knowledge that he'd shocked her.

He washed her hair, her body, and took good care of her clitoris in the enormous marble-lined shower. She was like his drug, the only thing that filled the emptiness he felt inside. Sarah provided his soul, he mused, as he took her again, this time from behind.

James had always considered himself a solitary man, content with his rather nomadic lifestyle and constant need to prove himself in the eyes of the public. He'd never really given much thought as to why fame provided his oxygen, or what was lacking in his own psyche that required public adulation. He just knew that there was something wrong with him, deep inside.

He had always felt a failure.

He was a wealthy man, especially after wrestling control of his finances from his father. He was revered as the most handsome man alive by media outlets. He'd broken into Hollywood, the most difficult of closed shops, and risen through the ranks.

But he still felt a failure.

The only time he felt like a man, or indeed felt anything at all, was in Sarah's arms. The way she looked up to him, let him lead her. It was heady stuff.

She didn't think he was useless, or weak, or not as good as dopey daytime telly actors.

She thought he was worth following half way across the world and saving from a religious cult.

James made a decision.

As they lay side by side on the vast, emperor-sized bed, getting their breath back from their third orgasms, James grasped Sarah's hand and turned his head to face her. "I'd like to get married soon."

"Me too," she gasped. She hadn't quite got her breath back, not being as fit as him.

"Fancy going to Vegas next weekend?" He beamed his movie star smile, knowing full well that she was always helpless in the face of it's luminescence.

"Our parents?" Sarah reminded him. She knew hers would be livid at them if they did it without them, Besides, she wanted them present.

James pulled a face. "I'm happy to fly them in, but my mother"...he trailed off. Sarah sat patiently, waiting for him to speak. He sighed. "You know what she's like. She'll bitch that nothing is right, cause a fuss, make a scene. She did it at Jonathan's wedding. The only reason it actually went ahead is because my sister-in-law, Hannah, is the most forgiving person I've ever met."

Sarah could see the pain written on his face. She debated what to say. "You realise your mother is a classic narcissist, don't you?" She said gently.

James nodded his head. "I had therapy during those years. They mentioned it."

"In psychology terms, we call people showing the same traits, Narcissists. They often rule a family in the way your mother does. They're very common in show business. I often have to deal with them."

"Am I one?" James asked, intrigued. Sarah didn't often show off her degree.

"No, but you are the victim of one. Listen, I don't want to do the pop-psychology thing, but your mother is the person who instills your early inner voice. All this 'not as good as the neighbours' bullshit is just that, bullshit."

James took it all in, turning it over in his mind. He'd always known that there was something wrong. It had been concealed by his youth and inexperience as a child, just a wil'o'the wisp of an idea that other mothers didn't dislike their own children as his mother had with him. Nor was their relationship purely measured in money "owed" for his upkeep until he left home at eighteen. His mother had constantly told him what a failure he was, despite the rest of the world claiming otherwise. "If that's true, then I gotta be as stupid as she says for not spotting it, or standing up to her," he said.

"Why would you spot it? What were your terms of reference? You probably thought all mothers had a favourite and a scapegoat."

"Don't they?" He asked. She shook her head before kissing him. "So what do we do about her?"

"We manage her. It's all you can do with people who have narcissistic personality disorder. That and minimise contact. A lot of experts recommend no contact at all, especially for the scapegoat child."

"You mean stand up to her?"

"Or let me do it."

"You don't know what she's capable of. I'm enough of a black sheep as it is," he said ruefully. The thought of his mother ruining his wedding day was depressing. She'd probably whine that she was too hot/cold, or that she felt unwell, so that he'd cancel it for another day. At his first premiere, she'd refused to smile, complained that the red carpet was too far to walk, and had wanted them both dropped off at the back door of the theatre instead, claiming she was too embarrassed to go in the front. In short, she'd ruined it for him. He'd never taken her to another despite her insistence that he owed his fame entirely to her for some reason known only to herself.

"You, my wonderful husband-to-be, are in no way a black sheep. You're just the one that got away. She lost control of you, which is why she punishes you. She'll tell you that so-and-so's wedding was wonderful, far, far better than ours, but once you know her game, it just morphs into yadda yadda type noise. It was how I used to cope with all the narcissist actors and actresses and their pathetic demands."

"Hmm, wait and see, anyway, I don't want to wait to do this. I just want the world to know that we're forever. I don't care about all the hoopla that people do for weddings, unless of course you've got your heart set on a traditional one?" He sounded a little anxious.

"Not at all," she reassured him. "I'd be happy with a shotgun jobbie in Vegas."

"So this coming weekend?"

"Yeah, OK."

Sarah called her own parents first, putting the call on loudspeaker so that James could join in. They lay on the huge bed with the phone between them as she prodded the screen. Her mother answered. "Hi Mum, got some news for you. Is there any chance Dad could take Thursday and Friday off next week?" Sarah began

"Is this what I think it is?" Linda asked, excitement evident in her voice. "Course he can take a few days off."

"Yep, we decided on a secret wedding, in Vegas. I'll sort everything, just check your email tomorrow for the plane tickets." There was a loud squeal down the phone. James smiled at her, gratified by Linda's response.

"I'll get a dress. Who else is coming? I must get Tom's suit cleaned, and he'll need a new shirt."

"Just James's parents. It's a secret wedding and we don't want the paps arriving or worse, James's fans, so no mention to anyone at all, not even the rest of the family. If it gets out..."

"Secret squirrel," Linda said, which was their code for privacy, named after a cartoon of a spy squirrel that Sarah had loved. Sarah blushed slightly, which James thought was adorable. "So my baby girl is getting married," she sounded a little wistful. "Mind you, after what you two have been through together..." She paused. "He's a good man Sarah, I think he proved it. Your dad thinks so too, he'll be delighted."

"Where is he?" Sarah asked. She calculated that it was early morning in Hertfordshire.

"Popped out to fill up my car and get the papers."

A pang of homesickness hit Sarah, she could just imagine the scene. Sunday mornings were always her dad's time for car care. The only time he went anywhere near a shop was his weekly visit to the petrol station, whether the cars needed filling or not. "He'll be so excited when I tell him. We were just talking about you last night, wondering when you'd name the day."

"Are you disappointed we're not doing the church thing?" Sarah needed to know.

"Not at all. It's whatever makes the two of you happy darling. You know us, we'll fall in with whatever. If this is what works for you, then we're delighted." She paused, "will it be hot in Las Vegas? Only I need to know what sort of dress to buy. Will I need a hat?"

"It'll be hot Linda," James interjected, seeing that Sarah was a bit choked up, "and only wear a hat if you want to. It'll be very informal. We'll all stay in a nice hotel though, so you'll need stuff for that."

"Hello James, didn't realise you were there as well love," Linda said, "I'll make sure I pack a selection."

When Sarah finally pressed "end" on the call, tears were flowing freely down her cheeks, dripping in large, grey splotches onto the snowy white cotton. James pulled a tissue from his bedside table and handed it to her. He too felt emotional, but not in the tears of happiness way that Sarah did. More of a warmth permeated through him, a realisation that his new family would be different, more accepting. He could envisage a time when successes and triumphs could be shared freely with Linda and Tom, not hidden away shamefully in case they enraged anyone.

When Sarah had regained control of her tears, it was time to tackle James's parents. "Brace yourself," he told her as he prodded his phone, also set between them on the large bed.

"Don't worry," Sarah reassured him. She grasped his hand. She'd be his strength.

"Hi Mum, I've got some news," he began after she answered.

"Let me guess," she said. "You finally got around to remembering to call your mother. It's about time too. Joan Robinson's son calls her every day, mind you, he's a bit of a mummy's boy. Needs his nose wiping still..."

"I'm getting married next weekend, in Las Vegas. Do you and Dad want to come?" Sarah saw him cringe slightly.

"Oh, I don't know what we're doing next weekend. Lesley Patterson said she might be having a drinks party to show off their holiday snaps from their break in Majorca, not that it'll be much fun looking at photos of her in a bikini. Who are you marrying by the way? Let me get my diary." The line went quiet.

"I'll take it from here," Sarah whispered. They waited for Marion to come back on the line.

"Hmm, we might be able to make it, I'm not sure what your dad's got on," she began.

Sarah cut her off. "It's fine Marion, my parents are flying out to be our witnesses. My mum loves a five-star hotel, so it's not imperative that you come, seeing as you're both too busy." James could hear the sarcasm dripping from her voice, as could Marion, who panicked a little.

"I didn't say we wouldn't come," she protested.

"It sounded like it," Sarah challenged. "If you decide to grace us with your presence, it's imperative that it's kept totally secret. If word gets out, even to family and friends, I'll change the venue and just have my mum and dad as witnesses. I don't want the paparazzi or fans spoiling my day. Is that understood?" Marion realised that Sarah was totally resolute.

"Absolutely. I won't tell the boys. What about afterwards?"

"Afterwards is fine. If you want to attend, I'll email your flight tickets and details over tomorrow. Has James got your email address?"

"Oh yes... Will we be flying first class?"

"Of course. I'll book you a suite too, which in Vegas will be pretty spectacular." Sarah paused. She knew that she needed to dangle one more carrot to satisfy Marion's overblown sense of entitlement. "Shall I drop some money into your account so that you can get some new outfits? I know we've not given you much time to shop."

"That's very thoughtful of you Sarah. I will need a new dress and shoes. James won't mind will he?"

"I'm sure he won't," Sarah replied. She glanced up to see James staring at her in utter admiration. It was the first time he'd ever seen his mother faced down.

"Are you sure you don't want to wait, do it here on the island? The church is very pretty and the function room at the back is very reasonable," Marion said, the prospect of being queen for the day slipping further and further away. Only one of her sons had married, for some reason none of the others had taken the plunge, preferring to live in sin. She couldn't work out why they'd all been so resistant to big white weddings. Jonathan and Hannah's had been marvellous, once the guest list had been revised of course, and the venue altered. All her friends from knitting club had congratulated her on how wonderful it had all been. Marion had practically basked in the glow of admiration from the women at her flower arranging class once they saw the fabulous arrangements Marion had pushed for. Lucky that Hannah's father had footed the bill.

"We're doing it next weekend in Vegas," James interjected. "It's what both Sarah and I want."

"Is she bullying you into a shotgun wedding? Is she pregnant?" Marion demanded, under the impression that she was just talking to James.

"No, I'm not, and no I'm not," Sarah told her firmly. Marion cringed a little at being caught out. "I'll email you tomorrow."

With that, she pressed "end" on the call.

"You, my little dragon-slayer, are magnificent," James told her. He marvelled at the way his normally obstructive mother had cowered at Sarah's firm but resolute stance.

"Years of practice dealing with spoilt actors." She kissed his lips, before swinging her legs out of bed to trot off to fetch her laptop. She wanted to research Vegas weddings.

CHAPTER 21

Sarah sprang into action the moment James was collected from the penthouse on Monday morning. Her first job was to organise some flights for both sets of parents, plus of course, themselves. Within an hour, she had everything booked and paid for, on James's credit card of course, and everything emailed across to both sets of parents. James had already dropped a thousand pounds into his mother's account.

She turned her attention to her own outfit. She found a rather sweet, lacy white dress on Net-A-Porter, and some pretty lingerie, which she ordered in a couple of sizes. James had a gorgeous navy blue Tom Ford suit that he planned to wear, with a crisp white shirt and cerulean silk tie. They would all be staying in suites, three of the five available at the Four Seasons. Sarah knew her mum would love it. They were meeting them there on Friday evening, flying out after filming finished for the day. The only person in Illinois who knew about it was Martin, who was sworn to secrecy. James had only told him because they needed to make sure no filming that included James ended up scheduled for the weekend.

For such a small, simple wedding, it seemed to Sarah another whirlwind week. She managed to get her hair and nails done, a tan applied, and treated herself to some new cosmetics. She'd spoken at length with the manager of the hotel, promising him a back-hander if it all remained secret, and organised cars to take them to and from the venue, which was a tiny little chapel. She'd declined the offer of an Elvis look-a-like to conduct the ceremony.

Thankfully the Net-A-Porter dress was perfect.

James barely stopped grinning all week. With the shoot nearing its end and the thought of Sarah busy organising their wedding, he felt on cloud nine as he struggled into the heavy Titanium Rod costume and swung around on wires for hours at a time. It had been a long shoot, longer than usual, but the Cosmic Warriors franchise was big-bucks stuff. The CGI on each movie alone took over a year to do. He'd have just a month off after Illinois, then it'd be back on the road promoting, which would take them both all around the world.

And Sarah would be with him.

There'd be no more lonely meals in even lonelier hotel rooms, no more empty hook-ups with women who'd filled him with even more self-loathing for leading them on, letting them believe that one night of anonymous sex would result in them being the first Mrs Morell.

They'd explore the world together, first-class of course, at the studio's expense. For the first time, he'd be able to enjoy it, knowing Sarah would be guarding his back, checking interview questions and ensuring he didn't put a foot wrong.

Sarah's dad pulled her into a hug as soon as he opened the door to them. They'd arrived the day before and had settled in nicely. "I can't believe my baby girl is getting married," he said. "It only seems five minutes ago I was your favourite man in the whole wide world." She noticed his eyes were a little glossy.

"You'll always be my favourite man, Dad," she reassured him. Linda kissed James on the cheek.

"I'll take good care of her, don't you worry," James said to Tom, shaking his hand.

James's parents joined them ten minutes later, clearly delighted with their hotel suite. Marion was on best behaviour, having been warned by her husband that Sarah wasn't a lady to be trifled with. The happy couple were hosting a dinner in the dining room of their suite, so it was a happy, relaxed affair. Both sets of parents seemed to really hit it off.

"It's really quite romantic," sighed Linda, "running away to Vegas to get married with only a few family members."

"It is," agreed Harry, "far better than the hoopla they'd have suffered if they'd done it traditionally. Can you just imagine the security they'd have needed?" James nodded. They'd only taken two security personnel to Vegas. Having checked online, nobody had gotten wind that they were there and what was planned. It had been another reason they'd kept it to just their parents, the fewer people who knew, the better. Both sets had been asked not to breathe a word to a soul, even other family members. They needed it kept secret until it was done.

The following morning, James dutifully took his suit and stuff across to his parent's suite to get ready there. Sarah spent the morning alone, having a long, slow bath while she collected her thoughts and got ready for the ceremony at one. She pondered how it would feel to be Mrs Morell, to join the gang of Morell daughters-in-law and be part of such a large family. She hoped that getting married so privately wouldn't cause a massive backlash from James's fans. Although nothing they said really mattered, it wasn't easy being slated online. She could only hope they remembered how happy they'd been at her return and the horrified outrage they'd expressed about the attack.

At ten-to-one, they all set off in two cars from outside the back of the hotel. The manager had made sure no photographers were around before they stepped out of the service entrance and into the blacked-out cars. Ten minutes later they pulled up outside the little chapel, Linda looking around nervously for reporters. "I don't think they hang around wedding chapels on the off chance a celeb will show up to get married," James laughed. He was right, they were safe.

Sarah gazed into James's beautiful blue eyes as they said their vows, promising to love each other for the rest of their lives. She meant every word, and so did he. She could always tell when he was telling the truth. It felt to Sarah as though we were the only people in the room, nobody else existed, just James and her, telling each other how much their love meant. It felt as though her heart would explode with happiness.

'This beautiful, handsome man is mine,' she thought. He had flaws and was human, but he loved her, she was certain of that. What they had together was real, nothing to do with movies, publicity, or fame. It was just him and her, two halves who had found each other. By the end of the ceremony, they were both grinning at each other like kids.

After some pictures, snapped by Tom, they all stepped outside and back into the cars. This time, James and Sarah had one to

The Fixer

themselves. They were finally alone. He slid up the privacy screen. "Happy?" He asked.

"Ecstatic. You?"

"The same. I can't believe we just did it, Mrs Morell."

"I know. Feels surreal. Well Mr Morell, you just got yourself a wife."

He pulled her into his arms and held her tight. "I know, good isn't it?"

Being married brought them even closer together than before, which Sarah didn't think would be possible. James was happier, more relaxed, and more certain they were together for the long haul. They didn't announce it straightaway, but his fans were like hounds, and as soon as both sets of parents were spotted in Vegas, searches were done through all the chapel records. The news was broken for them. Sarah swore she could actually hear hearts breaking all around the world.

Eventually, the time came to leave Illinois. For Sarah it had been a marathon, made endurable only by James. They would have a break in the Caribbean for the Christmas holidays, before returning to London to embark on promoting Cosmic Warriors 1. Organising it all kept her blissfully busy while James wrapped up his filming.

She'd chartered a private yacht, which would leave from St Thomas. With only an extremely discreet crew on board, it ensured they would have total privacy. It would effectively be their honeymoon, so she planned lots of sun, sea, and sex. James was pretty enthusiastic about that idea too, ordering a secret package online which Sarah was forbidden to open until they were on the boat.

They flew down to St Thomas on a private jet. It was extravagant, but such a treat to have the plane to themselves. "So, Mrs Morell, there's a club we should join..." James said, his naughty smirk making an appearance. She smiled at him and played innocent.

"What club would that be?"

"If you go to the back of the plane, see that door there?" He said, pointing down the plane. "Go in there and take all your clothes off. I'm just going to get you some more champagne, I won't be long."

She sashayed down the aisle and stepped into the bedroom,

which was small, but perfectly fitted. She slipped out of her jeans and top and was just about to unclip her bra when James arrived bearing two glasses of Krug. "I came just at the right time," he murmured, casting an appreciative eye over her black lace Lejaby lingerie. He pulled out his iPhone and prodded the music button. Instantly, a deep bass filled the room. "Tease me," he commanded. He sat back on the bed and sipped his champagne, watching her intently.

Sarah put on a floor show, giving him glimpses of nipple, before turning away, hiding the parts he liked to see. They had hours till they landed, so she was in no rush, and she knew James liked to be teased. When her bra was eventually thrown on the floor, she dipped her fingers into his champagne and dripped it onto her nipples, before letting him lick it off. She could tell by the way he was fidgeting that she was having the desired effect.

As she dipped down to kiss him, he grabbed her shoulders and threw her onto the bed, before dragging her knickers down her legs. Seeing him lose control was thrilling and a huge turn on in itself. Before she had time to register what was going on, he had her legs open and his face thrust between them, giving her lush, deep licks. She thought she'd come on the spot.

They spent the entire flight in the bedroom, setting the tone for the whole honeymoon. With no work or schedules in front of them, they both relaxed and got back to their more wild lovemaking.

Three hours later, both slicked with sweat, they lay side by side getting their breath back. "I think you've actually broken my dick," James told her. "It's exhausted."

"Your fault for being so damn sexy," she said. He smiled and pulled her into his arms. She nestled into his chest hair and inhaled his scent.

"Will it always be this good?" She asked. She was blissfully happy.

He stared at the ceiling. "Yes, I think it will. If anything, it'll get better the longer we're together. I've never felt so close to another person as I feel with you." His arms tightened around her.

They lay in silence for a while, enjoying the feel of skin against skin. Eventually, Sarah shifted, only to discover he'd dozed off, no doubt worn out by all their shenanigans. Smiling at his angelic sleeping face, she jumped into the shower and cleaned up. She'd brought a sundress to change into before landing, so pulled that on and left him snoring gently while she went back to her seat to read her Kindle.

Sarah had to wake him a half hour before they landed, so he could shower and dress before they had to be in their seats. She figured he was shattered after nine months of non-stop filming and the stresses associated with being on set all that time. With the privacy of the boat, he'd be able to fully unwind and switch off.

They got their first sight of the boat walking along a busy, bustling quay. It was a sleek, pristine Sunseeker, far larger than she'd expected. "Wow," said James, clearly as impressed as she was. They were welcomed aboard by the captain, a jolly man called André. He introduced them to the rest of the crew, who'd be taking care of them. With their bags safely on board and being unpacked in the master suite, they set sail.

The Caribbean Sea glittered as they ploughed through it towards open sea. The two of them stood on deck watching Dolphins race the boat, leaping out of the water in almost perfect synchronisation. Islands dotted the distance like tiny emerald jewels in a turquoise and diamond ocean. "This is beyond perfect," James sighed, sipping a mojito. "I can feel the tension slipping away. Two weeks of just you and me, nobody else, what could be more perfect?"

She smiled at him, happy he felt the same way she did. It felt as though she'd run a marathon in Illinois, coping with her job in an unfamiliar place, dealing with the attack, and struggling with the isolation. She needed the holiday too. She slipped her arm through his, needing to feel his skin against hers, reassurance that he was real, not a figment of a dream. He glanced down at her. "You OK?"

She nodded. "I'm just so happy, it feels like I might wake up any moment," she said. He beamed a smile and kissed her gently on the lips.

"I know exactly what you mean, because I feel exactly the same way. That shoot went on forever. I feel like I've been living in a bubble."

"To an extent you have," Sarah agreed, "but we've got two whole weeks of this gorgeous place ahead of us."

"I've got two whole weeks of my gorgeous wife ahead of me you mean," he laughed. "I have a surprise for you."

"I love surprises," she said.

"Go down to the bedroom and wait for me there," he instructed, a naughty smile teasing his lips. She grinned at him and skipped off to the master suite. Sarah loved naughty, sexy James. She sat on the end of the bed waiting, wondering if it had anything to do with the secret package he'd hidden from her.

He strode into the bedroom a few minutes later, holding the brown box, which she noticed he'd opened. He placed it on the cabinet, too high for her to see what it contained and fished about in it. He pulled out a blindfold.

James stood in front of her, dangling it from one finger. "Take your clothes off," he said. "I bought us some toys to try. Are you up for it?"

"I'm up for anything," she said breathlessly. She loved it when he took charge, and it excited her when he showed his slightly pervy side. James could be quite the dirty boy at times. She threw off her sundress and knickers.

He circled her like a predator, his gaze appreciative. Standing behind her, he whispered in her ear, "I think you've seen enough, Mrs Morell." She felt his warm breath on her neck. He slid the blindfold over her eyes. "Is this exciting?" He asked. She nodded, her body responding to his close proximity. He kissed her neck softly, making her shiver with desire.

Sarah felt the loss of his body heat as he moved away, back to his secret box. She heard him throw his clothes on the floor, then some rustling as he found the items he was looking for. She jumped when his hot mouth enveloped her nipple, followed by his hand sliding between her legs. His fingers felt slippery, and as a warm tingling spread over her already sensitive flesh, she realised it was some form of exotic lube.

Her arousal ramped up about a million gears. She normally liked to see his beautiful face when they made love, to look into the expressive blue eyes that had gained him millions of devoted fans, but in her blindfold, for the first time, she felt him. Sarah felt his desire to please her, his passion for her body and the love which poured out of him. With her eyes covered, she could finally see the man behind the beautiful face, and she loved him.

His next trick was to lay her onto the bed, on the edge, so he could slide into her. She was almost mindless with the need to come, but in that position, she needed some extra stimulation. He kept a fairly gentle pace, teasing her.

Then she heard a buzzing.

He pressed something against her. It felt mind-blowing, as if it had three prongs, perfectly placed to work on the areas needed to make her explode.

The orgasm made her scream, it was so intense. James held her legs open in a show of merciless domination. She just couldn't control the pleasure as she convulsed around him, arching off the bed violently. It went on far longer than any orgasm she'd ever experienced before, and as it began to subside, he sped up his thrusts and turned up the device. Another orgasm hit without warning, making her see stars. Sarah could only lay helplessly as it rearranged her insides. She could hear James's breathing get heavier and more ragged as he pressed into her and let go, his cock pulsing as he pumped into her.

Eventually, he switched off the buzzing, and there was silence. She pulled off the blindfold and squinted up at him. "Wow," she muttered. He looked extremely pleased with himself.

"Did you like that?" He asked. She could only nod. "Want some more?" He asked, giving her a playful thrust.

"Nooo," she cried, "I need to recover first. That was death by orgasm."

He laughed. "I've got plenty of toys for us to try out."

"You're trying to kill me," she said.

It set the tone for the rest of their honeymoon. They spent lazy days sunbathing, talking, and swimming, while evenings were spent feasting on each other. In short, it was blissful, and probably the happiest time in both of their lives. Neither of them wanted it to end.

Eventually they returned to St Thomas, where they would spend a night before heading back to London. For the first time in a fortnight, they could check emails. All seemed fairly quiet, as people had realised they were on honeymoon and left them alone. Sarah logged into the fan sites and read the despondent posts from his broken-hearted fans, smiling at some of the more nutcase ones who seemed to think James was some kind of asexual virgin. '*If only they knew what a stud muffin he really was,*' she thought.

Her fond memories were interrupted by James reading an email, his hand flying up to his mouth. Even under his tan, she could see he'd paled. "What's up?" She asked.

"That woman... Mitch's ex-wife Erika... She's doing a kiss and tell on me, pretending we had an affair. It's gonna be called 'Titanium Rod was super-bad in bed.' I never slept with her Sarah, I barely knew her, I promise."

Sarah frowned. "Who's printing the story?"

"National Enquirer."

"OK, I'll get into them and give them a better story in exchange for them not printing that one." She couldn't see what the fuss was about.

"It went to print today. We're too late to stop it."

They went into panic mode. James called his lawyer while Sarah phoned her contact at National Enquirer. "You're printing a story which is wholly untrue. He hasn't slept with her, she's just a fan who's wishful thinking," she said without preamble. Ranchez, the journalist on the celebrity desk groaned.

"I did try and call you ten days ago, but you weren't picking up and you didn't call me back," he said.

"We were sailing round the Caribbean on our honeymoon. I could've given you a far better story, which incidentally, wouldn't have landed you with a lawsuit. You can't print lies, Ranch."

"It hit the stands this morning Sarah, there's nothing any of us can do. Besides, I've only got your word for it that she's lying. Maybe your man isn't telling you the whole truth?"

"Well, he's on the phone to his lawyer as we speak, so we'll soon find out."

"His lawyer?"

"Yep."

Ranchez went quiet. He knew full well that stars didn't involve their lawyers unless a lie had been printed. Sarah wondered how much he'd paid for the story. "Print a retraction on your website, and an apology in next week's magazine, and I'll see if I can calm him down. I'm not promising anything though."

"My boss'll go nuts. He'll tell me to stand by my story."

"If that's the case, expect a writ this week," she snapped. "Tell your boss we're prepared to go the whole way."

She slammed down the phone and went online. Sarah checked all the fan sites. It was being mentioned, but not really believed, due to the events leading up to the attack having been printed in such detail. They were dismissing the story as the ex-wife trying to make money out of James. On IMDB, they hadn't even mentioned it, being too busy ripping each other apart. She could see a pair of trolls were causing mayhem on there, clearly causing a huge row. She left them to it.

James finished the call to his lawyer. "I'm issuing a writ tomorrow. He's also going to issue to the woman making up this story. As her husband was an employee of my gym, he signed an NDA which covered his family, so even though this is a pack of lies, she's in breach of it. Mr Bush always advises hitting hard and hitting fast. He'll get it prepared today. In the meantime, he advises no comment. We simply remain silent about it all."

"Agreed," she said, snaking her arms around his neck and kissing him gently. He softened slightly at her touch, gazing down at her, his beautiful face inscrutable.

"You do believe me, don't you?"

"Of course I do. Now, I suggest we don't let this spoil our last day. There's a pretty, and private pool on our terrace. The sun is shining and the view is fantastic." He smiled and looked down her cleavage.

"Yeah, the view is pretty good from here."

Laughing, she smacked his arm and led him outside. They had a whole terrace to themselves, complete with a small but lovely pool, sun loungers, and immaculately-kept garden. It was like Eden itself. James had mixed them both mojitos at their little minibar, so Sarah sipped hers and squeezed his hand.

"This doesn't seem such a disaster with you by my side," he blurted out. "I'm just tired of fighting these fires, sick of everyone having an opinion or wanting a part of me. It just seems easier with you around."

"Team Morell," she said, which made him smile. "Don't forget, I share your surname now. If it affects you, then it does me as well. A silly woman trying to make a few quid out of a kiss-and-tell won't rip us apart. From what I've seen, nobody believes her anyway."

"Really?"

"Yes really. Someone on Who Dated Who remarked that she'd shagged so many people in Quinsville, she probably couldn't remember which one you were, and on Datalounge, they're adamant that it was you shagging your trainer, so the ex-wife must be lying."

He laughed like a drain. "Can always rely on Datalounge for

some unbiased opinion."

"Exactly. Now, all the gay slurs, they've not upset you; you just ignore it. This woman's slurs are in the same vein. We know it's not true, and only my opinion on the matter counts."

He pulled her into a hug, seating her between his legs on the lounger, wrapping his big arms around her. "Only you Sarah," he said, kissing her neck, "can talk the sense required."

He pulled them both back onto the lounger so she was laying on top of him and kissed her deeply. For that moment, the world disappeared and only the pair of them existed, complete with each other. Scented breeze rippled over them as they lay in the sunshine, reminding themselves that they were forever irrevocably joined both by love and by declaration. James knew it would take far more than just a girl to pull them apart.

The next day they flew to London. Landing at Heathrow, a sense of relief washed over Sarah. She was back on home turf, comfortable with her surroundings. Driving over to James's house, she had the feeling of coming home.

He insisted on carrying her over the threshold, claiming it was traditional to do it for a new wife. He carried her right through to the kitchen and sat her down on the island unit. "We need some welcome home champagne," he announced, before opening his gargantuan fridge and pulling out a bottle of Laurent Perrier. With practiced ease, he popped the cork and grabbed two flutes from the cupboard. They toasted their new life, their marriage, and everything else, before drinking the pink, bubbly nectar. It was one of the things she loved about James, he treated everything like a celebration.

Sarah was like a pig in muck being in her familiar surroundings. While James dealt with the pre-production details of his next film, she caught up with all her old contacts and friends, lunching every day on somebody's expense account. As James's wife as well as his fixer, doors opened which had been previously closed, and she was able to really promote his charities in exchange for snippets of information about him. It never failed to amaze her how fans would lap up any bit of insight. When she accidentally-on-purpose let slip that he used lip balm, in exchange for a write up about the Furry Friends charity, the fandom went nuts, with his Facebook pages running polls to decide which brand he used. He thought it was hilarious.

The Fixer

Erika sat in her lawyer's office as he read the writ that'd arrived that day, having been handed to her personally by a young, suited man. She looked at the shelf of files, piled haphazardly behind him and thought of the last time she'd been there, when he'd read her father's will.

She tried to gauge his reaction as he read through the papers. He was a good attorney, having gotten her a great settlement from Mitch during their divorce, which she'd already spent. He'd gotten it all done fast too, luckily before her father had breathed his last. Erika was a relatively wealthy woman. He turned the final page and peered at her over the top of his glasses. "Did you sleep with him?"

She shook her head, chastened by his penetrating gaze. "Not as such, no," she admitted in a small voice. Other people sold kiss-and-tell stories to the National Enquirer all the time, so she hadn't expected a writ. It had been a big shock.

"How much were you paid for the story?" He asked, his voice a little softer. Erika had thought it was just easy money, quick cash while she was waiting for her inheritance paperwork to be sorted.

"Twenty thousand bucks," she admitted.

"So let's get this straight, you sold a false story to a national paper for twenty Ks, and you just got a writ for two million in damages from the other party. There's no truth in your allegation, so you can't prove it in court? No photos, saucy texts, nothing?" She shook her head, panic rising through her body. She'd believed it'd be easy, that James wouldn't hit back. "I think you just spent every penny of your inheritance, plus a bit more. If you're really lucky and he's feeling generous, you might not end up bankrupt."

Sarah noticed James had something on his mind, he was mulling something over for a few days. On a rare night off together, she'd made them dinner, which they were eating on their laps in front of the telly.

"Are you upset about something?" She asked. "You seem very quiet."

"No, not upset."

She swallowed her food. "So what is it?"

"I've been thinking, I just keep mulling something over, but I'm not sure how you'll feel about it."

"Go on," she urged. She was intrigued.

"I really want a family. I'd like to start trying for a baby."

Sarah had believed that James had lost his ability to shock her. Together they'd discussed and tackled mad stalkers, kiss and tell attempts, a narcissistic mother, and a religious cult. They seemed tame, almost run-of-the-mill compared to this latest revelation. He saw her surprise. "A baby?" She spluttered. "Aren't you forgetting we start promo at the end of the week, then after that, you begin pre-production of Cosmic Warriors 3? The next three years are fully diarised. I'm not sure we can pencil in a baby."

"Or two," he said. It had been on his mind a lot, especially after discovering why he'd had such an unhappy childhood. He'd shied away from family life, believing it brought only conflict and misery. Sarah, and her parents, had shown him that it needn't be that way. It would also give him a great excuse to buy a house in the country. He'd always liked Oxfordshire, with it's picturesque villages, or a large farmhouse in the Cotswolds that they could fill with children, none of whom would be subjected to the bullying and torment that he himself had experienced. "I'd like to give my children a happy childhood," he said absent-mindedly.

"A laudable aim," Sarah replied. She knew abuse survivors often healed by giving to others. James was a fairly classic case. She knew he'd move heaven and earth to create a secure and happy family life. She'd just have to make sure she kept Marion away.

"Other actors have children. It didn't seem to hold Orlando back," he pointed out.

"True." She took a mouthful of chicken. He was staring intently at her. She hadn't screamed or point-blank said no, which in his mind meant yes. She swallowed. "I'll give it some thought."

"So you'll stop taking your pill then?" He subjected her to his very best winning smile.

"Maybe, maybe not," she told him. She needed some time.

CHAPTER 22

Marion was in a foul mood. Harry was oblivious as he sipped his Asti Spumante at the Parkinson's drinks soiree a few weeks after they'd returned from Vegas. Everybody had heard all about James's quickie wedding and despite Marion's long and detailed stories about first class flights and the suite at the hotel, complete with stolen dressing gowns, they'd moved on to other topics. Ariadne Parkinson was regaling the room with the news that her son, the daytime telly actor, had paid for their swanky new bathroom and was treating them to a fortnight in Majorca as a thank you for all the help they'd given him. What Ariadne didn't let on was that the bathroom was renewed due to her son breaking the shower screen and the basin in a drunken rampage during a rare visit home, and the holiday was a cheapo, last minute affair that he'd spotted in the teletext bargain bucket section when searching for a birthday gift for his father. It was still enough to enrage the green-eyed monster in Marion.

She'd also had a call from Miles that afternoon, complaining that he was again short of money. Almost all the money Harry had "earned" from looking after James's earnings had gone in that direction. Poor Miles had explained that his son, Archie, wanted a new computer for his eighth birthday. Apparently it was called a MacBook Pro, and would cost around fifteen hundred pounds. Miles had pleaded poverty and asked them to buy it. Marion had said yes, of course. She couldn't bear to disappoint little Archie on his birthday. When she'd asked if they were coming down, Miles had explained that they wouldn't be able to as his car had given up the ghost and he couldn't afford a new one. He told her to just send the money for the computer, he'd go and get it and give it to Archie on the day. It broke Marion's heart to hear that her best boy was in such a pickle. Miles always seemed to have it so hard despite being the best of the bunch when it came to her boys.

The following day she called James. "Hello dear, just a quick call," she began. James's heart sank at the sound of her voice. "Your father and I have made a decision. It's not right that you have all that money to waste on first class flights and fancy holidays when Miles is struggling so much and we need so much done in the house, so we decided that you can give us a third of the money you make and we'll distribute it around the family." She held her breath.

"Perhaps Miles should learn to live within his means," James began. His mother soon cut him off.

"I might have known you'd be nasty about poor Miles. You always were a selfish boy, greedy could be your middle name. Your dad and I are getting old you know, and our bathroom isn't designed for old people. I feel *frightened* when I have to get in and out of that bath. Your dad'll break a hip if he has a fall..." She could sense that she wasn't winning, so she tried a different tack. She sighed loudly. "I'll call Archie and tell him that he can't have a birthday present because his uncle James is too mean to spend his money."

"What is it he wants?" James asked. He was resigned to sending something, even though he thought Archie was a bit of a spoiled brat. He wondered if there was a branch of GAME nearby so he could buy a fifty quid gift voucher to send.

"It's called a MacBook Pro. Some sort of computer that he's set his heart on."

James laughed. "He's what? Seven? What does he need one of those for?"

"He's eight. See, you don't even know how old your own nephew is. You should be ashamed. He needs it for his schoolwork."

"Where's he going to school, NASA? Bit over the top for an eight year old. Anyway, why is Miles promising him stuff like that if he can't afford it?" It was a straightforward enough question, but it prompted another deep sigh.

"To fit in at school. They all have them nowadays." Marion

didn't know if that was true or not, but Miles had insisted on an expensive private prep school, which was taking up all his money, well, what the mortgage on his large farmhouse in a top village in Hampshire didn't guzzle. Still, James could afford to support the family, so it was his duty to look after his parents and brothers. Marion genuinely regarded James's money as "family money."

"Ridiculous," he said. "And you're as much to blame. If you keep bailing Miles out, what's he gonna do when you're gone?" For some reason it made him inordinately angry. As a child, he'd never been spoilt. His mother had insisted that asking for too much was greedy. It hadn't stopped Miles though. His parents had bought whatever had been on Miles's wish list at Christmas, with the explanation that he'd share. Miles had always been a selfish bastard and had whacked anyone attempting to play with his expensive toys or watch the telly in his bedroom that everyone else had been denied. The two eldest had also scarpered at the first opportunity, leaving home the moment they could. They were both quite a lot older than the youngest three.

"You're a very selfish, greedy man," Marion spat, making James wince. He tried Sarah's advice, yadda yadda, she'd called it. He tried hard to be immune to Marion's tactics. "I'll tell everyone how mean you are, that you don't care if I fall and break my hip."

"How much will your bathroom be?" He caved in a little, not too much though as he'd already paid off their mortgage and had a direct debit set up to drop a couple of thousand into his father's account every month. He often wondered what they spent it all on.

"Thirty grand should cover it."

If James hadn't been sitting down, he'd have fallen to the ground in shock. He realised how she was trying to manipulate him, guilt him into handing over more money than a lot of people earned in a year, *'probably so that she could play Lady Magnanimous to Miles,'* he thought ruefully.

"No way. I won't get paid for Cosmic Warriors 1 for a few months yet. A bathroom doesn't cost that. You'll just give it to that ponce Miles, then hold your hand out for more. Well, the answer's no." He prodded his phone to end the call before she had the chance to call him a failure again, or worse. His hands shook as he thrust the phone back in his pocket. He'd never put the phone down on her before. It was a strangely liberating feeling. He wondered if his dad was taking the brunt of her wrath at home.

It was satisfying to finally get one up on the beatific Miles, the train wreck of a man who could do no wrong. On a superficial level they got on OK, although James hadn't agreed with most of Miles' life decisions. All his life, James had been second best, or third or even fourth best most of the time. He'd had no voice within his family, just a little boy ignored.

Now he was only bothered with because they wanted his money. He knew that and it saddened him as to how low they'd stoop. Miles had bullied him, with their mother's blessing, so badly as a child that James had left home on his 18th birthday. Nobody had been particularly concerned, after all, his mum had moaned so much about having mouths to feed and chores she had to do. He figured that he'd done her a favour by getting out from under her feet. When Miles had given him a black eye on his sixteenth birthday purely for being the centre of attention, his mother had told him that he probably deserved it, and that "if you just kept your mouth shut, he wouldn't have to hit you so hard." She'd said that to his ex too, when Miles had beaten her up. Suzy had, quite rightly, run for her life. Marion had called her every name under the sun for leaving Miles bereft and heartbroken. She was completely clueless as to why Suzy had dumped him when he didn't break all of her fingers, only a few, and she made him do it by complaining about him spending their savings to the bookies.

As soon as James started earning good money, they'd all crept back, reminding him of his duties. His mother was fond of telling him how much he "owed" her for bringing him into the world, for letting him live in her house until he was 18. Her threat was always that she'd tell everyone about the time that his dad had had to cart him off to the Priory, how he'd let himself be brainwashed by a cult. James really didn't want it becoming public knowledge.

Now he had Sarah, fixer extraordinaire, who could squash pretty much any story, or spin it to turn it around completely. Marion had lost her power. He related the call to Sarah over lunch that day. She listened as he grew angry at the way his mum had behaved.

"You did absolutely the right thing," she soothed, "Just be aware that she'll punish you in some way." She thought for a moment. "When a narcissist loses control of a person, they try to control how other people see them. Chances are she'll tell everyone at her Women's Institute what a bad son you are and how you ignore your family now that you're famous. I saw a similar thing happen once before."

Marion was still in a bad mood when she attended her WI meeting the following day. "Saw a poster with that son of yours on it," said a slightly wizened lady who had a whiskery moustache, "Quite the looker isn't he? You must be very proud..."

"Good looks don't make up for a bad heart," said Marion, "He stole all of Harry's money you know. Left us penniless."

Word spread around the community centre hall. People came to commiserate and get the gossip on James, who had become the island's famous person. The ladies were so kind to Marion, crowding around her to hear about what happened. Enjoying the attention, she found herself embellishing the story. He'd stolen the money Harry had saved for their new bathroom, spending it recklessly on his expensive wedding and his demanding new wife. The big diamond she was wearing should have been a new shower cubicle with built in steam function. Only Shirley Davenport hadn't believed her, but she kept her mouth shut and just listened.

The women all lapped it up. Nobody challenged her story. Five of the ladies invited her for coffee the following week. Marion re-told the lie so many times over the following weeks that she herself began to believe it. Even Harry agreed that James was mean. He'd seen how much he'd been earning, knew that he could spare a bit. It wasn't fair for poor Archie to be going without simply so that Sarah could buy fur coats, they reasoned. (Not that Sarah would have been seen dead in a fur coat). As James and Sarah jetted around the world promoting Cosmic Warriors, Marion became angrier and angrier, convinced that they were just on holiday, probably flying first class using *HER* money, which could have paid a month's mortgage for poor Miles or a term's school fees, especially after Miles had told her he'd been conned out of a month's salary the day after he'd been paid. Apparently an acquaintance had invited him to invest in a very lucrative business, which should've secured him for life, only it had gone wrong, and the man's other business partner had run off with all the money. According to Marion, there was no way that Miles could've foreseen it. It was just another example of the world being against her best boy.

The truth had been that Miles had gone on a bender and had gambled and drank his salary over a long weekend. His long-suffering partner, who was stressed about their finances as it was, had been forced to pawn her late mother's jewellery to pay the mortgage, and was about to find out that he'd run up her credit card when she tried to use it to buy groceries. She was threatening to leave and take Archie with her.

Marion was fretting about poor Miles so much, she strong armed Jonathan into lending him some cash to tide him over. She didn't particularly care that it left Jonathan short for the month, but it hadn't been enough, so Harry had cashed in one of their ISAs to make up the shortfall.

She pondered the problem of how Miles would cope once they'd gone. Realising that James was being controlled by that Sarah, she set about making an appointment with the solicitor in the nearby town.

James was nestled between Sarah's legs, carefully shaving off her pubic hair, the pair of them giggling like naughty schoolchildren, when his phone rang. They were in Tokyo enjoying a rare night off from the madcap world tour that the studio had set up to promote Cosmic Warriors 1. The Japanese premiere had been a roaring success, as the pundits had forecast, and the film was predicted to have the biggest opening of any movie worldwide that year.

He glanced at the screen and grimaced. "What does Miles want this time?" He said, abandoning the razor and swiping to answer. "What's up?" Miles only ever called him when he wanted something.

"There's been an accident," he said, "a car crash."

"Mum said your car was off the road," James butted in. "I'm in Japan, there's nothing I can do to help." He glanced up to see Sarah watching him. He sat up, for some reason not wanting to be staring at his wife's vagina while talking to his brother.

"Not my car, Muppet, Mum and Dad's. They crashed on the A36."

James's blood ran cold. "Are they alright?"

Silence.

Miles voice cracked as he spoke eventually. "No. I think Dad had a heart attack at the wheel, died instantly. 'Drove into the central reservation,' the police said. No other casualties, just him and Mum. The police are here. They had my address programmed into their new satnav."

James sat stunned, trying to take it all in. Eventually he managed to croak; "Do the others know?"

"Yeah, I've called everyone. Just thought I'd better let you know too. The police have told me to go secure their house. Jon said he'll formally identify their bodies. He'll drive down to do it."

"How will you get to the Island?" James asked.

"Mum bought me a new car a few weeks ago. Archie couldn't get to school otherwise," he replied, thinking that James was always nosy. "You didn't nick all her money you know," he added mysteriously.

"What are you on about?" James demanded,. "I didn't nick anything, you know that. I paid them money every month. Where else do you think it came from?"

Miles ignored him. "I'll call you when I know more," he said before the line went dead. Within seconds it rang again. This time it was his younger brother, Jonathan, who was wondering why he had been told by Miles to drive to Hampshire, near Miles' house to do the identification of their parent's bodies. Miles had said that he was driving to the island to their house instead. It was all a bit strange. Adam and Steven, the two eldest were both abroad as well, so all the stuff to be done was being left to the two of them. Jonathan was convinced that Miles was up to something.

"He said a funny thing to me," James confided, "accused me of nicking money off them."

"Mum told everyone that you stole her money and spent it on Sarah," Jonathan said. "Personally I didn't think it was true. I mean, why would you? How would you? But you know what Mum was like, if it was hers, it was Miles's, if it was yours, it was hers too, then Miles. Lazy bastard had a thousand quid off me last month 'cos he pissed away his salary. Mum made up some stupid story, but we all know what he's like."

"She told you I stole her money?" James was incredulous. "I paid off their bloody mortgage. Maybe she thought that when I said no to her latest demand, it was me stealing my own cash." The familiar bubble of indignation rose through his belly. He felt Sarah's hand on his arm, a calming presence. He remembered that his mother was dead.

"Well, I didn't want to be the one to tell you," Jonathan said quietly. "I knew exactly what she was like. I never forgave her for the way she treated Hannah at our wedding. Still, we shouldn't speak ill of the dead." He thought back to his wedding day, his mum wearing a pale cream outfit, lacy to the point of bridal, playing the munificent host, having invited a ton of people neither he nor his bride even knew, telling him how *important* each person was. She'd treated his wedding like a networking opportunity, a chance to show off. She'd even brow-beaten Hannah's dad into reducing the dress budget in order to spend more on flowers to decorate the church.

"No, we shouldn't," James agreed. He was reeling. He wondered who else thought he'd stolen money from his aged parents.

When he finished the call, he relayed it all to Sarah, who shook her head sadly. She hoped that Marion hadn't lied to their wider circle, but didn't put it past her. She hugged James tight, all thoughts of their randy night off forgotten, as it was getting late. He'd have to fly back for the funeral, which would be disappointing for the fans who queued up to see him at his premieres, but family was more important, even dysfunctional ones. She calculated that it would be held during the Australian leg of the tour, given that the coroner would need to be involved. It made it even more of a shame because two of his brothers had been scheduled to share in his big night.

Miles stood in the kitchen of his parent's house. The clock sounded louder than normal, filling the silence with its unrelenting noise. He checked the fridge and found it filled with the usual cheeses and condiments that they always liked. Home-made chutney jostled for space with Women's Institute piccalilli, bought for reasons of political friendship rather than because anyone ever ate them. He'd stopped on the way for milk, so set about making a cup of tea, the kettle feeling alien in his hands. Only Marion ever made tea.

The little room they called "the study" looked out over the garden towards his dad's greenhouse. It had an IKEA desk, an elderly computer, and a shelf full of files. His father had been one of those neat and tidy people who'd filed every piece of paper carefully. He scanned the shelf. Bank statements, pension, guarantees for household appliances, will.

He pulled the box file containing their will from the shelf and opened it. He saw straightaway that Mr Forester, a local solicitor,

The Fixer

had drawn up a new one only weeks before and held the original. He opened the copy and began to read.

Sole beneficiary.

They'd left him the lot. He smiled for the first time that day. He'd hoped to get a bigger share than the others, they'd all got plenty of money, well, Jonathan's new wife had a very good job. It had been only himself struggling. He stroked the desk, it was all his now.

Financial freedom.

He'd be able to take a year off work and kick back a bit. The house had to be worth a fair amount. He knew that James had paid off the mortgage. Idiot. If he'd have had that sort of money, he wouldn't have wasted it trying to get in their mother's good books.

He was interrupted by the doorbell. He opened the front door to see a smiling old lady holding what appeared to be a bunch of twigs. "Hello, is Marion about? I brought these round for her flower arranging class. She wanted structure you see," she said, as if Miles was remotely interested.

"Mum and Dad were killed in a car crash this morning," he told her, so bluntly that she dropped her twigs, which made a mess on the porch floor. Concerned that she too might have a heart attack, he helped her into the kitchen and made them both fresh tea. He discovered that his mother had always spoken fondly about him to her friends, calling him her "best boy." He puffed up proudly. He also found out about the lie she'd told about James.

"Everyone was very angry about it," Mrs Withenshaw told him. "Poor Marion was so upset that he turned out so bad, wondered if she'd done something wrong herself. We all reassured her though. I mean, the rest of you are all fine young men, although I think the two eldest live in Australia, don't they? Leaving behind aged parents isn't very fair is it? I know the others at our flower-arranging class thought so too."

"Jonathan and I both live near-ish," he told her.

"Wasn't he the one with the wife who was rude to Marion after she took over the arrangements for their wedding? The poor girl was clueless. Marion did a marvellous job. Didn't get a word of thanks though. People can be very selfish."

The old lady left after promising to assist with the funeral tea. Miles spoke briefly to the solicitor, the funeral director, and the coroner before he began trawling the house for valuables. He was interrupted by Jonathan calling.

"It's definitely Mum and Dad," he said. He sounded upset. He didn't feel the need to explain to Miles that while their father had been in one piece, their mother hadn't. It'd been traumatic. He wasn't sure whether to drive down to the south coast or back up to South London.

"I wasn't holding out any hope that it wouldn't be," Miles replied. "I've sorted the house. I'll probably stay here for a few days; there are lots of arrangements to make, funeral, that sort of thing." He fingered the gold brooch he'd found in their mum's jewellery box. Worth a few bob.

"Want me to come help?" Jonathan asked. He didn't relish the thought of spending any time with Miles, but felt it was his duty, what with the other three being so far away. It wouldn't be fair to leave all the work to one person.

"I'm not sure if it's a good idea," Miles began. "Only I just found out that I'm sole beneficiary. I gather the rest of you upset mum so much she cut you out. I'm not certain how welcome any of you would be if you came here. Apparently everyone dislikes the way your wife treated Mum at the wedding. I can't upset people when I need their help with the funeral..." He trailed off. This was easy.

"Are you shittin' me?" Jonathan demanded. "Can I at least get my personal possessions? Baby photos?"

"Like I said, all left to me, sole beneficiary. I can't go against that. People are upset enough as it is."

James was asleep when an irate Jonathan had called him to relay the news. He'd already spoken to the eldest two, who'd both decided that Miles could get stuffed. They wouldn't bother coming back for the funeral, nor would they bother fighting the will. There was a twenty year gap between the eldest and himself. Jonathan wondered what his mum had done to them to make them both run so far away from her.

James had listened to Jonathan's rant, his insistence that it wasn't fair, Miles had always been treated better, loved more. He had to agree. Sarah had woken up and was also listening in. "It should've been split between us, equally," he'd said. "Lazy bastard's always been rewarded for being a failure. Wanker still owes me money." Jonathan was scathing.

"You won't see that back," James told him. "He's owed me

The Fixer

money for years. Doesn't see why he should pay anyone back. Mum always taught him that what was ours was his, remember?"

"Why'd they do this?" Jonathan demanded. "Why cause all this upset and hassle? Why not just be fair?"

"She lost control of all of you, so she's punished you, created conflict. It's what narcissists do," Sarah told him. "The only one she had control of was Miles, partly because he's weak, and partly because he was dependent on them. They controlled him financially. Bred him to be greedy, then fuelled that greed."

"That's her to a 'T'," exclaimed Jonathan. "Your missus is very clued up," he told James.

"She is indeed," he replied, gazing at her in admiration. She was delightfully mussed up, laying on her side, facing him. They had the phone in between them on loudspeaker.

By his side. Always.

"Are you gonna challenge the will?" Jonathan asked.

"No," James said, "but I won't tell Miles that. Let him think he's got Mishcon's finest on his back, willing to eat up the entire amount in fees. That'll make the greedy twat sweat." He heard Jonathan laugh.

Sarah butted in. "We will need to see the will. It's a public document, so if it gives reasons why they made this decision, I might need to slap a lid on it. If it doesn't, but it gets out, I'll spin it that there may have been 'pressure' from within the family." She did air quotes around the word pressure.

"Do your worst," Jonathan told her.

Marion and Harry had a joint funeral, a very small affair with just a handful of people present. Those that attended were predominantly Harry's friends from the bowling club, who hadn't heard about the scandalous sons, besides. It was a matter of etiquette to attend a fallen member's memorial.

James stayed out of public view for the three days around the funeral, thus avoiding the accusation that he was out having fun while his parents were buried. Indeed, nobody could be sure whether he attended on the down low or not. The sad part was that he could have attended. Only Miles insisted that the villagers would attack him, having painted a picture of furious people bearing pitchforks, ready to drag him out if he dared show his face in the chapel. In reality, it wouldn't have happened. For all their kindness to Marion when she was alive, in truth she'd been regarded by the majority as a nasty piece of work who'd driven away her beautiful sons with her sharp tongue and nasty ways. Those women had just enjoyed hearing the gossip, regarding it as they would a soap opera with weekly updates. They'd all lived long enough to know that chasing two sons away to the other side of the world showed that something was seriously amiss.

Sarah and James spent those three days holed up in their hotel room, talking for hours, Sarah coaxing out all the memories that James had hidden so firmly. As his understanding grew, he confessed that he wished he could go back and tell the lost, ignored little boy, who hid under his bed for hours at a time, that he'd be OK. He wanted to reassure his younger self that it wasn't his fault that Miles tortured him so much, and that he'd survive and thrive. It was an emotional time.

Shirley Davenport emailed Sarah and James their condolences. Along with everyone else, she'd heard what Marion and Harry had done and she fervently hoped it wouldn't mean the end of James's patronage of the Furry Friends. Thanks to Sarah, she had a Just-Giving page, a video blog, and donations had jumped enough to build a new Hedgehog hospital, with the local vet coming in four times a week. The sanctuary had been transformed.

In Illinois, Erika meekly signed the cheque for two hundred thousand dollars in damages that her attorney had negotiated on her behalf to save her going to court. He thought she'd got off lightly given the damage the lie had done. She'd also had to pay the Enquirer back their fee. She wasn't bankrupt, but it had eaten an enormous chunk of her inheritance.

The cheque was made out to the "Furry Friends Rescue Centre."

CHAPTER 23

The Australian premiere was a raging success, as were the premieres in LA, New York, and London. It was a week after the funeral. Sarah had pulled out all the stops to fly in Jonathan and Hannah, who stood alongside Steven and Adam, James's eldest brothers, and their partners.

The press had gone crazy when the "Morell men" and their ladies had walked up the red carpet. Four handsome men, all in perfectly-tailored tuxedos, showing off their elegantly-attired women. It was a show of strength, of unity, the press declared. Nobody mentioned Miles, who was watching proceedings back in England on his father's elderly desktop. Archie had already smashed the MacBook Pro in a fit of pique when he couldn't work out how to use it. Miles seethed at the sight of his brothers claiming the limelight, and the comments on the Daily Mail website espousing how handsome they all were enraged him. Every time he'd tried to comment saying how lame/awful/thieving they all were, his comments were moderated out. He gave up in the end and fished a bottle of whisky out of his secret stash. He decided not to mention it to his girlfriend.

Sarah clasped James's hand tightly, trying to remember to look up, not slouch, and hold her stomach in. He glanced over to her and smiled, before giving her hand a little squeeze in return. She beamed widely for the cameras.

It was his night. Along with the other premieres, it was his night to gather up the adulation that she realised he needed. The brothers he'd retained wouldn't try and steal his limelight. They understood that they only had walk-on parts in his big night, were there to share the fun, the after party, and his success. They all stood back as James signed autographs and took selfies with his fans. His fans, nobody else's.

It was the first time he'd taken family to see one of his movies and not had it criticised. His mum had always found something to dislike, or told him he'd over- or under-acted his part. It was quite a revelation to hear only how much they'd enjoyed it. The press also felt the same and declared it a massive hit. Martin was walking around like a peacock.

They got back to their hotel just as the sun was rising over Sydney. The after-party had been a raucous affair, carrying on much longer than was usual, but as they were flying by private jet that night, nobody worried too much about sleeping. She'd loved seeing James party with his brothers, although it was interesting that none of them were really grieving. If anything, they all appeared liberated. It was a concept she'd have liked to ponder properly once the festivities were out of the way.

"You OK?" She asked him as he read the texts on his phone when they'd finally got back to their room.

"Better than OK," he told her, his eyes shining. "Alan texted his congratulations, as did Danny Laker. The figures are out, and apparently Cosmic Warriors is the highest grossing opener in LA history. We have officially got a hit movie." He beamed like an excited child.

"I don't think I can drink any more champagne," Sarah said, "But I'm quite willing to have a go."

"Stick with me kid," he said in his American accent before pulling another bottle of champagne out of the minibar and efficiently popping the cork. He poured two glasses and handed one to Sarah.

"Cheers. Here's to success," he said, tipping his glass towards hers.

"Success," she agreed. They both drank. "Tonight, yesterday, I'm confused as to when it was, the premiere, it was fun." She was feeling a little woozy.

"Partying with you is always fun," he replied. James was a soppy drunk, prone to extreme sentimentality when he'd had too much champagne. He'd never done anything worse than embarrass himself whilst under the influence, which he figured was a good way to be. He regarded angry drunks as the worst, especially when they hid their violence behind alcohol and absolved themselves of blame. "The boys too. I liked that dress you got for Hannah. Think she did as well." He graced Sarah with a soppy grin. "Although she didn't look as gorgeous as you, my lovely wife."

"I'm getting you well-trained," she giggled. "Seriously, it looked great tonight, the Morell men. It'll make great copy tomorrow. Today," she corrected herself.

"Got a make the most of my bit of remaining family while I can," James said, becoming more serious. "It's not like I've got a lot left."

"Then we need to make our own," she said before she could check herself. Several weeks had passed since James's admission that he wanted a family. She'd come round to the idea, especially now that Marion wouldn't be a presence in their lives. Interestingly, both Adam and Steven had decided to get married to their long term partners. It was as though all of them were suddenly free.

James beamed his devastating smile. "Tonight just gets better and better," he said. "Shall we have a ceremonial burning of your pills?"

"You're drunk," she said, laughing as he rummaged around in her vanity bag for them. Drunk or not, he didn't intend to let an opportunity like that pass him by. She watched as he threw them off the balcony.

"Now, let's make a baby," he said, pulling his shirt off.

****

Eighteen months later, Sarah sat on the patio of their house, gazing at the rolling fields stretching down to a glittering river, which meandered along through the rolling fields of Oxfordshire. It wasn't Devon, which they'd both deemed too remote from London, but it was rural, peaceful, and beautiful. James sat holding his son in his arms, who had finally fallen asleep.

He'd refused to take any movies between Cosmic Warriors sequels, meaning that he had time before promo to enjoy the house they'd bought and planned to fill with children. The timing hadn't worked out too well, as Sarah had given birth in California during

Cosmic Warriors 3 filming, but she'd handled it with her usual aplomb, organising everything to work like clockwork while she was indisposed, balancing her laptop on her enormous bump. She'd even managed to find their house, a large, rather rambling place, with an Aga and an enormous inglenook fireplace. He often wondered how she managed to keep track of everything, especially when she was watching his back constantly.

He loved her being pregnant, from the first little signs of a bump, right through to when she was like a beached whale, having to be hauled into his trailer each day. He'd enjoyed all the planning, the anticipation of their new arrival. Sarah had morphed into a sensual, voluptuous mother, a real mother, one who would love her children properly.

Life had gotten crazy after the first Cosmic Warriors, more so after the second, but she still monitored his online comments, handled his publicists, and managed his diary. He'd offered to employ someone else if it got too much, but she'd laughed at his suggestion and got on with arranging the renovations she wanted.

"How come he drops off the moment you hold him?" She said, eyeing the sleeping bundle. "Hollers the place down if I try."

"It's a gift," James quipped, glancing down at the mop of dark curls peeking out of the pale blue blanket. If anything, it was a nuisance that Louis dropped off if he so much as picked him up. He liked making his son smile, watching his gummy mouth curl in delight. He was fascinated by his bright blue eyes, so much like his own, but not yet jaded by the things he'd see in the world.

In the months following his parent's deaths, Sarah had talked a lot about healing. She'd instinctively understood that the damage his parents had done ran deep. It'd explained his fascination with cults, why he'd been an easy target for predators who wanted to use him, his fame, and his money. He'd spent his life being programmed to feel like a failure, almost accepting that he'd have to constantly strive to feel like a success, and that other people were more worthy. The first time he held his son in his arms, he knew he'd come through.

The End

ALSO BY D A LATHAM

Also by D A Latham
A Very Corporate Affair Book 1
A Very Corporate Affair Book 2
A Very Corporate Affair Book 3
The Taming of the Oligarch (Corporate Affair Book 4)
Salon Affair
The Beauty and the Blonde
The Whore of Babylon Cay
The Debt
All available from all good e-retailers
Find out more at:
Facebook: The Novels of D A Latham
Twitter: @dalatham1
dalatham.com
Please consider leaving a review for this book on the site you purchased it, or on Goodreads. Reviews help others discover new books.

Do stick around for a bonus chapter from
Salon Affair

Chapter 1

I finished up my last client, taking her through to reception to recommend her products, and hand her over to the receptionist to pay her bill. I said my goodbyes, and hot-footed it through to the staff room to claim my glass of wine, and a chair, ready for the staff meeting. The entire staff were there, with it being Saturday evening, and we just had to wait for the receptionist to lock the front door and join us, and we could find out the reason for the impromptu meeting.

Damien, the salon manager looked ill at ease when he stood to address us. "Guys, as you probably realise, the salon isn't doing quite so well lately. We've tried various marketing schemes, even a coupon offer to try and get new clients, but our accountants have told us that we're carrying too many staff for the revenue." *Well, if you stopped giving it away for next to nothing on Groupon, we might make a bit more profit*, I thought. I kept quiet. "So I have to inform everyone that we're having to make three people redundant. Everyone will be put into the pool, and scored based on performance over the past year, then the three lowest scored will be informed. The process will take around a month. I'm sorry guys."

I looked around the room at my workmates. They all looked uncertain. Personally, I felt quite safe. I'd trained there originally, and worked to the 'Gavin Roberts' method. I also had an enormous clientele, and was usually the second biggest revenue earner in the salon.

"So who's gonna get the push?" asked Belinda, our newest, and dopiest stylist. *Probably you.* "I don't think it's fair, I haven't had time to build up properly yet, I've only been here a year." She seemed blissfully unaware that a year was more time than most stylists got when it came to building a following. I wanted to tell her it was probably her habit of talking non-stop about her boyfriend, and his various issues with commitment, rather than her client's hair, that was the problem. Her refusal to retail didn't help either, as she assumed everyone was too poor to afford anything, which was quite rude really. Damien ignored her.

"Next week, each person will have a meeting with me, and asked if they'd like to opt for voluntary redundancy, so give that some thought, and I'll see you all next week." Damien dismissed us, not meeting anyone's eyes.

I pulled on my flat boots and coat, ready for the walk to the station. "I bet it'll be you," sneered Holly, the über-bitch. She never wasted an opportunity to be nasty to me. Unfortunately, she was the most popular stylist in the salon, and the only one to make consistently more than me.

"I'm sure there's other people in the firing line in front of me," I pointed out, smiling at her bitchy, rather put-on, pitying look.

"Not on your pay scale. Just think how much they'll save sacking you, and sharing out your clients. At least my clients insist that they'll only have me, and nobody else. My clients are totally loyal, unlike yours," she pointed out. About two years previous, I'd broken my ankle and been off for three months. During that time, the other stylists had looked after my clients. She'd taken that as clients not caring who did them, rather than them being understanding of my predicament.

Matt was waiting for me at the station when I got off the train. "How was your day?" he asked. He only worked office hours, and seemed to think me working Saturdays was strange, even after a couple of years together.

"Busy, all fine, until last thing. Damien told everyone he's going to have to reduce the staff by three people. All those cheap deals he did have dented profits."

"Do you think you'll be ok? Or could you get made redundant?"

"I doubt it. I wouldn't mind changing salons though, somewhere a bit more creative and high end. He said we could take voluntary redundancy if we wanted."

"I don't know if that's a good idea Lil, you have certain protections due to long service. If you changed to another salon, they could just sack you." *Oh thanks, believe in me why don't you?*

Matt followed me into the semi I shared with my parents and younger brother. He made himself comfy at the kitchen table, and listened as I told my mum what had happened. "Why not start looking for another job, just in case," Mum advised, "if nothing happens next week, then all well and good, but at least you'll have a back-up plan."

"Mark, can you get off the computer for a little while please?" I asked my little brother. He sighed loudly, and slid off the wheelie chair, to give me access to the family desktop. I closed down YouTube, and googled 'hairdressing jobs, London'. There seemed to be pages of them, I flicked through, several catching my eye. "There's loads, look, Sassoon, Trevor Sorbie, and Gino Venti are all advertising for stylists. That's just on the first page."

"You should get Lisa to check over your CV, update it a bit," advised Mum. Lisa was my best friend, and was a secretary in a recruitment company. She was bound to know about CVs.

"Are we going out tonight?" I asked Matt, knowing full well that the answer would be 'no'. Matt was in the throes of buying his first studio flat, and was saving obsessively. As I predicted, he shook his head.

"Sorry Lily, even with a two for one coupon, dinner at Zizzi's would still be over twenty quid. I had to pay for the survey today. *There's always an excuse*, I thought, determined not to offer to pay. Recently, I paid for everything so that the tightwad could squirrel his money away for a flat that would be solely in his name. In his defence, we'd only been together two years, and I had an appalling credit rating due to not earning for those three months in a plaster cast, and a boob job that I'd struggled to pay for. "Your Mum's chilli is better than fancy restaurant food anyway," he asserted, as Mum plonked plates of chilli and rice down in front of us.

Matt borrowed my iPhone to see what was on telly that evening, announcing the programs that he wanted to watch through mouthfuls of rice. "I might give Lisa a call if you're just gonna be watching telly all evening," I told him. He looked a little hurt.

"These are the programs that you like to watch Lily, what would you prefer to do then?" he demanded, a little edge to his voice. If I was being truthful, I would've said that I wanted to go out clubbing in London, after listening to Holly all day, telling her clients about some fancy bar and club she'd visited, which had sounded impossibly glamorous and fun. *I bet she doesn't sit indoors watching x-factor on a Saturday night,* I thought. I knew it would be pointless expecting Matt to take me to the Kensington Roof Gardens. All that'd happen would be him asking for tap water, and bitching about the prices. Even Lisa, my very best friend, wouldn't go somewhere like that, claiming to be too uncomfortable about her weight to get dolled up.

She turned up that evening, wearing a onesie and slippers, repeating her delight that she didn't have to get 'dressed up' to visit, having been coming round to ours since she was three. We left Matt sitting with my parents watching Ant and Dec, and sat at the computer to write a killer CV.

Between Lisa and I, we really jazzed up my résumé. I listed out all the courses I'd attended since graduating college, and Lisa thought up an excellent mission statement along the lines of me wanting to continue growing professionally. She even found a great photo of me on Facebook, efficiently cropped Matt out, and added it to the top corner.

Once it was all done, I sent it off to five salons, filling in their online applications as I went. "One of those has gotta get you an interview," said Lisa, "I can't see you having any issues finding a new job, what with being the best hairdresser in the world 'n' all that."

I smiled gratefully. Lisa had been my very first client/victim, patiently sitting for hours as I struggled through my first ham-fisted attempts at cutting. "Do you think I'm doing the right thing?" I asked.

"Course you are. You're way too good at your job to hang around in Gavin Roberts forevermore. I know it's near Victoria, but it's not true West End hairdressing. There's no way you should be doing groupon Tuesdays and student Wednesdays. You should be doing hipsters and celebrities."

The program must have finished, because Mum came in to make cocoa, and Matt came to see what we were up to, and remind us that Big Brother was just about to start. He read through my new CV, smiling at the photo, and agreed with Lisa that it was really good.

He stayed over that night, as was normal on a Saturday night. I snuggled into him, careful not to 'crowd him', which he hated. He had issues with intimacy, and although he enjoyed sex, it had to be on his terms, with everything staying the same, done in the same order. Thankfully, I quite enjoyed our little routine, and Matt often remarked that we shagged 'efficiently', both successfully reaching orgasm with minimum effort on his part, or disruption of sleep on mine. If I was truthful, I'd admit that it was a little 'pipe and slippers', but I couldn't muster up the enthusiasm to change it.

So there we were, lights off, fumble fumble, tweak tit, condom on, then a bonk that generally lasted around ten minutes. I'd come, then him, and he'd pass me a tissue. Afterwards, he'd roll over and doze off. Matt didn't do cuddling.

I lay awake in the darkness, trying to analyse what was bothering me. Nothing had changed, Matt was just doing what we did every weekend. Lisa was just being Lisa, my fat, funny, best friend. The problem clearly lay with me. *Maybe a new job will provide all the change I'm craving.*

The next morning, Matt went off to his usual Sunday morning football practice, and I joined Mum in a trip into Bromley for a mooch about. We were sitting in Café Rouge, having a latte and a sit down, when I pulled out my phone to check my emails, seeing straightaway that there was one from Gino Venti. I opened it, and read through it, skimming past the pleasantries. "I have an interview, Mum, and it's tomorrow!" I squealed, thrusting my phone into her face for her to read it. She took the phone from my hand, and read it through carefully.

"Tomorrow at three o'clock. Lucky it's your day off. Where is it?"

"Bond Street, well, South Molten Street. Right in the heart of the West End. It's a really glamorous salon, think they feature in hairdresser's journal on a regular basis. They win all sorts of awards. I'll have to look really trendy."

"Best we have a look in Karen Millen then. Just don't tell your father."

"You're the best," I beamed. Mum had always wanted to be a hairdresser, but had never realised her dream, mainly due to marriage and babies getting in the way. She was a great supporter though, and we enjoyed secret splurges on dad's credit card every now and then, usually when I needed to look the part for something.

Two hundred quid later, I had a new outfit, and new shoes, ready for the following day. We smuggled it all into the house, past Dad, who was snoring on the sofa. I carefully cut off all the tags, and hung it all up to keep it pristine.

Mum and I nipped round to see Aunt Doris for an hour after dinner, taking a bag of food, and some Tupperware boxes of dinners that mum had made and frozen for her to heat up during the week. Strictly speaking, she was my great aunt, my Mum's father's sister. She hadn't had children of her own, and after her

The Fixer

husband had died, relied quite heavily on Mum. She was a game old girl though, quite good company, and still had all her marbles, even though she was in her eighties. In recent years, she'd got a bit wobbly on her pins, so needed a bit more help than she used to.

Mum sorted out the kitchen, and put a wash on, while I quickly hoovered and dusted. It wasn't a large house, so we were able to get it freshened up quite quickly. I told Doris all about my interview, and my new outfit, while I carefully dusted all the knickknacks on the mantelpiece.

"You aim as high as you can Lily. You're going to be a long time sitting in front of a fire when you're old. Do as much as you can now, while you're young. I'm grateful for all the good memories I have." She gazed wistfully at her gas fire as she spoke.

"Out dancing on a Saturday night?" I prompted.

"Of course, and more besides. I was a bit of a girl in my day you know. The war was over, and all we wanted to do was have fun. So many people had been killed and maimed, that we felt as though we had to party even harder, you know, to make up for what they missed out on. Plus of course, we'd all grown up with the rationing and deprivation, so it felt wonderful to drink, eat and dance without a care in the world." She smiled to herself, before whispering; "of course, the men were all sex starved, and desperate. It was a great time to be a pretty girl."

"I bet. Mind you, it was all a bit more staid in those days, wasn't it?"

She laughed. "Not really, the only difference was that you had to get married if you got pregnant. Human nature never changes Lily, it's why you should grab life with both hands, and never settle for second best." She changed the subject when Mum came in bearing a pot of tea, and a plate of biscuits.

Matt was sitting watching telly with Dad when we got home. He smiled at the news that I had an interview. "That's great, at least if the worst happens, you won't be out of work. Your fares'l be a little more though. Bond street's a tube ride as well as the train, so don't forget to factor that in when you're discussing pay."

"I won't. Tell you what, shall I meet you from work tomorrow? Seeing as I'll be up there already. We could go for a drink before we come home."

"Nah, costs a fortune for a pint up there. Better off getting a pack of Buds in the supermarket." He went back to his telly program, not noticing me pulling a face at him, and slumping down onto the sofa next to him. I was getting seriously ticked off with his 'every penny counts' philosophy, which he'd always had, but had become magnified with his flat purchase. I couldn't really understand it, he earned great money, had loads of savings, and would still have plenty left after paying his new mortgage each month. He was behaving as though he'd be poverty stricken.

I was quite relieved when he went home, saying he needed an early night, in preparation for the week ahead. "Are you and Matt alright?" Mum asked, frowning.

I sighed. "Yeah, I'm just getting a bit fed up with how tight he is all the time. We seem to sit indoors every night. Feels like we're an old, married couple."

"I'm sure he'll be better when he's actually got that flat, and got used to paying a mortgage. He's probably just a bit nervous about it," counselled Dad.

The next day, I awoke with a tummy full of butterflies. I spent an inordinately long time doing my hair, and was ready by mid-day, and pacing around, waiting till it was time to leave. My phone chirped, making me jump. It was only Lisa, wishing me luck, and saying she'd be round later to hear all about it.

I decided to leave early, just in case a train was delayed or cancelled, or I got lost. I checked my bag, making sure I had my purse, keys, phone, and travel card, and debated whether or not I needed to take my scissors. They hadn't said I'd be trade testing, but they also hadn't said I wouldn't. I slipped them in anyway, just in case. Satisfied that I was organised, and looked suitably fashionable in my new outfit, I set off.

I'd got used to the noise and dirt of central London during the years working at Gavin Roberts. Compared to the area around Victoria, South Molten street seemed quiet and genteel. I was still early, so found a little coffee shop to sit in, and watch the world go by, until it was time to impress. I sipped my latte, as my nerves really kicked in. As I watched impossibly groomed, beautifully dressed women wander past, carrying designer shopping bags, I felt gauche and provincial. *Snap out of it Lily, these women need people like you to keep their polished personas alive,* I told myself.

At five to three precisely, I walked down to Gino Venti. I hadn't been sure whether or not it would even be open on a Monday, but I could see that it was indeed open, and buzzing in there. A

The Fixer

Mediterranean looking woman was behind the reception desk. She greeted me with a broad smile. "Hello, welcome to Gino Venti, how may I help you?"

"I'm here for an interview with Gray Parker," I said. She looked at her screen.

"Lily Hollins?" I nodded. "Gray's expecting you. Please take a seat, and I'll tell him that you're here. Can I get you a drink of anything?" I shook my head. I really didn't want to have to manoeuvre a cup and saucer as well as my handbag and my feet. She went off, presumably to get Gray. I sat down on the cream leather sofa, and looked around the reception area, checking out the products. There was only one product line that I wasn't pretty expert on, the rest I'd already done extensive product knowledge training with. The rest of the reception area was pretty swanky. The desk itself looked as though it was carved out of limestone, with a brushed steel G V logo mounted on the front of it. The magazines were all this month's Vogue and Tatler. Not an old or cheap one to be seen.

"Gray won't be a minute," the receptionist said, making me jump. I'd been so engrossed in checking out the salon, I hadn't seen her come back. A few moments later, a tall, lean, man walked though with a client. He reeled off a list of her services to the receptionist, and picked a few bottles off a shelf to place on the desk in front of the client. I watched as she kissed him on both cheeks, and turned to pay her bill.

"Lily Hollins? I'm Gray Parker, pleased to meet you." I stood up, and shook his hand.

"Nice to meet you too. Her hair looked lovely." I nodded towards the client.

"First compliment, and you haven't even left the salon yet, Maggie," he called out to the glamorous blonde, "that's an extra ten quid on the bill."

The client giggled. "You're such a tease Gray. Alright, I'll pop an extra tenner in your tip jar. Do you pay that lady to say nice things?" *An extra tenner? Jeez.*

"Seriously, your hair looks lovely," I told her, "the colour's beautiful." For all her cut glass accent, and designer clothes, the woman seemed really friendly and nice. She smiled and thanked me, and I followed Gray through to the main salon. There were two stylists working, and a few clients sitting with colour taking.

"I wasn't sure if you'd be open on a Monday," I said.

"Oh yes, we're open seven days a week. There's only so many clients we can fit in the salon in one go, so we have to open long hours to accommodate everyone."

I followed him through to a tiny office, taking a seat opposite him. He was one of those rather beautiful looking men, tall and lean, but not thin, with a crooked smile, and extremely stylishly cut, short hair. He was also wearing head to toe Prada. I guessed his age at around forty. "So, Lily, what made you apply to us?"

"I need to progress as a hairdresser, and your salon is pretty well known. I saw the article in Hairdressers Journal, and figured that this salon's where it's all happening right now."

"You've been at Gavin Roberts a long time? Trained there, and all that. It's a great salon, so why do you want to leave?" His eyes bored into me. I couldn't exactly say 'because I'm bored, because I hate Holly the bitch, because I'm doing five pound Groupons due to my fuckwit manager accidentally selling two thousand of them to every tightwad bargain seeker in London'.

"My ambition is to be a top West End hairdresser, and I need to move out of my comfort zone to be able to achieve that." *Good answer Lil, pat on the back for that one.*

"I see. What's your specialism?"

"Cutting, but I vardered in both cutting and colouring. I can do all of it to an extremely high standard."

"I saw that on your CV. How come you vardered twice?"

"I had the opportunity, and took it. I wanted to be able to do every aspect of hair, not just one thing. It's also why I took on so many additional courses," I said.

He nodded. "It's very impressive. Must have taken up a lot of your spare time?"

"I didn't mind. Most of the courses were so interesting that it never worried me, doing them on my days off. I don't have kids or anything to worry about, so can purely concentrate on my love of hair." I slipped that in, in case he wanted to ask, but was wary of the rules governing asking about kids.

"I see. Have you got a portfolio?" I pulled the file out of my bag, and handed it to him. It held all my precious certificates, as well as photos of the work I did to achieve them. He flicked through it, pausing at a picture of a colour I did as my entry for Redken young stylist of the year contest. "This is good. What did you use?"

I reeled off the formula, and placement technique. He seemed quite impressed. "Did you win?" He gestured to the picture.

"Came second," I replied, feeling a blush rise up my neck. I wished I'd been able to boast being 'young hairdresser of the year', but I wasn't.

"So the judge was a blind arsehole then?" He smiled at me.

"The winner's style was beautiful. If I'm honest, he won fair and square."

Gray looked up, and regarded me intently. "He works here. The one that won."

"Really? He's fantastic." I remembered a bleach blonde, slightly tubby feminine boy, screeching when the winner had been announced.

"Don't tell him that, he's bloody impossible as it is. We'd need a crowbar to get his head out the door." Gray smiled. "So Lily, what about your expectations?"

"I don't really know what to expect to be honest. I'm a hard worker, a team player, and a good hairdresser. I can build a clientele pretty fast, and my client retention runs at about 90%."

"Ok, let me tell you about how we work. It's fairly unique because we don't have strict hours as such. Everyone works on a 40% commission, so we all work long hours. There's no basic, so if you sit around in the staff room, or take an afternoon off, there's no pay. Bear in mind a cut and dry starts at a hundred quid, you can see why we all put the hours in. We all choose our two days off each week six weeks in advance, so that bookings can be made ahead."

"Is it busy?" I was beyond curious.

"Extremely. We turn people away every day, which breaks my heart."

"Sounds brilliant."

"A lot of people like set hours, set pay, and the same days off every week. It's not for everyone. I take it you can be quite flexible?"

"Oh yes. There's nothing holding me back."

"Good, now, trade test. I don't suppose by any chance you brought your scissors?"

"Yes I did. Would you like me to stay and work this afternoon? Show you what I can do?"

"That would be brilliant. I'll show you where to put your bag, and orientate you with the salon."

I stowed my handbag in a locker, and followed Gray back out to reception, where he introduced me to Paulina, the receptionist, and asked her to book me some clients. "What time do you need to get away?" He asked.

I shrugged. "I don't. Book what you like."

Paulina beamed at me. "Great. I've got a list of people waiting on cancellations. Anything I shouldn't book?" Gray shook his head.

"She's an all-rounder. A rare breed." He smiled at me, and wandered over to greet his next client, who was waiting patiently on the sofa.

Within half an hour, I was working on a head of highlights, then another client while the colour was taking. I was painfully aware of the other stylists watching me closely, and Gray assessing everything I was doing. I just tried to relax into it, and work as if I was in Gavin Roberts. In total, I did three clients, each one getting a restyle, advice, and a bag of retail added onto their bill. By the time I'd finished, it was nearly seven, and the others were all finishing up too.

"Let's go over the road for a drink and discuss how you've done," said Gray, as I put on my coat, and said goodbye to the others. He spoke briefly to Paulina, before steering me out, and a few doors down to a swanky looking wine bar.

"I'm meeting my husband in about half an hour, so what would you like to drink?" *Husband? Oh, I geddit.*

"Could I have a white wine please?" I wondered if I should offer to pay, but Gray had gone to the bar before I could say anything. While I was waiting, I tried to tot up my takings in my head, but as I didn't really know their prices, it was impossible to work out.

Gray placed a glass in front of me, and sat down opposite. "So how was that for you?" he asked.

"Good thanks. I enjoyed it. The salon's lovely to work in."

"You looked comfortable. Your work's very good by the way. I think you're a bit wasted working for Gavin Roberts."

"Thank you."

"Your takings today were 440 services and 180 retail. You get ten percent of retail by the way." I nodded. "We take off the VAT, then you get 40%, so that's 140.80 plus 18 retail. I make that

158.80. Not bad for three and a half hours work." He pulled a wad of cash out of his pocket, and counted off a hundred and sixty quid.

"I didn't expect to get paid for a trade test," I spluttered. He shoved the money across the table to me.

"So, when can you start?"

"It depends. They might want me to work my notice, they might want me to go straightaway." I paused, "So does this mean that I've got the job?"

He smiled, "Of course. Quite a coup, getting first and second place winners of the Redken hairdresser of the year. Tomme, the winner, he's fantastic, but he's more of a princess than you'll ever be."

I sipped my wine, and looked around the bar. It was one of those achingly trendy places that I'd been desperate to try. The other patrons seemed wealthy and hip. I was grateful for my new outfit. Gray chatted about the other stylists, who were all male. I'd be the only girl. "Does Gino still work?" I asked.

Gray shook his head. "He retired a few years ago. Paulina's his niece, she looks after the salon for him, and I manage all the staff and clients, the actual hairdressing part really. Paulina just handles the money. She's quite good though, for a non-hairdresser, runs the reception really well."

I finished my drink just as a handsome, suited man approached us. He bent down to kiss Gray's cheek. "Chris, this is Lily, our new stylist." I shook his hand, and stood to leave.

"I'd better be getting off. I'll call you as soon as I know what date I can start."

"You don't have to rush off, if you'd like another drink?" Chris said. I glanced at my watch, it was nearly quarter to eight.

"I'd better get going, they'll all be wondering where I am."

As soon as I got on the train, I switched on my phone, to find various text messages from Mum, Lisa and Matt, all wondering where I was. I called Mum, and told her the good news, and see if someone could pick me up from the station. Apparently, Lisa and Matt were both round my house already, waiting for news.

Over a celebratory cup of tea, I told them all about my afternoon. Lisa and my parents were all made up for me, but Matt had to pour cold water over my triumph. "I don't think commission only is legal Lily, they need to fix proper working hours, and at least pay minimum wage. Are you expected to pay your own tax? Or do they put you on PAYE?"

I gave him a hard stare. "I just earned £160 in three hours Matt, I hardly think I should be whining about minimum wage, and Gray made it quite clear that there isn't fixed hours."

"You should be paid double time for Sundays," he said, rather sulky at my refusal to take his advice.

"Don't be ridiculous, I'm not on an hourly rate. Listen Matt, are you pleased for me or not?"

"Of course I am, I just don't want to see you exploited."

I exploded. "How can 40% of everything I do be exploitation? You once worked out that if I worked mobile, it'd only be 50% profit after the costs, so how on earth do you think that providing a salon in Bond street and a hefty price list, along with as much retail as I can possibly sell, and a steady stream of clients equals exploitation? Would you rather I carried on in Gavin Roberts at seven quid an hour?"

"At least it's pay if you're quiet."

"I slog my guts out. I'm never quiet, so your argument doesn't stack up."

"I just can't see you earning much, 40% of nothing is still nothing Lily, and I'm not having you sponging off me."

I stood up, feeling my fury rising. "I think you'd better go. Considering I've never asked you to pay for anything, and you're way too tight to even offer, I won't accept being called a gold digger."

"Lily, calm down," said Lisa, who was watching proceedings.

"No I won't calm down. I put up with sitting in every night, so that he can save every penny for his stupid flat, and when I finally get the chance to realise my dream, he behaves as though I'm not good enough." I turned back to Matt, "I think you need to go and find a nice girl, who won't outshine you, and is happy to sit indoors counting pennies with you. This isn't for me."

"You're making a big mistake, nobody will ever care for you as much as me. I guess I didn't realise my affection was measured by how much I spend on you," he huffed.

"Just go, please. Take your stuff too. I've had enough Matt." I sagged into my chair, relief flooding through me at finding the excuse to end it. Mum and Dad stayed silent, rather wisely not getting involved. I knew they liked Matt, but seeing as they didn't try and talk me round, it appeared that they agreed with my decision.

Hope you enjoyed that excerpt from Salon affair, available at all good e-book stores and in paperback.

Printed in Great Britain
by Amazon

58628039R00129